THE HERRENHAUS FORFEIT

CHASING MERCURY
BOOK TWO

Paul Phillips

I QUATERNI BOOKS

For Roz, Thomas and Freddie,
who put up with a lot...

CHASING MERCURY:
A NOTE ABOUT THE SERIES

The Herrenhaus Forfeit is the second book in the Chasing Mercury series and the story begins shortly after the events described in the first book, *The Borodino Sacrifice*.

However, it is designed to stand alone as a separate novel, as well as being a continuation of the story. While certain key plot points may be recapped here, there is no requirement to have read the first book before starting this one.

I hope you enjoy it!

Paul Phillips

CHAPTER ONE

The men who had set off up the mountain before daybreak were not professional killers, although two were gifted amateurs and the other four eager to impress. With tools across their shoulders their long shadows took on the look of workmen, particularly when the mule path narrowed above the grotto of the Madonna della Rocca and they began to ascend two-by-two. But these were no labourers. They wore hats, suits and waistcoats. The tools were guns.

In the villa on the edge of the little town that perched on the crags, the three crazy Americans were arguing, as usual. It had taken Nino many days of watching and listening to understand that they were not truthfully arguing at all but he kept such knowledge from his face, knowing best that what the crazy Americans wanted from him was big eyes, a bigger smile and an even bigger appetite. These things were easy to provide.

Mamma had lit the fire beneath the range and was preparing breakfast. Nino crept into an empty storage niche to observe.

Schaefer, the junior in age if not rank, had emerged from the bedrooms to find the others already at the kitchen table. As Nino would have put it – as indeed he had reported about the neighbourhood – Schaefer was a Capitano with a neat moustache and a certain quality about him. Not quite like the *crucchi*, despite that name of his, but more than a little reminiscent of Il Duce's pig-defiling *squadristi*. He worked in an office, down in the big town. There Nino's comprehension deserted him.

"Anaheim, Azuza and Cu – camonga! Say Bradley, gotta train to catch?"

The bigger man flashed Schaefer a forced grin and said nothing. He was lacing his army boots, but since he wore only his singlet you didn't have to be Fearless Fosdick from the funny papers to see he was just heading out for his morning's exercise.

Stockinged feet up on the table, a book in his lap and an unlit pipe between his teeth, it was the third of Nino's crazy Americans who answered.

"Sergeant Bradley doesn't feel he's earned his chow until he's conquered a couple of mountains." The older man, the nose-poker, Nino called him, raised the glass of almond wine that was perpetually at his side and added in his terrible Italian: "*Salute.*"

Captain Schaefer shook his head and lit a cigarette.

"You oughta find yourself a girl, Bradley."

"Oh, he found one. And then he lost her."

Bradley tied a knot he'd need his jack-knife to undo.

"Tom, you're forgetting the conditions of your room and board."

"Fuh-geddin? What am I fuhgeddin?"

The two younger men exchanged a look.

"You promised not to ask us about our work," Schaefer said.

Tom Cabot sniggered into his *vino di mandorla*.

"I'm a reporter. I had my fingers crossed. And I wasn't asking anything, I was telling. I'm sure you got it all on file how he was wounded on a secret mission behind Russian lines after VE Day. Czechoslovakia, wasn't it Bradley? But did you know it was all about a girl? He sprung her from under the noses of the NKVD. And then she pulled a Houdini on him."

"Story of my life," Bradley grunted.

"Story of mine, when I get to the bottom of it. All this…" Cabot waved his pipe-stem. "How Schaefer's no more a public health advisor than I got a can of DDT up my caboose. How he's really Navy Intel and you're here to clean up the mess you made putting the Mob back in charge of this place… Phooey! Sidebar on page eight, tops."

And with that, Nino's incomprehensible nose-poker sat back and poured another large one. Breakfast of Champions, they called it. Bradley shrugged.

"I told you he wasn't as stupid as he looks."

"I can fix that part about the DDT though," Schaefer said.

Through a combination of the bomb damage it had sustained, its position on the cliffs and the all-importance of its tumble-down roof terrace, the villa had a tendency to seem inside-out, upside-down and back-to-front. With a small bow to Signora Greco, Bradley limped up the steps to the hallway and wrenched open the front door. Beyond the arch of stooping pomegranate trees, in a glare of dusty light, stood a man with a submachine gun.

*　　*　　*

They had been billeted in the villa for two weeks now and after a shaky start with the locals that had seen their jeep stolen and stripped bare, they had thrashed out a kind of truce. Like everything else it revolved around food. Once they had demonstrated their bottomless reserves of K-ration cheese, chopped meat and cigarettes, the eggplants, tomatoes and fennel started appearing and it was now an established fact that Signora Greco kept the kitchen open – and the almond wine uncorked – all day, with all-comers welcome. The jeep was miraculously restored to full health and sat unmolested every night in the olive grove between the house and the road. Just as swiftly, Tom Cabot appeared, and his easy manner made him an instant hit with the townsfolk. Everyone from Nino's gang to the local priest would stop to chew the fat with Tom, even the older guys with their card games and their secrets. These rumours of forced DDT treatments on the island's coastal plains were unpleasant, *certo*, but such unfathomable American business could be left at the foot of the hill each evening. On the roof terrace, with a full stomach, playing 'donkey' and sipping *ficodindia* moonshine as the sun sank behind the Etna, such concerns were far away.

Which was just copacetic, given their real mission, which came down to food just the same. The food and other supplies that vanished from the docks at Naples and Salerno, Messina and Palermo, ninety percent of it, every ship. And the cause of that? It was marked nightly, on every wall, in the fresh death notices, the ass-backwards Hammer and Sickle and the outraged slogans – *MAFIA ASSASSINI!* Cabot the newsman had cut straight to the point: the shameful deal that Naval Intelligence had done with Luciano in New York, to get his capos over here to play ball for the invasion, never caring how it would become the island's future, to be dragged back into its racketeering past. Word was that Schaefer Senior had been one of the geniuses behind that stroke. Word was that Luciano was on his way home to the old country. So Junior was here ahead of him, working out of Army CIC in Naples and independent of the Naval Detachment at Palermo, to schmooze local dignitaries in the areas that had not yet been handed wholesale to the Mob.

Supposedly. And for Bradley, a soft posting while his knee and shoulder mended.

Supposedly. Seemingly not.

As he flung his weight against the door, he was conscious of three imperatives. That the gun firing had to be a different gun firing from a different position, or else he would have been perforated. That something had been tossed through the door as he closed and bolted it. That in all probability he had once again dislocated his shoulder.

A German stick grenade, skittering down the steps. In that instant of revelation he had frozen. In the next, Time did the same. Bradley reached the kitchen with a hop, skip and jump. As he overtook the grenade he vaulted the kitchen table feet-first, felling the astonished Cabot. He had just enough puff left to heave the table onto its side and bulldoze it forwards before

4

the thing detonated.

"Sonofabitch!"

Why did I ever come to Sicily, he thought – why didn't I…?

He shook his head and it felt like they'd clamped his brain in a vice. His ears were singing – and somebody wailing. Two people, Nino and Signora Greco.

Cradling his useless arm, he got to his knees. The table was in pieces, along with every bit of glass or crockery in the kitchen. He could hear tiles still falling, inside and out. He could smell olive oil and lamp oil mixed in with the burnt explosive. And something else, close by. Almond wine.

Tom Cabot was clawing at him, pointing at the stable door that led to the vegetable garden out back. At first Bradley thought the old war correspondent was proposing a swift retreat, and almost considered it, before noticing the boy and his mother huddled together in one of the wood storage holes at the side of the oven. Then he realised that the door had blown open and Cabot had spotted another intruder at the rear. It took two crouching strides to get to the range and the cast iron skillet the Signora had left in there, another two to reach the back door. The top half of the door was ajar. When the face appeared, Bradley ignored the pain in his dead arm and swung the other with all his might.

The results were impressive. It could only have been the oil and fat spilling onto the bottom of the skillet with the impact but the intruder's face didn't just flatten, it went up in smoke.

Again Bradley slammed the door and latched it. He knew better than to try for the guy's weapon. That kind of thinking was greedy. That was how you got your head blown off. And for the moment, and very belatedly, he needed his to think with.

He sat down again as the pain sapped the strength from his legs.

More gunfire from outside the front of the villa. Excited voices coordinating a further attack.

"Gotta get my shoulder back in," he said to Cabot.

—

5

"How do you do that?"

"Not me. You got to do it, Tom. I got to relax."

As he lay back on the debris he saw Cabot clamp down hard on his pipe-stem. He looked like he was trying not to sneeze.

"Relax. Sure, why the hell not?"

"Stretch my arm out to the side then kind of push it up and back behind my head, like a pitcher winding up. I might pass out for a while there, but you should feel it click back in alright."

"Which pitcher?" Cabot's strained voice and face were shrinking to nothing as the pain rolled over him.

"Uh... Carl Hubbell..."

"Knucklehead! Hubbell's a southpaw and this is your right arm. Under the circumstances, I'll make it 'Dizzy' Dean..."

When he tuned back in he was propped against the remains of the table with Cabot fashioning a sling from the tablecloth.

"Reckon you'll be able to move?"

"Reckon I'm gonna have to."

He wasn't here for his charm. He was here to ride shotgun for Schaefer on their trips down to Taormina and Catania. But his side arm and tommy gun were tucked away on top of the wardrobe in his bedroom, out of Nino's reach. He'd already found the kid making free use of his smokes and had no desire to see him with a .45.

Schaefer, the diplomat, had dressed for duty without a side arm, of course.

Bradley frowned.

"Where the hell is he?"

Cabot's nod indicated the way to the downstairs bedrooms.

"Scooted along there when that potato masher came down the steps. Jeez, I thought I was a goner!"

"You still are, probably. I think there's a whole bunch of them out there." Bradley had taken a couple of shaky steps towards the passage when three pistol shots rang out and the captain reappeared in the doorway.

"Someone breaking in through your bedroom window!"

"Did you get him?" That was Cabot, always wanting to know more. Bradley took one look at Schaefer's face and used his left hand to take his pistol instead. There was no resistance.

"Four rounds left?" He had to say it twice before Schaefer nodded. Bradley could understand him going for the pistol not the tommy gun but leaving behind the holster with the spare magazine pouch, even for an officer, was something else. Not that he'd be able to reload it or rack the slide one-handed. Nor hit anything with his left hand anyhow.

"What do you want us to do?" Cabot asked.

"Pile whatever you can over the back door and window. And find some knives." He couldn't think of a way to defend the front entrance. There was nothing to barricade the door up there and in any case the stairs from the roof terrace came down into the hallway. Better hope their assault on the front of the villa was confined to his bedroom.

He knelt where he could see both the steps and the passageway.

Just for a second, he shut his eyes again and felt his heart pounding. Just for a second he thought *Wish you were here.*

Out at the front, a machine gun opened up. His hearing was still scrambled but it sounded strident enough to be a German MG 42, firing wildly. The door he had slammed and bolted began to fly apart in chunks but they didn't have the angle to fire down into the kitchen so the only real danger would come from a ricochet.

The only real danger to *us* anyhow – he marvelled as the MG ripped through another belt without pausing.

The question was whether these jackasses were covering an assault or shooting up the place for the hell of it. And if it was an assault, had they switched entry points? Surely not even they would be fool enough to come down from the roof at the same time as blasting the hallway, although he'd be happy to watch them try.

There came a different-sounding bang from out front, which was either a different weapon being brought up or some kind of catastrophic malfunction in the overheated machine gun. Shrill cries suggested the latter.

Whatever had happened, it was the distraction he needed. He snuck up the two steps into the passageway and listened for movement as he approached the front bedroom. Nothing, only the shouting or wailing up top. He stuck his head around the doorjamb.

Two intruders. One sitting on the bed cradling a wounded arm, the other halfway through the heavy shutters with a finger to his lips, eyes comically wide. The window guy had a sawed-off scattergun so Bradley took him first, nearly missing despite the point blank range. He aimed more carefully for the other man's shirtfront and tore a flap off the top of his skull.

Tucking the pistol into his sling, he stepped onto the bed and tried to reach above the wardrobe for the Thompson and the rest of the ammo. No dice. The paralysis in his injured shoulder had crept around to the good one and try as he might he couldn't raise his arm without losing balance and nearly blacking out. In desperation he stuck a hand behind the wardrobe and heaved it over.

No-brains had toppled backward to spill his last onto the bedspread. Shit-for-brains was still draped over the windowsill, groaning. With a groan of his own, Bradley retrieved the gun, whacked the guy with the buttstock and went back out into the passage.

In the kitchen he let Schaefer take the pistol and reload it. He asked for Cabot's help to cock the Thompson.

Heavy breathing all round. Four ashen faces. The sound of cursing and clashing metal from up front was terrifying.

"It's gonna be OK now," he said.

Spooked though he was, at least Schaefer didn't do anything dumb like pull rank. Instead he and Cabot listened while Bradley told them how to defend the kitchen. As he spoke, Bradley found his gaze drawn by Nino's horrified expression. He tried to give him a reassuring wink.

"And where are you going?" Cabot wanted to know.

"Up there," Bradley indicated the hallway by the bullet-riddled front door, where the staircase ran up to the main bedrooms and the roof terrace. "Someone's got to finish this."

*   *   *

The others were just staring now. Tom Cabot, Captain Schaefer, Signora Greco, Nino. They were seeing someone as if for the first time, someone quite different from the injured, inward-turned man they had known. A stranger, a phenomenon.

Nino watched in wonder as Bradley prepared himself. From the way he turned his head and half-turned his body, from the way his eyes narrowed and swept the room, the boy could see he was thinking about his path up the kitchen steps, past the front door, and up the stairs to the roof landing. Planning it, picturing it. After a few seconds, grasping for the understanding of what he was watching, he saw Bradley go over to the bench alongside the flue. There was one of the Americans' miraculous cans, one of those drab green cans with the little key attached, with the biscuits and coffee powder and, wonder of wonders, the chocolate inside. They had been about to open it for breakfast, but now Bradley picked it up and turned it around, half-smiling. Then he wedged it between his body and the bench and reached for one of *mamma*'s cooking implements, a pasta-cutter Nino's father had made, so she said. In astonishment the boy watched Bradley force the cutting blades into the end of the green can. But if he wanted a piece of chocolate so badly (and Nino knew that one could feel like that) why hadn't he used the key?

The answer came as Bradley turned and stooped to hook his arm through the strap of his submachine gun. With its thick wooden handle and even the loop of cord on the end for hanging it on the wall, the thing in his hand looked exactly like the *crucco* stick grenade that had come through the front door all those endless minutes ago.

Crazy Americans, certainly. All this – the fact that it had

9

been bound to happen – confirmed that diagnosis. And one not-so-crazy American too.

And he was going, gone. Nino found he had unlatched himself from his mother's arms and crept halfway out of the hole to gaze after him. He knew now what Bradley's preparations had reminded him of. The priest and his attendants in the sacristy, robing for the procession. Tales of Saracens. And borne aloft, the statue of San Giorgio.

*   *   *

Bradley stood on the landing, hidden in the strong shadow from the hole in the rafters. From here he could tell that the rooms Cabot and Schaefer had been using as their bedrooms were shuttered and still. After a minute, hearing nothing from them, he decided that they were empty.

The roof terrace was a different matter. He could have sworn he'd heard voices – two voices, hissing urgent whispers at one another – from out there. Of course it might have been the neighbours, or a trick of the villa's erratic layout funnelling the sounds from below, but his instincts said no: two men, gunmen, covering the arch that led out onto the roof from two well-chosen positions several yards apart.

He knew which positions he would have chosen.

He knew which positions they had chosen.

What he needed was a real grenade, not a goddamned B unit. But it would have to do.

He closed his eyes. He exhaled. The next breath he took might be his last.

And then, like Cabot, he laughed inside at what he'd thought. What a crock. Not even Cabot would come up with something like that, not even Cabot's colleagues. Because even if both intruders plugged him the instant he swung out there, even if they got him in the head like the guy downstairs, even if they took his head *off*... still he'd take another breath, try to move his eyes and mouth, try to scream. That was what you remembered, what stuck with you in your nightmares. That was why you started shaking, and sweating, like this. And why you had to do it, right now, before your knees gave way, before you messed yourself, before you puked.

He found he had thrown the can of coffee and candy. He swung out into the sunlight. One man was rising from the jumble of stone pots and planters where the figs and tomatoes were ripening. He was wearing a cheap suit and a cap and carrying a Carcano rifle. A young man, not yet twenty. The uncontrolled hip-shot from the Thompson took him in the legs and backside and sent him tumbling over the uneven edge of the front porch roof.

The other man had gone to ground behind the rickety stone stack that half-supported the wrecked pergola of dried-up grapevines and bougainvillea. Bradley ducked back around the arch again and they took turns keeping each other's heads down until the Thompson's magazine was empty. He was reaching for the spare down the back of his waistband and wondering how the hell he was going to load it when his opponent threw aside his own submachine gun to make a bolt for the low parapet at the rear. Bradley hefted the Thompson like a club as he went after him but in the end, gritting his teeth, he simply charged him. The man yelled in terror as he tipped over into space, catching the edge of the outhouse roof with a familiar clatter of loose clay tiles but missing the *bastardoni* cactus that was the only real barrier there and tumbling off to land somewhere further down the mountain.

No sign of anyone else up here, nor on the adjacent balconies and rooftops. Although the sounds were coming back now, the sounds of women and children, dogs and roosters, the neighbours were smart enough to keep their heads down. Between the political unrest in the towns and the bandits in the hills it might be days before a force of Carabinieri was mustered to investigate. As for the attackers at ground-level, the tiles and timbers made this a poor vantage point but it seemed like they'd been routed. All he could detect from below was a sobbing and a sort of death rattle.

11

He went back downstairs, having to support himself on the walls. The shattered front door refused to budge until he tore it apart. In the shade of the cypresses and olive trees lay the young man who had fallen off the porch roof. It didn't take an anatomist to see that the fall had done something bad to his back. The death rattle was his. Although his eyes seemed to follow Bradley, the bullet wounds in his legs and buttocks were scarcely bleeding and the sound was the sound of him drowning now his body had lost its swallowing reflex.

"Look at you," Bradley said. "Look at you."

The other man was the one who was weeping. He sat propped against the low orchard wall, hands to his face, blood seeping between his fingers to stain his forearms and shirtsleeves. In front of him on the lava flagstones lay the machine gun, with the chamber fragged. Bradley guessed the missing pieces were in the gunner's eyes.

He limped back into the villa and descended the kitchen steps.

"It's OK, it's all..."

He stopped. Nobody looked at him. They were kneeling around Tom Cabot, who lay twisted on the floor. A bit like the boy up top, Bradley thought. Too much like the boy up top.

"Who got him?"

Then there was anger in Captain Schaefer's eyes. No, not anger. Hatred.

"His heart got him. We were all listening to you, up there, and he just..."

Nino too now. And his mother. The look on their faces said it, and anyhow it was a look Bradley knew from way back. They were siding with Tom Cabot, against him. Ordinary God-fearin' folk, who couldn't handle what had happened, rallying to one another against the one who could handle it, or so they thought. Already they distrusted and disliked him for being able to handle it. Soon they'd have it so he'd somehow caused it.

He knew better than to argue, or to join them around the

dead man, his victim. Instead he sidled to the back door and unlatched the top of it. Skillet-man lay in bad shape where he'd dropped, lightly flambéed. No one was sitting vigil over him.

He pushed his way out and skirted around to the front again. That was it. Either they had only been six or the others had fled.

Only six.

"Jesus!" he said to himself.

He was still fighting his pants pockets for his smokes and lighter when Schaefer came out and lit one for him.

"It was his imagination, I guess. Hearing you up on the roof, I mean. It was all too much for him."

Bradley shook his head.

"It was just his time."

"What do you mean?"

He shrugged and drew on the cigarette. He was feeling light-headed now.

"He hit the beach with us at Omaha." He spat then, as he always did. "Second assault wave. Never wrote about it, not like his buddies who came in later in the day."

"I didn't know."

"I knew him from back then. We got along OK."

"No, I mean I didn't know you were there... Holy shit, Bradley."

"Forget about it." He stopped short. That wasn't what Schaefer had been reacting to.

The captain was standing over the youth with the broken back. He looked stricken. Again.

"What is it?"

"Don Ciccio's eldest," Schaefer said. "Fuck it, we're gonna have to get out of here. Off this whole goddamn island."

Bradley nodded.

"Guess I can kiss goodbye to the welcome home parade in Jersey too."

Beyond the town's promontory, the terraced foothills fell away and faded, merging with the cloud that shrouded the volcano. Above the cloud, or between the cloud and the newly overcast heavens, they could see the snow at the summit. It would melt no further. Fall had come.

They turned and went back through the shattered door. Nino and his mother would need sending away pronto, with a little something for their troubles. Then there would be Tom Cabot to deal with.

For now nothing stirred beneath the umbrella of the cypress and the wizened wreath of red-flecked pomegranates. A lizard had frozen on a stone, tasting the air. Soon the last flies of the summer would be gathering.

The men who had set off up the mountain before daybreak had not been professional killers. It had been their misfortune to meet one who was.

CHAPTER TWO

The headlights glinted off muddy puddles and rain-slicked rubble. Obstacles appeared to slide into view as though carried by floodwaters. It was impossible to tell whether the shrouded figures were refugees or Russians. If they were roadblocks, one simply drove around them with a half-hearted wave. What, after all, was another jeep sloshing through the mud with its roof up and its sides sealed?

Soon after leaving the village on the Gleiwitz road they saw the lights of their objective. The lindens that were meant to screen the building had lost their leaves early and many more had been cut down for fuel. The brick monstrosity rising behind them looked thoroughly forbidding.

Built in the last century as an *Arbeitshaus*, for most of its life it had served as the region's lunatic asylum, but once the lunatics had started running things around here, it had acquired a different sort of inmate. The Nazis had used it as an internment camp, people said. And now, of course, the tables had been turned once more.

As they drew up at the guardhouse a floodlight was switched on and everything beyond the stippled windows became a blue-white glare that got inside your skull. Helmeted and trench-coated figures gathered round the jeep, affording occasional glimpses of posters and slogans that extolled the virtues of vigilance and vengeance in Russian, German and Polish. Papers flapped, so many papers, in envelopes and folders, on clipboards. Matches were cupped and lit, telephones cranked, torches shone through the windows.

Then they were through and driving up to the front door.

Mila Suková leaned forward and squeezed the driver's shoulder.

"Well done, Vojtěch," she said.

*　　*　　*

The commandant looked like he had just woken up. While his *ordinarets* rekindled the samovar on the sideboard he skipped back and forth behind his desk as though stamping his boots on or shaking off an attack of pins and needles. At length, the tea served, he sat back and gestured for his visitors to avail themselves of the well-worn armchairs.

"Your arrival here is most inconvenient."

The lingua franca, it appeared, was to be German. The obstructiveness was all Soviet.

Seated on Mila's right, the man who purported to be their liaison officer from General Tiulpanov's office let out a grim chuckle as if to say 'I told you so'. Disregarding him, she turned instead to the man in the RAF wing commander's uniform and translated the commandant's words into English. She herself was dressed as a member of the British Women's Auxiliary Air Force, or a passable approximation of it. Only Vojtěch, standing by the door with their luggage, looked like a common Ivan.

The wing commander was examining his hat in his lap and hardly glanced up.

"Well I'm sorry about that, old man, but we all have our orders, don't we?" As he waited for Mila to catch up, he nodded toward the papers on the commandant's desk which, Tiulpanov's man had insisted, gave comprehensive authorisation for their visit from the Allied Control Council. "So if it isn't too much trouble…"

The commandant had not removed his hat, nor introduced himself. Unlike the liaison officer's dark green rifles cap, his was the maroon-banded, blue-crowned cap of State Security. His name, they knew, was Major Anatoliy Dyachenko.

"You must understand," he said. "This is a special institution, what is called a *Schweigelager*."

"A silent camp," Mila said.

"*Das stimmt*. The internees have no contact with the outside. They have no legal status, no legal documentation."

"And yet you know who they are."

"Hostile elements," Dyachenko said. "Spies, saboteurs, Hitlerites, counter-revolutionaries."

"Steady on, old boy," the wing commander came dangerously close to laughing. "I meant you know which actual chaps you have – and you know you have our one, this, um…?"

Mila consulted her files as she translated.

"Lamprecht. Gustel. Officer of the National Socialist People's Welfare Organisation, Egerland, and subsequently attached to various SS Special Action Units at the Forest Camp Bobruisk, region Russland-Mitte. Alleged to have been involved in the mistreatment of Allied POWs during the evacuation of Stalag Luft VII, January this year."

"We have this person," Dyachenko said. "But your enquiries will be fruitless since they refuse to co-operate."

What skulked behind that smirk, Mila wondered. Had the prisoner in fact co-operated? Was the commandant suggesting that the methods to which he had recourse would produce co-operation in even the most recalcitrant of prisoners, where theirs would not? Or did he simply believe that tracing the fate of one's missing aircrew, as the RAF had been doing since the war's end, was a sentimental indulgence of the petty bourgeoisie?

She found her eyes drawn by the poster behind his desk, which showed a heroic partisan bestriding a degenerate homunculus. In Polish (for Silesia was no longer German, even if its surviving populace might be) it read *The Giant and the dwarf of reactionism*. The dwarf being the Home Army which in resisting Nazism had dared to dream of an independent Poland.

No indeed, there was no place for sentiment here.

She began to rise and the wing commander was on his feet before her.

"Well, you never know, we may strike it lucky." From beneath the RAF moustache he flashed the commandant a smile and added: "Softly, softly, catchee monkey!"

Mila's German translation stumbled to a halt and the commandant raised an enquiring eyebrow. She felt herself begin to blush.

Fortunately it seemed their liaison officer spoke both languages idiomatically and with a sweeping bow that both apologised for the intrusion and scooped up their papers from the desk he drawled something suitably offhand about spit and mosquitoes, once in German for general consumption and once, fraternally, in Russian.

"I will have the prisoner brought to the gymnasium." The commandant regarded each of them without expression and shrugged. "You may conduct your interrogation there."

* * *

Major Dyachenko's deputy, a marginally less discourteous senior lieutenant named Golovatenko, had so far led them a merry dance through the darkened building. Giving his boss time to locate Lamprecht and bellow out a few fresh questions of his own, Mila surmised. She could only hope that he wasn't also reminding his prisoner to dummy up. At every doorway and every turn their cases knocked against railings and radiators, chains and padlocks tolled and footsteps echoed relentlessly from the marble floors, but not a sound came from the five storeys of wards and cells and washrooms.

A *Schweigelager* indeed. Silent as the settlements hereabouts, their German-speaking populations rounded up and expelled. Silent as those same folk had kept themselves on *Kristallnacht*, or when the asylum had been liquidated to make way for the internees, or in the face of further abominations. Silent, now, as the Soviet monolith itself, on the matter of whether it had appropriated merely the fabric of the Nazi camp system or its function.

And from this great absence she expected to draw out a single voice? Forcing herself to march ever deeper into the maze of freezing corridors and stairwells, she could not help but shudder. It was more likely that tonight she and her group would be swallowed up and silenced too.

And yet...

"It's the great paradox isn't it?" Stas, overloud and halfway plastered, had scoffed earlier this evening at the run-through.

In the back of the farm truck, the rest of the MERCURY network had rolled their eyes or cursed beneath their breath. Their coach and mentor, the author of this crazy stratagem, had decided that he couldn't handle it sober *and he wasn't even going on the mission.*

"What is, Stas?"

Stanislav Hrstka had been a theatre director for long enough before the war to recognise the impatient authority in her tone.

"I'm sorry. The irresistible force meeting the immovable object. The existence of the one disproves the existence of the other."

"The Soviet internal security apparatus is the immovable object?"

"Unless you, Slečna Slavík, are the irresistible force."

"And there's only one way to find out..."

"That, Miss Nightingale, is the reality of this paradox. And of mine."

"Yours?"

He'd met her eye and almost held it. A shrug. Another slug of wormwood vodka.

His shaking hand upon the candlelit script.

"The more afraid you are, the more there is to fear."

Yes indeed, Mila thought, recalling how she herself had nearly surrendered to the suffocating weight of that logic and remembering the man who had helped her to get out from under it. A different kind of mentor – an equal, and a fellow victim. I wish he could have helped you too, Stas, because that irresistible force of yours is eating you up every bit as fast as your wormwood and I can't allow it to spread to the others.

But that was for an increasingly hypothetical future. Right now she had another part to play.

Golovatenko's grumbling escorts had come to attention either side of a set of double doors. The senior lieutenant disappeared inside and re-emerged with another warder in tow.

"The prisoner is present. You may begin your interrogation."

Mila bumped the wing commander's leg with the case she was carrying. When he remembered his lines, she spoke over him as swiftly as she dared. Emil might have spent a year as a waiter at the Savoy in London, but his act was unlikely to fool anyone who had met a genuine Englishman.

"Now see here, old chap, I think we'll have a better chance of getting the prisoner to open up if they don't see you bring us in. What d'you say, eh?"

"As you wish. My men will guard the door. Let them know when you have concluded your business."

"Splendid! And you have seated this Lamprecht character facing away from the doors as we discussed, yes – to work on the nerves?"

Golovatenko's look was plain. We aren't beginners at this.

"Jolly decent of you. Couldn't ask for anything more!"

As Vojtěch, burdened with the other cases, opened the first door for the two 'officers', Mila was relieved to see that beyond lay a small antechamber. Perhaps it had been used as a cloakroom, or for selling tickets. Above the second set of doors the Cyrillic for 'Gymnasium' was stencilled over an older sign, in English, for 'Library', and either side of that spread the scar tissue of scraped-off playbills. Evidence of long-forgotten Smoking Concerts and the Christmas pantomime, *Cinderella*. Relics of the wartime internees and the need to 'keep your pecker up'. Vestiges of civilisation, snatched from the Abyss.

Easing shut the first doors, one finger raised in warning, she whispered: "Go."

While Miro, as Captain Khasin, handed out the props, the others quickly changed costumes: Emil reversing his blue trench coat and donning an NKVD cap like Dyachenko's, Vojtěch promoting himself from driver to Starshina – easy enough, even in these post-Bolshevik days, with the addition of different collar-tabs – and Mila swapping her RAF hat for a jaunty *pilotka*. None of it would stand scrutiny, but as Stas had impressed upon them this was the garnish. The *performance* was what mattered.

At her nod, Vojtěch let the doors crash open. Mila flinched.

On an upright chair at the centre of the dim-lit space, in threadbare plaid box coat, filthy prison shift and woollen stockings, sat her last hope of ever finding her son.

*   *   *

Gustel Lamprecht had also flinched. She knew why this hall was termed the gymnasium, and how the prison guards got their exercise in here. Now she pulled herself up as rigidly as she was able in her half-starved, half-frozen state and tried not to let her eyes follow the Russians as they set themselves up for her interrogation.

First a long trestle table was found and positioned in front of her, then three chairs, like hers, into which the three men settled with much rearranging of holster belts, caps, cigarettes and ashtrays. Finally the woman erected a folding stool and perched herself at the end of the table, placing some kind of portable typewriter on her lap.

No – despite herself, her eyes were drawn to it – not a typewriter. A stenograph.

Her tired old heart began to pound. Even in this cold, bare room, with the remnants of a storm battering against the shutters, she felt her sunken cheeks prickle. This wasn't another interrogation. This was her trial.

The fellow in the centre was ostensibly a major from their State Security, but whoever he really was, that proud moustache of his marked him out as one of the Party faithful. The other two prosecutors might be the military officers they seemed or they might not. Unlike those plodders in the Gestapo, these Soviet secret police were never quite what they said. But when they composed themselves into one of their confounded troikas like this, there was no doubt they held your life in their hands.

And the woman in the leather flying jacket on the end? Here to provide a semblance of legal process? Or to record the sentence of the supreme degree of punishment, to be carried out immediately?

The non-commissioned officer, if that was what he was, began reading from a file.

"Lamprecht, Gustel. Your membership of the NSDAP and NSV is on record – both proscribed organisations under Order 00315."

She met the chairman's eye.

"Like millions of others," she said.

"...and so detained in complete isolation under the special regulations, namely no contact with other prisoners, no outside work details, no notification of next of kin, not even in case of death."

The major returned her gaze.

"Like millions of others," he said.

The one in the captain's uniform addressed her in surprisingly fluent German.

"Fraulein Lamprecht – Gustel, if I may – this special commission isn't concerned with punishing Nazis for obeying their orders. We know how mixed-up everything got at Bobruisk, with the partisans and the Sonderkommandos and everything. We're just trying to piece together what happened in the Central Russian territory – to the kids."

"The kids?"

Now the captain, too, pretended to refer to his files.

"Oh, I'm sorry. I thought we were taking it as read that you were one of the 'Brown Sisters' assigned to kidnapping and resettling Aryan-looking children." He flung out his hands and seized one of hers, tearing apart the fingerless mittens to twist her finger under the light. "You never married, did you Gustel, and of course any jewellery you might have had would be long gone in here, but here's where you wore a signet ring for many years. That would be the *NS-Schwesternschaft* monogram, no?"

She pulled her hands free and placed them in her lap to stop them shaking. On an impulse she lowered her head and half-closed her eyes.

"Hände falten, Köpfchen senken – immer an den Führer denken."

"What's that?" she heard the chairman demand in some disgusting Slavic tongue.

"I believe it was the motto in their children's centres and in the *Lebensborn* of course. 'Hands folded, heads down – always thinking of Adolf Hitler'."

"What a charmer. But did you notice how she twitched at the word 'Lebensborn'? Ask her about that."

Cursing inside, she raised her head again.

"The 'Spring of Life' was a family welfare programme, an example of what everyone chooses to forget. The Nazi Party was committed to unity and fairness."

"The Lebensborn was founded by Himmler, for SS members and their families..."

"But also there were places in the maternity homes for unmarried mothers, to remove the stigma and reduce abortion rates."

"And so maximise pure racial stock."

"Of course. But to give those little children the chance of a better, healthier life."

"Growing up to be dutiful Nazi soldiers and Nazi mothers."

"I would not expect you to see the value in that."

The major laughed. The captain gave his mirthless smile.

"But you ran out of *Volk* to foster, didn't you? You had to spread the net wider. Germanisation."

"*Re*-Germanisation," she said.

"Finding kids with blue eyes or blonde hair, snatching them

away from their families – *killing* the families if they protested – and farming them out to childless German couples through the Lebensborn homes. Does that sound about right?"

"All I did was to look after the children's welfare," she said, which was almost true, in the narrowest of senses.

"What about the kids who didn't pass the tests for racial suitability?"

"I wouldn't know about that."

And no, I really wouldn't, she thought.

"What about the kids from Czechoslovakia?"

That threw her for a moment. Why would the Soviets or the Poles be interested in them? Then she realised what they were talking about.

"I believe that after the village of Lidice was liquidated, the surviving children were assessed by the SS Race and Settlement Main Office and a small number went into the Lebensborn. I wasn't involved in that."

"What happened to the others?"

"To my knowledge, they were not saved."

"They died in the gas vans at Kulmhof, Fraulein."

"As I say, I was not involved in that. My concern was always children's welfare..."

"You remember, though, who arranged for Czech children to enter the programme – not just the Lidice children but in general."

"Yes, I..."

It was quite by chance, but in that moment she found her gaze drawn to the young woman at the end of the table. Something had attracted her attention, she supposed, a flash of eyes (most unusual for a stenographer) or a sharp intake of breath. But it was enough.

"I see," Lamprecht said.

"What do you see, Fraulein?"

The flashing eyes, the furious eyes, met hers. The voice, when it came, was low and level, and in a Slavic language quite distinct from Russian.

Czech.

"Us, Emil. She sees us."

In an instant the woman was on her feet and before the toppled stool had finished clattering across the polished wooden floor there was an automatic pistol pointed at her head.

"Not another word," the woman said. "Not another sound, until you give us the name we want."

Lamprecht found that she had risen to a half-crouch, half-expecting this moment to be her last. Fighting her nerves – furious herself – she settled back onto the seat and smiled.

The woman also sat, although you wouldn't call it settling. She was like an animal, a predator.

"We saw Doctor Stransky," she said in German. "He couldn't give us the name of the high-ranking official who took Czech children in late '44, but he gave us three former colleagues who would know. You're the last on our list."

"I know who you are," Lamprecht said.

Funny, the little, unimportant details one remembered – details that might just save your life.

But not by talking. Not like that.

"You're looking for the professor's boy, yes? Professor... Lossner? Stransky said he came to him about a year ago, asking him to take his son off his hands. I remember wondering what kind of mother the boy must have had, to leave this great professor looking after him when he was so busy with the war effort. A real *Schlampe*."

A white scar on the woman's prominent cheekbone became more noticeable as her face flushed, but the white knuckle on the trigger told Lamprecht all she needed to know for now. She let herself relax.

"Stransky hadn't any contacts in the RuSHA or the Lebensborn – at least he didn't think he had – so he referred the professor to a few people who did. One of whom gave him a name. The name you're now asking me to provide for you."

"*Asking?* Jesus!" the one called Emil said.

The woman rose again and leaned across to force the muzzle of her pistol against Lamprecht's brow. Painfully. Pathetically.

"Give us the name and we'll have a word with the commandant," the younger man in the NCO's uniform was almost pleading. "We'll get you fair treatment."

"Get a letter to your family," the so-called captain added.

But the short-haired woman in the leather jacket only groaned.

"No we won't, and she knows we can't. She knows we've bluffed our way in here."

"Then she also knows that we have to kill her anyway."

The woman pushed Emil aside and took his place opposite.

"No, she's thought of that. While she knows the name, I have to leave her alive."

"Then what's to stop her blowing our cover the moment we leave this room?"

The reddened face was close. With that short, spiky hair and those broad, peasant features, she was like an animal all right, scenting for fear.

"Nothing, except this. We were allowed to interrogate her, even at this late hour, because as we know, she's scheduled to be shot at dawn. This was Major Dyachenko's last crack at her, as well as ours." The grey-blue cat's eyes were searching Lamprecht's face for something and, perhaps, they located it. "If she raises the alarm, we face the wall next to her, but if she doesn't, well, there's a chance we might find a way to spring her – or at least persuade the major to stay the execution."

Lamprecht discovered she had forgotten how to breathe. Trying to hide it left her heart thundering.

"Trust each other?" she said through gritted teeth.

For all her fierceness the woman looked ready to vomit too. "Yes."

They stared for a long time, perhaps like lovers. That wasn't Lamprecht's area of expertise. Then the fair-haired woman gave a last, desperate gasp:

"So tell me the name..."

But Lamprecht had already decided to say nothing more. Nothing except the thing that made the fair-haired woman let out a tearful squeak, and jab her lowered brow with the gun again, and almost pull the trigger.

Almost.

"Hände falten, Köpfchen senken – immer an den Führer denken."

*　　*　　*

Stanislav Hrstka, like many in his profession, was more of a talker than a listener. Without something fresh or compelling to engage his interest, or at least to create a certain tension, he tended to drift off. Casting calls had never been his strong suit.

So, not the best man to mind the base and monitor the telephone intercept, he had to admit, but with everyone else out on the mission or lurking damply if indefatigably beneath the mouldering forest floor like Krkonoš himself, the best available.

He came to his senses at the sound of their jeep struggling off the waterlogged farm track into the stand of birch. A quick glance around told him that both the truck and the extra telephone wire were still well camouflaged, that the bottle of *Babička* appeared convincingly untouched and that with any luck no one would guess he'd been asleep.

As the jeep slid to a halt he was taking off the headphones and waving brightly from the wings.

"Success?"

Miss Nightingale's face said otherwise. Her frosty stare went from his stupid smile to the bottle on the flatbed and back again.

"Nothing here either?"

Hrstka opened his mouth to reply and dried.

Had they said anything on the phone line? Almost certainly not. But could he be certain? No. So much of the Russian was so different from Czech that even a name might have passed him by. Added to which, lulled by the diminishing rain, he had nodded off more than once. Like St. Peter and the others in Beethoven's oratorio, or in the stained glass of the Vysehrad Basilica, in this dismal Gethsemane he had slept.

He shook his head.

The outlying sentries – Dušan of the fearsome stammer and that true *Leší* wildman, 'Uncle' Ludvík – had emerged from their hides with their wrapped-up rifles, still covered in stringy bark and rotting leaves. The others were clambering into the truck and shrugging out of their costumes. Dušan's brother Emil peeled off his moustache.

"It wasn't your fault, Stas. The Reds were convinced. But that witch back there... somehow she knew."

Hrstka raised his eyebrows. It was all he could do not to grab the *Babička* there and then.

"No, it's OK. Miss Nightingale couldn't put a bullet in her head but she spun her a line about getting shot at dawn to keep her quiet," Miro clapped him on the shoulder and squinted around in the misty half-light. "I'd say Fraulein Lamprecht ought to be feeling pretty nervous round about now."

"A fat lot of good that does for us!" Vojtěch kicked at the side of the truck.

Miss Nightingale, meanwhile, had slipped out of the sheepskin coat and military jacket. Suddenly she looked so small and slight. Beaten, Hrstka might have said from her posture, if he hadn't known her better.

"I suppose when it doesn't happen she might say something. Plus I forgot to pick up that stool and probably left a dozen other bits of evidence behind. We had better get going for the border..."

But he had found his voice at last. And – the faintest chance, he thought – something else.

"Wait, Miss Nightingale... Mila."

"What is it, Stas? Another paradox? No, no, don't tell me. In having to do what it takes, I couldn't do what it takes?"

"This isn't your paradox, this is mine."

With frankly stagey bravado, he began to rummage through

and toss aside the other gear in the crates, the things they'd got from kids in ruined buildings and a dozen other low-level black marketeers like themselves. Some were props from their previous productions.

Retrieving one of the Soviet officer's caps, he picked out a brass-tipped cane and a pair of taupe kid gloves.

And the bottle of *Babička*. Because I know myself, he thought. But also because this cup cannot pass.

"Sometimes you just have to go again," he addressed the assembled company with a grin. "Would it be alright if I borrowed the jeep?"

CHAPTER THREE

They had slung a sign across the short flight of wooden steps that led to the uppermost level of the observation deck. NO ACCESS.

Checking that none of the scattered tourists, lovers or sailors were looking in his direction, which of course they weren't, Bradley swung a stiff leg over the chain. The platform above was something of a construction site. Three maintenance men in denim overalls were fixing heavy-duty cables to a complex geometry of directional antennas that had been mounted to a ventilator outlet on the top of the elevator shaft, giving the building's elegant roof terrace, which was evidently designed to resemble an ocean liner, the ugly flying bridge of a warship.

A genial voice cut through the wind.

"Welcome aboard. Apologies for the mess. A few modifications, strictly for the Weather Bureau you understand."

Bradley held onto his hat with one hand, offering the other. "Doyle?"

"And you must be the estimable ex-Sergeant Bradley. What do you think of the view?"

Bradley shuffled past the workmen and went to the railing. From this corner of the platform he could see most of Manhattan, Central Park ablaze with colour to the north and the great spire of the Empire State Building silhouetted against the late afternoon murk downtown. That was where all the other sightseers were looking.

Westward along the prow of the rooftop, squinting out over a smoky Hell's Kitchen, he could see the piers, the Hudson and New Jersey. Home.

The last time he'd been in the city, before shipping out for North Africa three long years ago, there had been the enormous French liner on its side at Pier 88. That had been Luciano's handiwork as well, Schaefer said: a surefire way of springing himself from Sing Sing in return for no more 'enemy' sabotage on the waterfront. Which had been the genesis of the Sicily sell-out, and hence the reason Bradley couldn't have lit out for Hoboken if he'd wanted to.

"Helluva town," he said.

Doyle was also clamping down on his fedora against the gusts. He indicated a pair of Adirondack chairs that were set up facing opposite directions in the style of a courting bench.

Bradley sat and turned up his coat collar. The R.C.A. building might only be meant to suggest a liner, but the wind and moisture and the vertiginous height of the place were bringing back the last couple of weeks on the troopship. The ABs had scoffed how it was fair weather and it would have been three or four weeks had they still had to keep pace with the slowest ship, and zigzag, but it had been enough to leave him feeling simultaneously cramped and dangerously exposed. Permanently damp and chilled, which played havoc with his knee and shoulder. In no mood for any more bull.

So by the time Doyle had gone through the hoopla of lighting his pipe, Bradley was ready to throw him 70 floors down to West 49th Street.

Then the man's demeanour changed so completely it was as though a metamorphosis had taken place. Even the voice lost most of its Britishness.

"Fellas," he said.

The word was flat and emphatic. Although he'd barely raised his volume or glanced in their direction, two of the maintenance men packed up their tools and went unobtrusively to stand watch.

"A bit of background," Doyle began. "Several months ago, a Russian colonel took the rap for one of his boss's sideshows, a failed attempt to provoke a western incursion into newly liberated Czechoslovakia and justify continued Soviet occupation of the country. He was packed off to the Gulag, presumably to his death. Shortly afterwards, possibly as a direct result, the relevant directorate of the organisation he represented, commonly known as SMERSh, was quietly disbanded."

Bradley said nothing, but he was no longer looking at the view.

"I'm bringing this up for two reasons. First – and I don't expect you to confirm or deny it – I understand you may have had a part to play in the demise of this officer."

"What's the second reason?"

"I thought you'd be curious about that. Well, here's the funny thing. Last month, the same Soviet officer marched into one of the NKVD's secret camps in Upper Silesia and extracted information about a Nazi prisoner, under false pretences. Twice, possibly. The Reds aren't being any more specific but they're mad as hell and it's a huge international embarrassment."

"International?"

"Mmm. The conman – conmen rather – come from a former British-sponsored underground network."

"The con*men*..."

"Well, yes – and women. Or woman. Which rather brings me to the point of this meeting."

"I'll bet it does."

"We want you to go and get her. After all, you've done it before."

"Get her?"

"Bring her back. Shut her down. At the very least, find out what the hell she thinks she's up to grilling Nazis, so we can stop her stepping on any more sensitive toes. There are places in Europe where the western allies and the Soviets get along just fine – but others that are the proverbial powder keg."

"And who's 'we'?"

Doyle laughed.

"Isn't that the 64-dollar question?"

"You mean Take It Or Leave It."

"I mean nothing's quite as simple as Us and Them, not any more. Perhaps it never was."

Doyle might have finished fussing with his pipe, but it seemed he had a new amusement now and Bradley wasn't in the mood to play along. He made to get up.

"Want to hear my funny story? I put in for a transfer and instead I'm landed with an honourable discharge and passage back to the States. The ticket comes with travelling expenses, couple of days' board at the McAlpin and an invitation to meet a Mr Doyle on the R.C.A. Sky View – about a job, I reckon. Well, nice meeting you and thanks for the soft soap routine. Guess I'll have to keep looking for that job."

"You might find one, if you're lucky, and if you can make yourself stand out among ten million others in your situation, most of them rather more able-bodied. But it won't be the job you want."

"You got about five seconds, mister..."

"We're the good guys, Bradley. At least we're trying to be." Doyle spread his hands in a gesture of helplessness, or an imitation of it. "I'm a Brit, kind of. Irish, but posh as pudding. That's back home. Over here, folks seem to think I'm a genuine son of the soil."

"So you've been here awhile..."

It was the kind of taunt guys from the front reserved for guys from the rear, but Doyle wasn't biting. He simply nodded.

"Uh-huh. Start of the war, we established something called 'BSC', British Security Co-ordination, right downstairs in Radio City. Those were the days. A bit of running down Nazi sympathisers and dropping them in the East River. Some ever-so-subtly persuading America to up its war effort or even to come in on our side, which of course you did, eventually.

Along the way, we helped you set up some of your secret agencies and dirty tricks departments. Now we're helping you manage the institutional preservation of your clandestine capability, as I believe the current parlance has it."

"Preserving... OSS?"

"Much like SMERSh, and of course just like BSC itself, that's been quietly disbanded too. But there are elements that right-minded people don't want to see go to waste and need to be consolidated elsewhere. Again, much like SMERSh, I'm sure."

"Here in New York?"

"There are compelling reasons not to do all of this in D.C., if we actually want to get things done. That goes for the British side as well. Especially the British side. One of those reasons goes by the name of J. Edgar, the other, Joseph Vissarionovich."

Hoover and Stalin. Two men who'd certainly be motivated to stymie the development of a peacetime American spy agency. If any of it was true, of course.

"But why you and your 'right-minded' people? Why isn't this coming from full-blown British Intelligence, back in London? They ran her, during the war, and they're the ones she really stands to embarrass. She's still married to the former head of that department, for God's sake."

Doyle pulled a sympathetic face.

"In name, perhaps. But we're pretty sure it was a marriage of convenience. Anyhow, we can't ask Smith about it. He's long gone, vanished from the map. As for that organisation of his, let's say it's not just at the cocktail parties down in Georgetown that the jolly old Brits and Uncle Joe's boys have got a shade too close for comfort."

Bradley shook his head in a mixture of disgust and resignation. Already Doyle reminded him of a couple of other guys he had known.

"OK, dammit," he said, thinking back to that 64-dollar question and trying to drum out the nagging voice in his head, the voice of experience, that chanted like the Take It Or Leave It audience *You'll be SORR-REEEE!* "I'll take it."

"We thought you would, Bradley. Isn't it why you badgered your pal at USFET to reassign you to something murky, in the hope you'd be able to get on her trail again?"

Wally Sloane, I might have known, he said to himself. He had no doubt that the 'State Department' representative with the outsized office in Frankfurt's U.S. Forces European Theatre building had been in cahoots with the OSS, if not an active member.

"Sure, only I got the Mob after me instead. And you guys. Don't know which is worse."

"Well, this will keep you out of their clutches if nothing else. And you'll have the full support of whatever the Strategic Services bureau happens to be called this week."

"What's my cover?"

"That's the thing. We've no idea where MERCURY will next pop up. Upper Silesia is Polish now, and well under Soviet influence, but she has likely crossed back into Czechoslovakia, which as you know is one of those more volatile regions. If she's after Nazis, in hiding or otherwise, she may well move into Germany, but which zone – ours, yours or theirs? No good posing as OMGUS if she's going to turn up in Hamburg, or as one of your psych chaps setting up *Die Welt* when she's really after someone in Leipzig."

Bradley had no idea what 'The World' meant in this context but he got the general idea. Too many occupying powers with their own brands of military government. Too many zones and borders. Too many possibilities. He wondered why Doyle hadn't asked him what he thought the MERCURY network was looking for. And whether he'd have told him if he had.

"A roving reporter sprang to mind. Like your pal Cabot – my condolences, incidentally. That kind of stunt works a treat in the pulps, but we've found out the hard way you can't just drop a new face in among a bunch of horribly inquisitive and distrustful people, all of whom know each other, most of whom are sleeping with each other, and expect not to arouse their curiosity. So we thought we'd better make you some kind of Nazi-hunter too."

Bradley's sense of nausea increased. It was the motion sickness you got from the long, inescapable slide to inevitability.

"What kind of Nazi-hunter would that be?"

"The kind you've been before, Bradley, when you were a squad leader in one of the platoons attached to Project OVERCAST, sniffing out their rocket scientists and technicians. That operation is still live, it so happens, and about to enter its second phase, codenamed PAPERCLIP. The whole of Occupied Europe is about to be flooded with well-meaning flatfoots from your old buddies the U.S. Army Counter Intelligence Corps, all chasing their own tails and turning over rocks to find another Wernher von Braun – or indeed another Professor Lossner. Many will have their own cover stories of course, but what should help our cause is that they'll be slapdash at best. This is Military Intelligence we're talking about."

"So if anyone sees through my first disguise they'll assume I'm running rats."

"And you'll have a shiny gold Special Agent's badge to flash if you run into trouble. It's better than last time, when Smith's chaps crashed you in on a wing and a prayer. I mean – you were in UNRRA fatigues, skulking around hiding from the real UNRRA teams – I'm amazed you weren't captured and turned." Doyle raised his gaze to the darkening sky as if the thought had only just occurred to him. "You weren't, were you, Bradley? I gather she turned your head, this girl. Didn't turn anything else while she was about it?"

"My stomach. When she let on how all you people operate."

"Well, that's touching. When this is over the two of you can join a Friends' Ambulance unit. In fact, that might work as a first-level cover story… I'm joking. There's a whole envelope of identities waiting for you downstairs."

"What?"

"Floor 36. Go to the British Passport Control Office and give your name at the desk. There's also a ticket for tomorrow morning's flight to Lisbon from the LaGuardia Marine Air Terminal."

Despite himself, Bradley had to laugh. The thing about the long slide, the thing that let you cope with the dread of its inescapable outcome, was that wrapped up in the motion sickness was something else. Exhilaration.

In its way it was almost a substitute for hope.

"No rest for the wicked, huh? Say, you might have brought those documents with you – saved me some time for my last night in New York City."

As they got to their feet, Doyle squeezed Bradley's arm and grinned.

"But how would I prove to you then that we're really on the side of the angels?"

*   *   *

Once Bradley had descended to the setback observation decks and the elevators, Doyle quit the platform and ambled to the 70th floor's south-facing perimeter. Although increasing numbers of sightseers were gathering for the sunset spectacle, most had opted for the more accommodating deck below, where the viewing telescopes were mounted. He found a gap, knocked out his pipe on the limestone baluster, and waited.

When the third maintenance man, the one who wasn't any kind of maintenance man, joined him at the railing, Doyle's focus never wavered from the famous vista.

"He's on his way. I've done what I can."

The man bumped his shoulder, accidentally or otherwise. The voice was guttural but educated, American, but with strong traces of another, older accent.

"You have done us a great service."

As the last squall of the sinking sun shimmered across the windows of midtown, Doyle half-registered the heavy horn-rim eyeglasses and homburg at his side. A real workman would have worn a newsie or a trilby. Then his attention was diverted, as was everyone's, by the lights coming up on the Empire State Building. Not all at once, but in an unstoppable sequence that bespoke the march of American greatness as nothing else could, Manhattan clawed itself out of an unpromising fall day to become the *Novum Caput Mundi*.

"Based on what I could see and hear of your meeting, he seemed a good choice," Berman said at last.

"He's capable. I'm sure the physical problems won't hold him back..."

"No. His attitude, I mean. Cynical, but one of Nature's innocents at heart."

"If you'd seen his file, you wouldn't call him innocent."

"I have seen his file." Berman said. "What I have not seen is yours."

Doyle almost laughed along with him. Then he realised it wasn't a joke.

"There have to be limits, Berman. Even to this."

"Does he know what MERCURY is looking for?"

"I imagine so, but I didn't want him to know that we knew."

"...and who it is we think her quest will lead her to?"

"How could he? Despite what we think she found out in Silesia, she may not even understand the significance herself."

"Well, if the individual she is looking for turns out to be the one that we are looking for – and if your Mr Bradley tracks her down in time – you will have a man on the spot."

"Even if we have had to paint a target on his back."

"He doesn't suspect?"

"I'm sure he'll have time on the plane to wonder why he was dragged halfway round the world only to be sent straight back again, but he'll assume it's just the way we launch a new cover story, not that we're pretty certain he'll be watched from the outset."

"Speaking of which..." Casually, Berman's gloved hand detached from the rail to point out an unaccompanied figure on the deck below. Some of the other sightseers appeared solitary too. That businessman, stunned by his latest balance sheet, perhaps. That woman in the fur-trimmed plum, taking stock before her evening's work commenced. But only this one had turned away from the view.

"Red?" Berman sounded as though he were clearing his throat.

"Or worse than that," Doyle hissed.

He stepped back from the edge and gestured for his men to cut the target off. The danger was they'd lose their mark in the subdued light and the general drift towards the elevators. But before he could formulate a better plan of action he was aware of Berman's sudden, surprising absence.

By the time he'd made it down to the 69th and negotiated the flowerbeds, he could see that his erstwhile companion in the incongruous homburg was moving purposefully – no, unstoppably – toward the target. Whatever Mosaic look of determination he wore in addition to the semi-official overalls, it was enough to cause the crowds to part like water. Through breaking waves of scarves and feathers, sailor's flaps and dixie cups, Doyle saw that the mark had spotted him too. A hand plunged beneath the breast of the oversized overcoat. Fright twisted the man's thin features, then...

A bosomy secretary, lording it over her new recruits, blocking his way.

A stolen glimpse of Berman in silhouette, his gloved hands slamming the fellow's head against the cast metal panels beyond the railings.

Two businessmen, turning at the sound.

A gaggle of returning servicemen, fresh off the boat and three sheets to the wind.

Doyle was trying to get his bearings as he shouldered through. The railings there would be pretty much exactly at the spot where daring visitors discovered they could gaze straight down between the 68th and 67th floor setbacks. All the way down. But that was during daytime. Anyone peering over now would be staring right into the uplights.

He cleared the crowd. Berman was bending to pick up his hat. The other two maintenance men came to a disorganised stop and spun around, confused.

The target was nowhere to be seen.

"Jesus Christ!" Doyle exhaled.

Berman peeled off his gloves. Gingerly, Doyle thought.

"Undoubtedly Red – or worse, as you said. What did you mean? The Nazis?"

Doyle had to shut his eyes and take several deep breaths. The world spun a little, but it was time to get moving.

The four men made for the welcoming radiance of the elevators, sidestepping a few perplexed onlookers.

"They are not sure what they saw or even if they saw it..." Berman was panting as they went. "Lights were coming on, shadows leaping around... *Gey gezunt* – we want him followed but not yet, by God! What did you mean by worse than the Reds?"

Doyle cursed under his breath and kept his head down as he walked.

"Worse *politically* speaking, that's what I meant. For us and our ambitions in Washington. For you and your hopes for your country."

"Eh? What the hell are you talking about?"

"You might have really gone and done it now, Berman. I meant the FBI."

CHAPTER FOUR

Bad weather hung like a guilty conscience above the old kingdom of Hanover. A windswept frost had clung all day to the bare fields and empty roads and the few figures in the ruined towns were shrouded in coats and scarves and blankets, but so far this was not the bitter winter that everybody feared.

Tossed up and down by the shifty Nazi air, Jack Penny had retreated into his own dormant memories. He wasn't in this rickety box kite at all, he was handcuffed in the back of the Black Maria as it sped through Stepney, spouting from his bonce where they'd cracked it open with their truncheons on the bloodstained cobbles of Cable Street.

But he and his oppos had given the bloomin' Blackshirts a proper hiding too, not to mention the filthy rozzers who'd been ordered to protect them. They had sent their message loud and clear. No fascist would ever prance intact through the East End of London. Not an English toff with his band of cross-eyed mugs, nor Spics nor Krauts nor any other blasted sort. The Ikeys of *Vaytshepl* had seen to that. With a few Bolshies mixed in and, he acknowledged grudgingly, the bloody Micks.

Even now, half asleep, with the street battles of '36 all but forgotten – and half the streets wiped from the map – he chuckled to recall the carrot-topped Lancelot who'd come to his deliverance with a hatstand from the window display of Gardiner's department store. Without him to distract the rozzers from the pasting they were dishing out, Penny would have been brown bread, like the poor Paddy was shortly after.

41

Shame they weren't all so open hearted.

Thoughts of his present business partner brought him to his senses and left a taste in his mouth that was quite distinct from airsickness. Partner? That was one way of looking at it, Penny's way, or at least it had been when he'd first made the mistake of joining forces. The other way of seeing it, Jimmy Lonsdale's way, was that he was henceforth and for evermore the guv'nor of Jack Penny and his gang.

That was the taste, bitter as the venom of serpents. Because that pikey shicer hadn't stood beside his fellow immigrants at Cable Street, nor would he ever have. Had he seen the opportunity in it, he'd have fought alongside Oswald Mosley's thugs instead, just like he'd seen the opportunity at the Café de Paris, after the bombs fell right into the basement ballroom and left all that tomfoolery for the taking. Penny had never shrunk from an impromptu smash-and-grab – he kept a hammer in his pocket and had made them something of his stock-in-trade – but robbing corpses, while they were still smouldering, that took something else that only Jimmy Lonsdale had. Same as the 'Piccadilly Commandos' they'd taken under their wing when the Maltese wops had got themselves interned for the duration. It was one thing to send the girls to target the overpaid G.I.s, but quite another to go and roll them too. Bad business, in every sense.

In the days when he'd still been Jacob Pieniazek, Penny had cut his teeth keeping nix for Jewish bookies at places that were just plain dangerous for them, a case in point being Hurst Park racecourse way out west. He knew a bully when he saw one and he learned how to spot the evil bastards who'd do more than stripe you, just for fun. 'Jimmy the Shiv' was one of them.

Over the past years, to complement their extensive blackout enterprises, they'd worked a lurk lodging false compensation claims for getting bombed-out in Jerry raids – but only Jimmy had seen the opportunity to flog hooky certificates for jerry-built shelters too. Then, after Penny hand-reared his own tame quack to sign off military exemptions for shirkers, it was

Jimmy who'd had him switch to forging documents for deserters and brought the MPs down on top of all of them like one of his dodgy shelters.

A liability, that's what Jimmy was. Greedy as the great hog he resembled, dripping with the dreck of Seven Dials. But a flippin' genius for dreaming up new schemes. And so here was dutiful Jack Penny, sporting the schmutter of a REME Staff Sergeant and the bow-and-arrow badges of Anti-Aircraft Command, with papers from a workshop detachment that really did exist, just not in any order of battle, and a pass to the British Zone of Occupation. They were upping the ante on their biggest earner yet and taking the operation international.

Suddenly self-conscious, he glanced at his neighbour on the arse-numbing tube-and-canvas bench seats. He was expecting either a green face or the customary look of disgust and suspicion but instead he found himself greeted by a sympathetic smile.

"Never as pleasant as it looks, is it?"

"What ain't, missus?"

She was mid-forties with a streak of grey running through the front wave of her hair, attractive in her way, but tightly buttoned up, for a civilian. Her look turned a little quizzical, if still fundamentally benevolent.

Yeah, I know your sort and all, Penny thought.

"Why, flying of course. Or is this your first time?"

Insulted, to his own surprise, he squirmed back against the cabin windows. For some reason he wanted her to notice his unearned crowns and stripes, and his fancy red shoulder flashes. But of course those were for shooting the buggers down not for going up in them. Plus she was right. He'd never even left England before, or not by more than a couple of miles offshore.

"I ain't allowed to say, missus."

"No, I suppose not."

"What about you then, if you don't mind me asking. Come over a lot?"

He had already clocked the simple wedding band (Jimmy wouldn't have liked that) and the fingernails, neatly varnished, but somehow short and workmanlike. At first he'd had her down as another Christian do-gooder but now he wasn't so sure.

"Oh, this will be my first time in Occupied Germany, but yes, I have flown before, in my youth."

She wasn't flirting with him, was she? She must have had fifteen years on him, which was a fair few lengths in anyone's book. Maybe she was teasing him. He hadn't had much experience of ladies of quality. But he couldn't help thinking that no, she wasn't teasing, she was lonely.

It took one to know one, he supposed. But that was no ruddy help and the moment, if it had been a moment, had passed.

Instead he found himself watching the other passenger, the one forward of the wing spar in the single proper aeroplane seat that faced the cockpit doorway. Another middle-aged civilian, but this one so unremarkable in his drab raincoat and baldy Brylcreem you'd never clock him at all if he weren't sat up front on his Tod like Lord Muck. He had a wooden suitcase with him that he'd kept on his lap ever since Northolt, his boring brown trilby placed atop it. Some kind of travelling salesman, he looked like. Except for the snotty manner. And the hands on that box of his. Those weren't just workmanlike they were actual worker's hands. Docker's hands, ferryman's hands. Hands that worked with rope.

Penny shuddered as he realised what sort of ferryman he was thinking of. When the plane gave another lurch, his guts did too.

"...so frightful, all the details that came out," the woman was saying. Now he'd pulled himself together he understood belatedly that she'd been speaking to him for a couple of minutes about the latest news from Lüneburg. "Such a relief that the trial is over now, for the surviving victims and the families, I imagine. I'm afraid I shall have to visit the place

44

myself, as part of the study I'm conducting. They've turned it into a Displaced Persons camp of course but to the world it will always be Belsen."

Did the man's head tilt at that word? Had he been listening?

Yeah, my old china, Penny thought. I reckon I do know who you are and why you're in no mood to socialise. Can't say I'm too sorry about that myself. In point of fact I'll be doing all I can, and then some, never ever to be in your presence again.

*   *   *

On their arrival at Bückeburg, the mysterious third passenger was met by an army major who appeared to have the only jeep and driver. A secret agent, Marjorie Jessop wondered as the little vehicle was swallowed by the rain and dark beyond the runway lights. Tying a scarf around her head and squinting in the wind, she decided that the whole idea of people on secret missions wasn't nearly as exciting as it sounded.

Apparently just as much at a loss was the rather alarmingly uncultured staff sergeant from the Royal Electrical and Mechanical Engineers. Once the aircrew had deposited their baggage on the metal sheeting that seemed the only man-made feature of the entire airfield, he slung his kitbag over his shoulder and offered to carry her cases. But where?

"I'm afraid we're not really set up here yet," the pilot told them. "But there's a guard hut at the gate where they'll sort you out a brew – and, I believe, a local taxi driver who ferries chaps into town in return for ciggies and petrol."

"I have to get to Hanover," she said.

"Sorry, that's 40 miles or more. You won't make it tonight. But Bückeburg's alright. There wasn't much fighting in the end. Best thing to do is pick the least damaged house, go up and knock on the door. Chances are it'll be one we've already requisitioned. If not, well, requisition it." As the RAF officer looked the sergeant up and down his smile faded. "What about you, Staff? Army HQ at Bad Oeynhausen?"

"Er, yeah."

"Mmm. Well, that's a pretty place, or was. It's the wrong direction for you, Mrs Jessop, but it might be safer to stick together for now. All I can suggest, I'm afraid."

The two of them walked to the gate in freezing rain and a biting wind that beat at the winter coverings on the long line of Spitfires. Marjorie insisted on taking one of her cases from the sergeant.

"Ta, missus. Getting a bit hefty it was."

"Educational texts," she said. "Schoolbooks. Samples anyway."

"You're selling them?"

"In a way. I'm trying to sell an idea, to the Military Government."

"And what would that be?"

She rolled her eyes. She didn't want to talk about it, not now, not like this. But he'd been friendly to her and was still carrying the heavier of her cases.

"That the way to stop... all this... is to educate the Germans differently. Starting with the women."

"And why's that then?"

"Take a look around you. Who do you think is left? The men are dead, or prisoners, or sulking about how they've lost the war. But the war isn't over for the women. In many ways it's only just beginning." She was warming to her subject now, as she always did, and any kind of warmth was welcome, wasn't it?

"I take your point."

"Do you?" She stopped in her tracks and regarded him shrewdly. "Yes, perhaps you do. *Kinder, Küche, Kirche* – that's how German girls were always told to see their role in society."

"Children, kitchen, church..."

"Precisely. And if that's what they continue to learn, it's only a matter of time before the men find a way to do it all again." Hoping he hadn't noticed the crack in her voice, she set off briskly to hide her emotions. Howard had always said they

---

46

were written on her face.

But what had got her so agitated? It wasn't only what had happened to Howard at Amiens, and to Peter at Trondheim just twenty-two years later. It was also Lüneburg and the Belsen trial and the sentences they'd handed down, to be carried out as soon as arrangements could be made. The photograph in the newspaper of those women with the numbers pinned to their chests. The young one in the middle, Number 9, Grese. And the excerpt from the trial transcript. *A whip made of cellophane paper plaited like a pigtail – it was translucent like white glass...*

Oh, honestly, what did she think she was doing here? All those fierce intentions she'd had back home, all the bright ideas in those grand speeches to the Education Branch and the Women's Affairs Committee, were thin as gossamer in the face of this bleak reality – torn to shreds by an icy wind that cut like white glass!

"Mrs... Jessop?"

"What is it, Staff Sergeant?" They had nearly reached the guard hut. By its light, mercifully, Marjorie could see that his eyes and nose were watering too.

He looked even more sheepish, suddenly.

"I don't really want to go to the headquarters in Bad Oeynhausen."

"No. I suppose not."

"So I was thinking perhaps we ought to get this cabbie fellow to take us into Bückeburg, like the man said."

"I don't think I have it in me to turf someone out of their home, not on an evening like this." Observing his features soften, she guessed that he felt a similar reluctance to hers, not so much out of sheer timidity in his case as from a lack of the right sort of authority, perhaps. At least, she suspected, he would see it that way.

"So what do you reckon...?"

"It rather depends on whether this taxi turns up," Marjorie said as she made herself presentable for the gate guards.

"Assuming it does, we'll ask him if there's a guest house still standing. There must be some place that can offer us a room."

* * *

Stefan Düttmann leaned across with his right arm and used the extra-long leather strap to close the door of his '37 Olympia. In fact only half the car was his. He shared ownership of the dark green Opel with Georg, in addition to – in theory – the driving duties. In practice, Georg was never sober and Stefan often had to hide the keys to deter his older brother from even attempting to take his shift behind the wheel.

The reason he used his right arm to close the door was that his left arm was in a ravine somewhere 30 kilometres southeast of Smolensk. But if you could drive a *Schützenpanzerwagen* with one hand, as Stefan had whenever he'd needed to be shooting with the other, a simple 4-door saloon was child's play, even though spare parts had grown hard to come by since the night the British had levelled Rüsselsheim.

The car, of course, was named in honour of the Berlin Olympics. Which, as he told most of his customers nowadays, was when everything had started to go wrong.

Not that he had said as much to the last couple. Not that he had told them anything, apart from who to ask for at the improvised Gasthof and how many packets of American cigarettes they owed him. With the normal British soldiers and airmen, he'd have been practising his English all the way – *clocks, cameras, currency, nylons* – but with these two so tense, and one of them being a woman, it hadn't seemed appropriate.

Perhaps he was just tired. It was draining, driving in this weather, and it had been a long day. If he called it a night now, and if Georg hadn't hit the bottle early, he might have time for a chat with his brother before they got their heads down. Not about their military service, of course. Since his unexpected return in the last week of the war, Georg had never once mentioned his unit and what it did, or not until he was so drunk that his words were unintelligible howls. But about their parents, and their sister, and the good old days, perhaps. There was a jar of pickles hidden under the floorboards.

He made his way across town, tooting every now and then to warn the shambling figures that were returning from the forest, heads bent low, with sleds of damp wood that would never burn. Reaching their home on the outskirts, he went to tuck the car away behind the row-houses as usual. With the part-cleared rubble and Old Norbert's rusted-out Wanderer it was an awkward turn that would have been better suited to a man with two arms, or at least the differential steering on his two-fifty-one in Russia, but it meant nobody was likely to use the narrow back lane as a thoroughfare.

So the Allied jeep lurking in the shadows of the balconies could not have been there by chance.

Stefan put the car in neutral and applied the parking brake. If he'd been in his half-track he'd have had his personal weapon pointing through the vision slit by now. And a squad of *Panzergrenadiere* above and behind him, of course. And his arm.

After a minute, seeing no movement around the jeep, he switched off. The only sound was the whispering of the wind in the icy mass of overhanging juniper. When he twisted in his seat for the door latch, a flashlight exploded in his face. All he saw beyond the light was the muzzle of a submachine gun.

*   *   *

Mounting the few steps to the front porch of Holzgasse 18, Mila gestured for the others to disperse. She wore the modified British uniform of a corporal in the 'Pestki', the PSK or Polish Women's Auxiliary Service, while her team had badged themselves as soldiers of General Anders' 2nd Corps. Unlike the Czech army-in-exile, there was no chance of repatriating the Free Polish Forces safely now the war was over and so they had been scattered across the British Zone to guard Surrendered Enemy Personnel compounds, coal reserves and forgotten ammunition dumps. No one wanted them coming to Britain, or knew what else to do with them. It was a good enough cover for her motley crew from the east, but with only Marek, and possibly Miro, capable of passing for genuine Poles, they had to be careful who they ran into.

When she knocked there came a series of chinks and thuds before a slurred voice called out: "Stefan? Stefan?"

"Herr Düttmann?" she said politely. "Georg Düttmann?"

Silence. Pondering. And eventually: "You want my brother."

Mila took a step back, glancing either side. She had sent Vojtěch home to Marta and Emil back into hiding with his twin (what use was a bad British impersonator in the British Zone?) but Miro was there, in the darkness, and Stas, and 'Uncle' Ludvík too. The latter was much too old and grey to be a soldier, but there had been no dissuading him. 'Just tell them I'm twenty-one and have had a hard war!' he'd said.

Her hand went to her holster and unfastened it.

"Your brother? But you just called his name, didn't you, Georg?"

"Who are you? What do you want?"

"Only to ask some questions on behalf of the authorities." Despite her appeal to the German conviction that *Alles Gute kommt von oben*, she found she had retreated a further two steps down the stoop. In the countryside, shotgun blasts might also come from above.

But then the door opened and a big man stood silhouetted against his hall light. The locals were lucky, there was electricity here. Mila's hand moved from her holster flap and flattened into a signal to the others to hang back.

"Georg Düttmann?"

"What of it?"

"We are here under directive No.9 of the Allied Control Council," she intoned in appropriately accented German, seeking to give the impression of a lowly storewoman or mess orderly pressed unenthusiastically into service as an interpreter and interviewer. "It is a formality – a few simple questions."

"About what?"

"So, let me see..." She pretended to consult the notebook in her other hand. "About those we have been informed you served with in the Sonderkommando 'Pfeffer'. At Bobruisk."

"Never heard of it. Never been there."

"...and specifically your former Commanding Officer, SS-Standartenführer Konrad Pfeffer. Born Freistadt, Austria, in 1903."

"Never heard of him."

Mila bit her lip.

If this brute only understood how hard it had been to get that name – not just for her but for the others, and particularly for Stas, who had conquered his demons to bluff and bully it from the Russian files in the performance of a lifetime!

If Düttmann only had the wit to picture, as she had, the erstwhile impresario returning to the prison to play the part of an NKVD inquisitor and 'deduce', right there in front of Major Dyachenko, how he had been duped the first time – how the interlopers had changed their uniforms, how they had intimidated the prisoner, the extra props they had used – in order to demand that the humiliated commandant aid the 'investigation' by disclosing what she and her first group of impersonators had not been able to examine: Lamprecht's dossier!

If she could only have made this devil appreciate the audacity of such a subterfuge, from an undoubted drunk and self-confessed coward, or the ingenuity with which they had then fitted the pieces together.

If she could only have spelled it out to him, possibly with simple diagrams and a teacher's cane, how they had connected Lamprecht's role in the Nazi *Winterhilfe* appeal at Stransky's munitions factory in Moravia to the time that Stransky, as a chemist, had been asked to lend a hand in the production of pesticides by none other than Himmler's newly appointed delousing specialist: the former Lebensborn administrator lately dismissed from that organisation for gross financial

---

51

malpractice, Konrad Pfeffer.

If she could only have shared with him the moment when Vojtěch – his young brain a better stenograph than her fake one – had recalled how Lamprecht had let it slip that Stransky only *supposed* he had no contacts in the Race and Settlement Main Office, meaning of course that he had and was simply unaware of his acquaintance's subsequent appointment within RuSHA.

If she could only have drummed it into him, perhaps in the manner that one housetrained a dog by rubbing its nose in its own mess, how from that morsel they had identified Pfeffer's name in the files, and linked him to the *Aktion* to kidnap Byelorussian children, and finally tracked down a surviving member of his unit...

If there was only a way to make him see how far she had come and how much closer it had to – *had to* – bring her to her objective!

But of course it wouldn't have made any difference. Some people were beyond reason.

"Herr Düttmann, if someone were able to help us locate Standartenführer Pfeffer – or even a third party who might know what happened to him – the record of such co-operation might prove advantageous, especially for anyone hiding prior membership of an illegal organisation. It could even benefit an application for a clearance certificate..."

When he stepped up close to her she could smell the schnapps on his breath. When he spoke she felt the hatred in the fine spray of spittle.

"You can stuff your *Persilschein* up your arses!"

The 'Persil ticket' that would wash one's record clean. Evidently he knew that there was no cleaning his. Mila forced her lips to form a thin smile and stood her ground. She knew what was coming next. Up against a man of his own height, Düttmann would likely have progressed to bumping foreheads or chests, but being that much bigger than she, he would use his hands to push her back.

Had she waited even half a second she had no doubt that Stas or Miro would have been up the steps and on him, with Ludvík close behind. But she did not wait. The instant his right hand moved, her left shot out and the iron rod that was threaded through the loops of her notebook caught him in the throat. By the time he sank to his knees his face had already changed colour dramatically. In the dim light from the door it looked almost black.

Kein Persilschein for that, either, *Kamerad*.

She gave a whistle and Marek came down the hallway, pushing Georg's kid brother ahead of him with his Sten gun. She saw that one of Stefan's arms was raised, the other missing, and that his eyes were wide with fraternal concern.

You don't deserve it, you bastard, Mila thought as they dragged Georg into the house. The door slammed shut behind them.

"Let's start again," she said.

CHAPTER FIVE

The flight back to Europe from the United States had taken no time at all. The silver Pan American Clipper had scudded off the surface of Long Island Sound soon after sunrise and touched down at the Darrell's Island air station in Bermuda for lunch. Duly refuelled, the huge flying boat commenced the long leg to Horta in the Azores, arriving at daybreak the following morning. They'd been airborne again by 0800 and had finally caught sight of the red rooftops of Lisbon in the warm glow of sunset. Even with the time difference, it was shy of two days since Bradley's briefing on the R.C.A. Sky View.

Then everything slowed to a crawl. The ancient Portuguese capital might be unscarred by the war but Doyle had warned Bradley that its winding alleyways were brimming with spies of every stripe and five days' waiting for the rumoured reinstated express across Franco's Spain had left him hiding from his own shadow. *Expresso* proved a misnomer also, as the journey was followed by another long delay while a train was found with the proper gauge for France. Here and there between Hendaye and Irun skulked shady refugee groups. Jews? Bradley had asked a local who spoke some English, wondering what other displaced persons would be traversing war-torn Europe not for home but for some further banishment. The Basque had laughed. Despite wearing a prodigious moustache himself, he'd placed a straight finger beneath his nose to imitate another sort. Nazis on the run, sneaking across the Bidasoa bridge into Spain. Exactly the kind of thing a real CIC Special Agent would have been interested in.

But Bradley was not a real agent, not for CIC, BSC or whatever the Strategic Services bureau was called this week. He had decided long ago that he had his own mission and he was reminded of it every time he lit another cigarette with the little gold lighter. He was going to find her again and then he was going to help her find what she was looking for. That was as much as he could foresee and as far as his loyalties went.

The Sud Express had barely got up to speed before it was pulling in at the blustery seaside resort of Biarritz. All at once, Army garrison uniforms were everywhere. It seemed they had set up an American University in the town to offer demobilising G.I.s a boost back into civilian life. And in case you still thought that sounded like all work, no play, Marlene Dietrich was at the Hotel Miramar.

On the way to Bordeaux, the furtive-looking Frenchman in the facing window seat told him about a German naval officer who had been ordered to blow up the entire port after D-Day and had detonated the stockpile of explosives instead.

"Like von Choltitz saving Paris, but only the *maquisards* know this one. Now, when you see Bordeaux still standing, you'll remember him. And me."

Bradley had nodded and smiled. He had been in France before, long enough to disregard none-too-subtle hints at having served in the Resistance, and to know that those who dropped them had something else to hide, especially when they combined them with a yarn about not all the occupiers and their enablers being so terrible.

Side-lined again and again to make way for military transports and freight trains, sometimes for eight hours or more, it had taken the 'express' another night and day to reach Paris. Here was another place he'd been before and had no wish to linger, since he knew both OSS and MI6 had maintained missions there. He caught a *velo-taxi* direct from Gare de Lyon to Gare de l'Est and flashed his gold badge at the Railroad Transportation Office window to finagle his way onto the next sleeper for Frankfurt, the 'Main-Seiner'.

As he was boarding he noticed a civilian couple, two carriages along, who were having trouble passing up their baggage. They had changed their coats and hats, and the woman had changed her hair, but they had been at the Bidasoa bridge.

Bradley cursed. In his guise as Charles S. Fisher, an advisor from the post-Morgenthau Treasury Department to the Office of Military Government – U.S. Zone, he had planned to stay on the duty train from Frankfurt all the way to Berlin and cross officially into the Soviet Zone from there. His cover story involved investigating the setting up of local 'barter rings', partly as a way to regulate the black market, partly to fight currency fraud and counterfeiting. Since much of the latter originated in the east, allegedly with official blessing, it was plausible he be permitted to travel there, even if only to give OMGUS the runaround. He had been prepared for a tail once he'd entered Soviet-controlled territory, but not now, and not, potentially, all the way from Lisbon. That had very different implications. So once the night train from Paris was across the German border and picking noisily through the ruins of Saarbrücken, he'd pulled out his smokes, made his way to the observation car and followed his suitcase into the darkness.

It might even have worked, in the old days, without his trick knee and shoulder. As it turned out, he was found shivering on the ballast by French occupation forces, who picked him up, patched him up and roughed him up again for good measure. Once they'd satisfied themselves that he wasn't a *Werwolf* out to sabotage the railroad (no SS blood group tattoo, American dentistry and, of course, that miraculous gold badge, the number on which checked out over the phone line to the CIC detachment in Berlin), they'd thrown him in the back of a ½ ton weapons carrier and driven a hundred miles on unmade roads to hand him over to U.S. forces across the Rhine, on the outskirts of what had once been Karlsruhe. The drive had nearly finished him.

He spent a week recuperating at the Kurmärker Kaserne in

Stuttgart, watching the DEFs fix holes in the walls of the barracks blocks. There were a lot of holes, but a lot of DEFs to fill them: re-designating them Disarmed Enemy Forces or, as the British had done, Surrendered Enemy Personnel, removed any obligation under the Geneva Convention to feed the POWs properly, which had been deemed unsustainable. For these men, volunteering for a pioneer detail on the promise of extra rations, be it a rebuilding project like this one or a *Minenkommando*, could make the difference between life and death, one way or another. Tough, perhaps, but more than fair, Bradley reckoned, and in many cases better treatment than they deserved.

Anyhow, what was so different about these clean-up operations than the work of the rubble-women? Why should these guys, of all people, get fed for nothing? It was a puzzle all right and he was thankful that he wasn't really one of the thousands of serious-minded officials who had been planning for the postwar reconstruction of Germany since even before the tide had turned at El Alamein and Stalingrad – or even one of the supposed law enforcers who had to decide what to do with the worst offenders. All the while he was waiting for the inevitable visit from a genuine counterintelligence agent.

When the man had showed himself in, he'd slammed his gold badge down next to Bradley's with a triumphant flourish.

"Schnipp-schnapp!"

"Yeah, about that..."

But despite his taste for fun and games, Lieutenant Hoffman had turned out to be a stand up guy. At first, Bradley had stuck to his story. He figured even if the Treasury Department wasn't really investigating currency fraud, maybe Army CIC was.

"When they set the rate at one Allied Military mark to one Reichsmark – and ten AM marks to the dollar – that kicked off a whole new black market. Our boys are buying old Reichsmarks by the bundle and exchanging them for AM marks and dollars..."

"Nice try," Hoffman said. "But we put a stop to all that weeks ago. Now if you were trying to prevent the Reds from printing AM marks like toilet tissue..."

"Well, it's funny you should mention that..."

"Relax, Fisher, or whatever your name is. I'm not here to give you the third degree. I've been told to help you – if you want to tell me what it is you're really after."

"They teach you that one at Camp Ritchie?"

"The Mythical Institute of Total Confusion?" Hoffman grinned, no doubt surprised that Bradley had even heard of the Military Intelligence Training Center in the mountains of northwestern Maryland, which he only had because of those lazy evenings drinking with the wily Tom Cabot and loose-lipped Schaefer on another mountainside, what seemed like months ago. "Shucks, yeah, probably. But this is on the level. The 70th level, if you get my drift."

Bradley had got his drift.

"I'm looking for specific gen regarding an impersonation con that was worked recently at an NKVD camp in Silesia. Failing that, I need to track down someone who knows about a former resistance group that has sunk without trace in Czechoslovakia."

"Well..." Hoffman, who Bradley suspected was never accidentally loose-lipped, made as if he were deliberating whether or not to show his hand. Which, presumably, he'd been ordered to. "If it's intel from the Soviet sphere of influence that you're after, we've got a little game going on down in Munich, and in Austria. The NKVD are very proud of themselves for recruiting a whole bunch of ex-*Abwehr* to spy on us, mostly poor bastards with families left behind in the Soviet Zone – you know how the Reds operate. Naturally, what these former Wehrmacht intelligence officers want more than anything is to get their loved ones out from under the sword of Damocles. Promise to do that for them and we can run them back against the Reds. Which we do."

"So?"

"So if we want to find something out, we just get one of our ex-*Abwehr* doubles to inform them that we're on the case. When the Reds brief him on how to dig deeper to find out what we know, we find out a lot about what *they* know... back and forth, forth and back... and they never realise we started off knowing next to nothing."

Bradley had laughed. He liked the gawky, bespectacled Hoffman and, if it was true, his was a pretty big secret to lay out there on the mess hall table. He decided to risk telling him a version of his own.

"OK – I think the prison camp is the one at Tost, or Toszek, I guess it's called now. What I need is the same information obtained by the man impersonating Colonel Andreev, whatever that was. I was fixing to snoop around the area, try to make contact with an ex-prisoner or an off-duty guard. Maybe this way I don't have to."

And there he had paused. That part of his secret wasn't really secret at all. In fact, given Hoffman's reference to the 70th level of the R.C.A. building, there was every reason to suppose that he and Doyle were working together. The next part was different though. Even if Hoffman had been briefed on this part also, it was personal.

The way they used those *Abwehr* doubles, they might indeed dig out a clue that would put him back on her trail. Or they might put the NKVD back on it too.

"The underground group is the MERCURY network," he said.

"The ones that foiled that SMERSh plot to stay put in Czechoslovakia?"

"If you say so. I figure the best way to freshen up the scent is to lean on a couple of untrustworthy characters who knew them before. A Czech called Zdenko Kovály, used to work in the Prague Housing Authority but has disappeared. Another who went by the name of Doctor Eduard Stransky, also a former war profiteer or resistance hero – likely both – and likewise AWOL in the wake of that failed plot you seem to know so much about. I spent the back end of August over there on R&R, chasing shadows. I can understand why MERCURY went deep again – the communists are worming their way into positions of power, so any former British-backed groups are basically outlaws now – but these two guys were in tight with the authorities. Perhaps they're the key..."

In the meantime they put him to work supervising the DEFs like some vizier to the Pharaoh, wearing a borrowed field overcoat with the 2nd lieutenant's butterbars and pinks-and-greens he'd brought along in his civilian baggage. By the third week of November he'd had them, and the barracks frontage, in pretty good shape.

Then Hoffman reappeared with a head cold and a sly smile that meant results.

"Buy you a cup of coffee?"

"Sure you're up to it?"

Hoffman sneezed. "Never better!"

"*Gesundheit.*"

They headed for the officers club, returning salutes as they went, which Bradley still got a kick out of. Halfway across the parade ground, Hoffman stopped and pulled out his handkerchief.

"Going to run that up the flagpole?"

"Wouldn't be the first time around here," Hoffman chuckled.

Bradley thought about all those holes he'd been in charge of filling for the past weeks. In many places there'd been more holes than stonework. Hoffman's verdict on his DEFs seemed a little unfair.

But the man wasn't looking around for fun, he was making sure there was no one else in earshot.

"Nothing solid yet on your Silesian masquerade, except that the prisoner the impersonators interviewed is dead and buried now. Heart problems. Not the only one, we gather. 'NKVD Tyurma-lager Tost' is being closed down and erased from the records."

"Dammit! They don't handle embarrassment very well."

"Ain't that the truth. But we've heard through other sources about a mysterious partisan band that snuck back into Czechoslovakia near Nachod, which has become an unofficial border town for west-bound refugees who are fleeing continued persecution across Poland. Word has it they even brought a bunch of refugees over with them in their truck. So I'm pretty sure your guys got away before the big lockdown."

"What sources? Word through who?"

"Through the refugees of course. They can be a great asset. And through an organisation that helps certain kinds of refugee follow certain routes to certain destinations."

"And if I asked, that would just be 'a certain organisation'..."

"Believe me Fisher, with this organisation, the more you ask the more uncertain it becomes."

Remembering Doyle's equivocations and those of others before him – and the long slide that linked them all together – Bradley shook his head in whatever it was that came between aversion and amusement. Self-knowledge, perhaps.

"What about the two names I gave you?"

"Zip on Kovály. Must have had a new I.D. ready to go." Hoffman's eyes rolled behind his wire-rimmed glasses. "But the other one? Boy do we have something on him!"

*   *   *

It was Sunday December 9th 1945, four years since Roosevelt's Day of Infamy. They had been four long years and now they were coming to an end. Company B of the 94th Division's 301st Infantry Regiment, pretty much the last remnants of the U.S. presence in this forgotten corner of the European theatre, were packing up and shipping home.

They had only ever been here by happenstance. The Reich across which they'd fought had included the infamous Sudetenland, annexed by the Nazis in '38 and now restored to Czechoslovakia. The latter, of course, was supposed to have been liberated by the Red Army, but in certain areas, particularly around Pilsen and Budweis, the rapid U.S. advance had even extended beyond the Sudetenland into the Bohemian Protectorate. Over the past eight months, the continued presence of Americans in this region had been regarded, variously, as a comfort and an aberration, but with all occupying forces pulling out, to east and west, the anomaly was finally being resolved.

If they had sought any further sign that the great adventure was over – beside the progressive thinning of their numbers, of the Soviets across the line of demarcation, and of the local populace itself – they might have found it in General Patton's pointless, probably fatal traffic accident yesterday near Mannheim. But among the irregular squad of soldiers who were blackening their faces and donning musty combat gear, only the two funny-looking lieutenants had heard that news and they were keeping it to themselves.

It wasn't quite the end, not just yet. There was time for one last mission.

As Hoffman checked and slung his grease gun, he threw Bradley a smirk.

"I heard about a churchyard near here. Back in olden times there were two local peasants who hated each other's guts and when they both died – of plague, I guess – they were buried side by side. Trouble was, no one in the village got any sleep after that, for the sound of arguing and cursing underground. It took the Pope to resolve the matter in the end."

"What did he do?"

"Got them to separate the headstones."

"And that worked?"

"Go find the church and the two graves side by side, with the crosses facing away from each other. See if you hear anything."

They crouched in silence, breath clouding in the pre-dawn gloom. Bradley saw that Hoffman's eyeglasses were steaming up again.

"Horseshit," he said. "Who told you that?"

"Some guy."

"Uh-huh? Gee, you oughta get a job in Intelligence."

"I tried. They wouldn't take me." Hoffman pulled out his handkerchief, wiped his glasses and checked his watch. "Come on, let's go."

With a combination of nods and pre-arranged hand signals, the tech sergeant sent his scouts ahead and had the rest of the riflemen fan out through the woods. Bradley and Hoffman followed up with the fire support team, strictly as observers.

The twelve men slipped between unseen outposts and across the invisible line of demarcation. For Bradley, this was not his first infiltration into Soviet-occupied Czechoslovakia, but here, now, in the snow-laced coniferous forests south of Budweis, with the local German-speakers expelled and the authorities seemingly in no hurry to repopulate the forsaken villages, it felt more like entering a different age. Elsewhere, the last maintenance elements of the 94th were finishing their work with the Czechoslovak army on the rebuilding projects. They were handing over responsibility for guarding facilities and running DEP or DP reception camps. They were preparing for final church parades and medal ceremonies with their Czech and Russian counterparts and getting on with making sure that come the new year, and the new age that it heralded, those tombstones would face unequivocally apart. But it looked like Hoffman and the squad leader had planned this well. With any luck they would be in and out before anyone had even noticed.

Of course, not all the work at the DP reception camps had been going smoothly, which was one reason why Patton had been removed from his command to go tearing around the Rhineland in the first place. At Camp Karlov, near Pilsen, he had sent back several hundred Jews who, having somehow survived the Nazis, had returned to their homes in Poland and Slovakia only to be set upon and driven out again. Supposedly he had even ordered his troops to fire in the air to keep them on the train while it was turned around.

Not that something like that would put them off trying to get through to the U.S. Zone: especially now it was obvious that the British element of the United Nations Relief and Rehabilitation Administration, mindful of official British policy not to enable any further Jewish exodus into Mandatory Palestine, would likely have sided with Patton. And with the boundary of the U.S. Zone poised to shrink westwards to the pre-war German border, this was probably their last chance to escape via a neglected backwater like this one.

Sure enough, the scouts soon drew their attention to the clumps of figures here and there among the trees. Some had lit meagre campfires to survive the night, others simply bundled together in heaps beneath the snow. Sunken eyes followed the Americans as they patrolled past with their fingers to their lips, and Bradley, who had seen people displaced and set to flight before, caught himself wondering what it was about these ones that was so different.

Then it hit him. The other refugees, the bombed-out Germans or expelled Sudetens, had divided naturally into the remains of family groups. In the absence of men of fighting age, women and children had predominated. But these were adults, many of them male, and although desperately cold and thin few looked old or frail.

There were no children.

Wiping off his eyeglasses again, Hoffman started gesturing to the people in the snow, directing them towards the American lines and away from the treacherous bulge of the Soviet-occupied Mühlviertel across the Austrian border. Fearing that he'd soon be calling out instructions, Bradley grabbed his arm and led him on into the forest.

After another hour they came to a woodcutter's track where an abandoned truck was half-hidden by the trees. If they had come upon it by chance, it was fortunate indeed that the derelict had air in the tyres, gas in the tank and juice in the battery; if not, Bradley knew better than to ask. They piled aboard and drove sedately until the track became a dirt road.

A few miles further sat the log cabin that functioned as the local police post. A sodden-looking VB flag hung from the eaves, denoting the Czech for Public Security, as the gendarmerie had been renamed.

Having signalled for his teams to cut the phone lines and cover the approaches, T/Sgt Grainger granted Bradley and Hoffman the access they had requested by the simple expedient of kicking the door off its hinges. Of the trio of half-dressed officers inside, one still on his cot and two at their late breakfast or early lunch, none saw fit to argue with the three submachine guns that were pointed at their chests.

The station was dominated by a wood-burning stove. On its far side was a wall of jail bars that might have served for the set of a Western if they hadn't also been draped with drying socks.

Behind the bars, between the socks, wrapped in restless shadows, Bradley saw a thin, dark man perched on the edge of his bed board. Deep-set eyes regarded him without recognition.

"Is it him?" Hoffman hissed.

"It's him."

"Stransky?"

Bradley heard the tension in his colleague's voice. He could almost feel the tension in his trigger finger.

"I said it's him. We got him. What's eating you?"

Hoffman's grease gun rattled as he jabbed it towards each policeman in turn.

"These are the same gendarmes who went with the fucking Nazis on their roundups."

"You don't know that. They're just three guys baby-sitting a government advisor who was found wandering the local farmland half-naked."

T/Sgt Grainger had removed one hand from his weapon to sift through the mess of paperwork on the only table. Evidently he'd used the past months to familiarise himself with the Czech language.

"...claims he was kidnapped off the street in Prague, held captive for months and forced to take in the harvest like an *Ostarbeiter*... Alleges he was interrogated vigorously on two separate occasions. Subsequent to the second, he claims he escaped through a drainage channel, although he is unable to identify the precise location..."

Despite the precarious atmosphere, Bradley had to laugh.

"She kept him on ice, in case the information he'd given her didn't pan out. I wonder why she came back and squeezed him again."

But he could tell how this was going to end if they weren't careful. So could Grainger. Quick as anything, the two of them trussed up Stransky for the journey, locked the policemen in their own cell and bundled Hoffman out of the station. Sure, it might have been better to conduct an initial interview on the spot, but that could wait. What mattered was that they had their quarry – and just maybe Bradley would have the lead he had been chasing.

Two weeks later, with Patton in the ground and the agreed withdrawal of all foreign forces from Czechoslovakia completed in time for Christmas, he was on his way to the British Occupation Zone of Germany.

CHAPTER SIX

Heiligabend in the Winter of Misery. In cavities across the ruins, candles and lanterns were lighting. Here and there, smoky-brown after all these years, precious lamp globes delineated the surprising rectangles of surviving rooms and doorways.

The little girl rolled her shoulder back to reach into the void, like her friend Rat had taught her to do. She let out a triumphant cackle as the leather sheaths she wore for fingertips encountered something that offered none of the resistance of rubble. *Ha!* It moved like tin, and a tin unbalanced by loose contents! She prayed to all those vanished benefactors – *Gott, Führer, Mutti*, the Rat himself – that just for once, on this holy evening, and with every other enticing hole in the collapsed building's *Adventskalendar* empty as an Egyptian's tomb, it might be biscuits.

The others called her *die Made*, meaning maggot or grub. Not just for the shiny new skin on her face and arms, although there was that, but because of how she seemed to luxuriate in the incomplete annihilation. After everything she'd seen, and seen destroyed, in the Big City, here was the life of a maggot in fat. Or so she had imagined upon her arrival two months ago, clinging like an icicle to the outside of the train. Lately the pickings had grown slimmer, the holes into which she was forced to squeeze tighter and deeper, her stake in the scant rewards even smaller. In the old days, in the Big City, working as a team, they had been better equipped to stand up to the gang's self-appointed *Blockwart* and to demand their fair share of the find. Added to which, she suspected that Rat had often let her have some of his. But now in Hanover she was at the mercy of every bigger kid, of the ever-growing numbers of ever more desperate grown-ups, and the piercing sleet and the endless cold and hunger.

Dear Saint Nicholas, let it be chocolate!

She gritted her teeth, stretching every last sinew. Her heart beat faster as her reaching fingers found the corner of the tin and rotated it several degrees towards her. Then, with a will of its own, it rocked back and toppled deeper into the void.

She swore and pressed her burning forehead against the freezing brickwork. So much for Saint Nicholas. But I might have known it would be no use praying to you, she thought. Where were you three weeks ago when we persistent little icicles, still clinging to our old memories of comfort and family, left our boots out for you on *Nikolaustag* and the Klagesmarkt Bunker Boys stole them instead? What fools we were! And what fools they are, the grown-ups whose pathetic warbling I can hear echoing through these caverns from your worthless bombed-out chapel across Goseriede.

Attention, Maggot! Pull yourself together, or it will be another beating for coming back empty-handed. If you can't squeeze any further down this shaft, you will have to dismantle it until you can: every half-brick, every charred piece of timber or twist of lead pipe, every hunk of plaster or mortar. It was Rat who had taught her how to do it without inviting a further cave-in and it was Rat who had shown her how sometimes, such as when you found servants' belongings in the remnants of a music room or shattered nursery toys in the wine-cellar, it seemed the various stories, even the various histories, of the collapsing buildings had combined to co-exist in the same space. Like archaeology. Like the sepulchre in the cemetery that they had shared.

Time is flattened too, he used to say, past, present and future. Food, footwear, shelter, protection, those are all that matters now. And wealth, of course, in various forms, to secure more of the above. But nothing else. Memories new and old are equally worthless.

Of course, for other girls of post grade school age, there remained other methods of acquiring security and other reasons to fear the acquisition of new memories. But not for Maggot, as Rat had known. In the Big City, when the Russians had come, there had been no choice for anyone, not even, it had seemed, for the soldiers themselves. But once that terrible onrush had subsided, and especially here and now in the British Zone, no one was ever going to choose her willingly. That was why Rat had taught her to fend for herself. And, she thought, why he had liked her.

Having cleared a bigger opening in the rubble she reached in again. Time, flattened or not, was of the essence now. Only the sickliest light remained in the sky and her precious matches were strictly for emergencies.

There was the tin, half-covered in soot, bird shit and brick dust. It was surely an old biscuit tin, but bound up with a ribbon in a way you wouldn't do for biscuits. Valuables.

She turned her head aside to stretch her arm all the way into the hole. Her fingers clasped on something, but it wasn't the tin or any kind of manmade object. What it felt like, as though a mirror image of herself were reaching through from a contrary world on the other side of the mound, was another set of leather-clad fingers.

She withdrew her hand and lit a match, offering it tentatively to the alcove.

It had not been her imagination. Protruding from the rubble there was a mildewed arm that began in the remnants of a floral print puff and ended in a mummified hand. Not leather-clad, just dry and black and leathery. She had shaken hands with Death again.

The woman must have gone back in to get the tin, even as the building was about to fall. Not during the bombing raids: the rubble had been cleared up from those and the dead laid to rest, eventually. Probably when the Amis had stormed across the Weser and overwhelmed the city's defenders. Or when the British, who had taken over the region, had organised the work gangs to pull down the more precarious ruins. Perhaps one of their number had recognised her house and snuck in to salvage something. But what?

Gingerly she reached past the hand and retrieved the tin. Whatever colour the ribbon had been, it was black with soot now and so she cut it with her little knife before prising off the dented lid.

Holding her breath, Maggot sacrificed another match. The wavy-edged photographs and onionskin papers sat sufficiently high in the tin to suggest proper treasures underneath, but as she delved she saw that the pile was being forced upwards by a single, creased card at the bottom. Transferring the flame to a wad of close-written letters, she unfolded the print to see a handsome man in a Nazi uniform with plenty of tinsel all over it. Pinned across the corner of the photograph was another black ribbon.

This had been a chimney, she realised. Hence the void, hence the soot. With the war ending and the enemy on their streets, the woman must have hidden her keepsakes inside the fireplace, including the damning evidence of her fallen husband or son. Had she taken the safer option of throwing it all on the fire, she might still be alive.

So much for valuables. One person's treasure was another's insignificant detritus. Or improvised torch, in this case. But there might still be hope. There was something heavier at the bottom and the reason it hadn't rattled or moved freely was because it was wrapped in black velvet.

Her own cold, mummified fingers were trembling as she picked out the solid gold wedding ring.

Nikolaus, I should never have doubted you. *Der Weihnachtsmann kommt!*

*   *   *

Marjorie Jessop walked as quickly as she dared past the sinister hulk of the Anzeiger high-rise and into the ruins of the Old

Town. Leaving the candlelit carol service in the roofless chapel, the darkness and stillness had at first seemed quaintly charming, but as the rapping of her heels on the icy cobbles rang around the rubble mounds and shadows flitted across stumps of brickwork in the corner of her eye, she clasped her handbag, kept her head down and hoped she looked no different from the German women she had come to know, namely outwardly disagreeable if not plain fearsome.

Gone was any sense of community now and in truth, even as she'd responded to the shy smiles and relieved handshakes from the families in church, she had already found it somewhat lacking. With the pastor's staccato emphasis on the phrase *Das Wort ward Fleisch,* she had not been able to clear her mind of the images that her committee had been screening for the Germans: the films from Belsen, where the Nazis' words had been made flesh for evermore. Even the lyrics to a supposedly shared sentiment like 'Silent Night' had grown menacing, as much for what they did not say as what they did. In German, the infant was merely described as having curly hair. Was the notion of being tender and mild so alien to them? And love's pure light – the dawn of redeeming grace – was here expressed simply as laughter from a baby's mouth. An engaging image, certainly, but where was the burning desire for redemption?

Her eye was drawn by a small flame that flared and died amid the rubble. A small shape, perhaps some kind of animal, scampered over the faint skyline of the mound. Marjorie realised that although she had stopped walking, the echoing footsteps had not.

She spun around and peered through the mist of her anxious breath. A slight, solitary figure was silhouetted against the reflection of the yellow-green glow that emanated from beneath the dome of the Anzeiger-Hochhaus. The figure of a woman.

When it was thirty paces away the figure stopped. Another small flash of flame, smaller this time, less desperate. A cigarette.

That kind of woman.

I knew you were waiting in the street,
I heard your feet, but could not meet...

"You're supposed to be underneath the lantern," Marjorie called out to the shadow, as much to steady her nerves as anything else. "By the barrack gate."

An exhalation of smoke, green as chlorine.

"Wie bitte?"

"Never mind. *Keine Sorge.*" Cursing her overactive imagination, she turned away to hurry on towards her own improper rendezvous at the Maschpark, only to be halted a few seconds later by a low whistle from behind her.

Six notes. A lilting, haunting refrain.

Marjorie took another step and then another, then stopped and turned again. The woman was following her, but slowly, matching her pace. One hand was thrust into the pocket of her long coat. The other cupped around the cigarette, briefly illuminating youthful features beneath the tilted brim of a felt slouch hat. Uncharacteristically slender legs took two steps closer in characteristically heavy socks and shoes.

That kind of woman. Possibly. But not looking for business. This one had something else on her mind. Recalling stories she had heard, Marjorie scanned the nearby rubble mounds for accomplices, possibly even for feral children like the *Wolfskinder,* or for one of the bands of former *Ostarbeiter* that still roamed the region. But the mimicking of the 'Lili Marleen' ballad suggested a degree of sophistication and that somewhat dismissive 'beg your pardon' had been pure *Hausfrau.* A German woman who had singled her out. That might mean a civilian of non-victim status who'd had all she could take of 1,500 calories a day and was looking to lash out at anyone associated with Mil.Gov. Or someone who had heard what the Education Branch was trying to do and wanted to help, even if only to qualify for a higher scale of ration card.

Or someone, like everyone else, who had something to sell.

The sound of a motor made her jump and then relax. The

only possible traffic this late, tonight of all nights, would be military. Perhaps redcaps rounding up revellers. Or perhaps he had come to fetch her.

Sure enough, a jeep was making its way through the ruins from the direction of the *Neues Rathaus*. As it rounded the bend, the headlamps swung Marjorie's shadow towards the woman and illuminated her face.

"You were at the carol service!" In her surprise, Marjorie forgot even to attempt to speak German.

The young woman raised her head. Beneath the brim of the hat and a fringe of spiky fair hair, the wide-set eyes and broad features stretched into an expression of amusement.

"So I was," she said, also in English. "We've been waiting to speak to you, Mrs Jessop."

We? Marjorie turned away from the enigmatic smile and saw that the jeep, with three soldiers in it, was hovering ominously. Her heart fluttered. Ordinary MPs on the drunk patrol would have been one thing. Special investigators were something else.

"I think if you don't mind I'll leave it to another time. I'm rather late..."

The woman stepped closer. The hand in the coat pocket was pointing something at her.

"Oh, I think Staff Sergeant Carter will wait for his 'Lili of the lamplight', don't you?"

Clambering up between the men in the back, Marjorie hoped the woman was right. Without that lift back to Bückeburg she'd be scuppered. And that was all supposing they were going to let her go again. As the jeep cut through the narrow streets and heaps of the obliterated *Altstadt*, she waited for the rest of the blackmail demand to be declared. After the woman's casual reference to Jacob she had no doubt that whoever these people were they were going to try to use her unorthodox domestic arrangements – and the threat of their exposure to her employers – to extort some service from her. What that might be she could not imagine.

She had known it was a bad idea, right from its clumsy

inception on that rain-lashed evening at the unfinished RAF station. She wasn't even terribly sure what she had seen in the uncouth staff sergeant that had led her to take him under her wing, and into her bed, nor exactly what it was that she saw in him now. To say that the last few weeks had been by turns strange, terrifying and overwhelming was an understatement and a half. But they had also been exciting. She had not felt so alive for years and years. More than that, she could not even begin to picture herself doing her day job at the Civic Development Section here in Hanover, or the Education Branch Headquarters in Bünde, without her nights at the little halfway house of Frau Lipke's *ersatz* Gasthof in Bückeburg. Coping with the Germans – with denazification, with the reconstruction of more than just infrastructure and industry, with the forced viewing of the Belsen films – called for something quite different from her well-worn widowly reserve. It demanded passion, a *Lebenshunger*, a lust for life.

Do your worst, she wanted to say. So what if I'm *shacking up* with an unmarried younger man who's probably a thief and a chancer? Take a good look around. Haven't you seen where we are? Didn't you hear those women boast about their white glass whips, before you put them to death? How can I be living in sin when we're all living in Hell?

Perhaps she had more sense than to try such a line of reasoning on her employers or Jacob's, but in this frame of mind she seriously considered calling the woman's bluff when it came.

Yet come it did not. When the jeep pulled into a shed on the edge of the shantytown at the ruined *Hauptbahnhof*, to be greeted by another not-quite-British soldier toting a submachine gun, the woman laid her hand gently on Marjorie's arm.

"I'm not sure we could stretch to *Glühwein* but can I offer you a drink? Whisky? Or a cup of tea?"

"I'll take a whisky." Marjorie followed the woman out of the shed and into a yard that appeared to be part of the unofficial refugee camp. Several blanket-swathed figures squatted around a campfire. Uprooted Germans who did not qualify as Displaced Persons, passing through to somewhere else, if somewhere else existed. A couple made way grudgingly, leaving unburned fruit boxes to sit on.

Across the camp, around other fires, people were singing. Some of the men had clearly been drinking. Most of the voices sounded close to tears.

"Let's have a chat, woman to woman. I gather that's your speciality."

Marjorie laughed and took the bottle.

"I wish it was," she said.

The young woman returned a sad, serious smile.

"The others still use my old *nomme de guerre*, Slečna Slavík – 'Miss Nightingale'. My real name is Ludmila Suková, but you can call me Mila, Mrs Jessop."

"Marjorie, please."

"Thank you." Now that she had said her name – if it was her name – the lilting precision of her English, the softness of the sibilants, made more sense. Not German. Given the sound of that pseudonym and its redolence of partisan bands, most likely Czech. "And please accept my apologies for the crude way we picked you up. I hate it that I had to pretend to threaten you. Or actually threaten you, I suppose."

"It's quite alright," Marjorie said.

"You see, I've lost my little boy." And there the woman paused, not for emphasis but, Marjorie understood, for strength. When the strength came it brought a certain earnestness and a certain carelessness she also recognised. It was the kind of carelessness that might make a man seize his rifle and raise his head above the parapet, she thought.

"I'm sorry."

"Oh, not recently. Six years ago. And as Stas back there would tell you, that presents me with a paradox. Now the war is over I'm prepared to do anything to find him. But if I do anything..."

"Untoward?"

Her eyes seemed to sparkle in the firelight, but not with mirth.

"Cruel. If I do anything cruel to find him, then how can I expect, how can I *deserve* to find him, amidst all this...?"

Her sweeping gesture might have meant the shantytown, the ruined city behind it, or the rest of the region behind that. It might have meant the whole of Germany, or all of Europe and much of the world beyond. Everyone was looking for someone in the darkness and in most cases, like the singers, or like this suddenly nervous young woman swigging whisky straight from the bottle as though it was going out of style, the only thing they were close to was tears. It had been a long time but Marjorie knew well enough how this night, of all nights, was not a good night for those who had lost the ones they loved.

"What is it I can do to help you, Mila?"

"I need an in with Mil.Gov and your Education Branch is perfect. Recently my enquiries led me to question two brothers, the Düttmanns. One of them, Georg, gave me the name of someone he had worked with, stealing children from the east."

"My God."

Mila shook her head as though to deny herself the same level of victimhood.

"My case is a little different but the officials involved are broadly the same. The man who took Pavel, the commander of the whole special action group, used to go by the name of Konrad Pfeffer. Georg gave up someone who might know where he is. A former clerk of his, called Helmut Ziegler. He was a schoolteacher in Münster before the war. And it so happened that the other Düttmann brother, Stefan, told us about two English who he'd just dropped off at a guesthouse in his taxi. One of whom was heard to mention that she worked for the Education Branch."

"I see, I see..." Except she didn't. Marjorie handed back the bottle with a querying look. At least that was what it was supposed to signify. Howard might have said it signified something else. "Sorry... do you think he works in our office or something?"

"No. But if he ever wants to work again as a schoolteacher, he'll need to pass denazification. And to do that he'd have to submit his *Fragebogen* to your section. It's possible that you have his questionnaire on file, including his current address."

"That's not my department..."

"No, but you could get us in there, perhaps, or get us the file...?"

Marjorie unwound the scarf from her neck and hair. She was feeling hot now. Dizzy. She saw the same warmth flush the young woman's cheeks. It had to be hard to rekindle such enthusiasm after so many years of searching, and yet she looked so fresh. Almost a child herself.

"How is it that you still have a... a gang?" There was no other way to say it.

Mila gave her a sly smile that accentuated the curve of scar tissue on her cheek.

"We're black marketeers. I need their help to find Pavel, so we help each other. When he's not hitting this stuff, Stas is a great designer of false identities and other subterfuges. Marek is a pickpocket, among other things, and Miro, the artist, our forger. 'Uncle' Ludvík is my rock."

"And you are theirs."

Mila shrugged, as though the thought had not occurred to her.

"I give them a sense of purpose, I suppose, and hold the group together. That's important, when a job requires an investment of time and money before it pays off. Or when we must win favour with people who can get things done."

Marjorie nodded. Woman to woman indeed.

"You're a mother to them," she said and saw her words sink in.

"In a way."

"And what are these jobs you do?"

"Why would I tell you that?"

"Because you need to trust me, Mila, and I you," Marjorie surprised herself both with the confident tone of her voice and with the content of what she was about to say. "And because if you can help me court some people with whom I need to win favour, I might be able to help you with your business operations, as well as your quest."

Mila wasn't looking drunk now. She was looking up at her with a new emotion. Not respect, perhaps. But not just surprise or – God forbid – amusement either.

Call it curiosity.

"Well... we try not to do anything too harmful, as I said."

"You said 'cruel'."

"I did. I suspect I have my own definition for that. I meant that we don't hurt people if we can help it, and we don't hurt anyone who hasn't asked for it. We're not above swindling Nazis on the run, but we'd never help them escape. We might let them lead us to some loot they've stashed away, but then we'll just take it, or even leave them for the authorities. We might break into someone's house or factory, if they were war profiteers, but we draw the line at robbing anyone who's going hungry, whoever they are."

"That's very noble of you."

"Not really. It means we're unlikely ever to bring the police down on us."

"So you acquire this merchandise. What happens then?"

"We try to turn it into the things we need. Equipment, food, bribes, mostly."

"You trade it on the black market, exposing yourselves to risk – and poor exchange rates – every time."

"What else can we do?"

Marjorie seized the bottle from her. Her hand was shaking.

"You need an 'in' with Mil.Gov. I need one with the local women. Leaders of women's groups, labour organisers, the people I'll never meet through our contacts in church groups and the bloody Women's Institute. The people *here*."

"And in return?"

"In return," Marjorie said. "I'll introduce you to someone who might take the merchandise off your hands, wholesale."

*   *   *

Jack Penny didn't believe in dybbuks or any other species of ghost. He didn't believe in the Golem either. He knew that Jews had to put up their fists for themselves. So whatever he had seen watching him a moment ago from the crest of the rubble mound couldn't have been some kind of disembodied spirit or animated matter.

It had just looked like that.

He took another nip from his hip flask and let out an appreciative grunt that clouded the air. Then he shivered anyway. Brandy was alright for warming your cockles and mussels but it wasn't much cop for frozen arses.

He was sitting in his jeep in the grounds of the imposing New City Hall, most of which was still standing. The same could not be said for its outbuildings, nor for virtually every structure of the Old Town spread out in front of it, save the scorched steeple and saw-tooth walls of the *Aegidienkirche*. Everything else was rubble.

A miracle they still found anything of value left under it, but they did. Making sure no beggars or snatchers were in the vicinity, he pulled out the duffel bag from beneath the dash and took a gander at tonight's haul. A blackened figure of a shepherd girl with her teats out: he'd get his Jerry pawnbroker to cast an expert eye over that because bronze had become pretty tasty, one way or another. A fancy china mantel clock, stopped but miraculously unbroken. An old book too, which wasn't really his thing, though Jimmy had told him to look out for something called the Gutenberg Bible. This one, very leathery and poncy, was called 'Goethe Faust' and dated 1790. There were also several pieces of tomfoolery, including an emerald the size of an eyeball and a nice fat gold wedding ring.

And all he'd paid the local gang-leader was two dozen tins of bully beef and one of his spare tyres. Not that the bastard had done anything to earn it of course, but he had his yung-uns to reimburse.

He looked around again for redcaps or, worse, for the German *Feldgendarmerie* they'd re-armed to serve as their guard dogs, complete with metal collars. So much for denazification! And so much, worst luck, for any chance of sending those same kinchins shinning up the *Neues Rathaus* for the copper on the dome. Which was a crying shame, because six years of global demand for electric wire and ammunition cases had left it a seller's market. That was why it was always a good idea to pick up any bronzes you could, regardless of artistic merit. Especially if your lads were running a smelting operation on the sly.

When the two women emerged from the stalagmites of the Old Town, Penny was busy berating himself for failing to cook up a raid on the roof lining to coincide with tonight, when all the redcaps and most of their square-head counterparts had their work cut out arresting pissed-up homesick squaddies. (There was always tomorrow, Christmas night proper, he supposed, although he wasn't really up on how the goyim did things and the Jerries seemed to do it all a full day early.)

But hang on. Two women? His old lady (no pun intended) had someone else in tow.

As he shoved the bag of treasures safely away again, he caught another blur of movement from the nearest rubble mound. Or not movement, not exactly, but a pallid sort of presence, like a face still fixed on him and yet still somehow blurred.

That couldn't be right.

He shivered again and shook his head to clear it.

"Evening, ladies!" For a crack he pulled out the big mantel clock and piled on a shirty look for Marjorie. "And what time d'you call this then?"

CHAPTER SEVEN

Bradley needed air. Pushing through the side of the tent, he set his hat against the freezing rain and fumbled in his overcoat for his Luckies.

"Tell me that again," he said.

Doctor Schlosser accepted a smoke and eyed the little gold lighter. His reply was more guarded, and not just because of his rusty English.

"The *Sonderbeauftragter* came to the B.A.F. works with a very particular request for assistance. He wanted a chemist's opinion on the possibility of modifying a certain brand-name pesticide, to remove the additive. Stransky asked me to help. I looked into it, but it was impractical, so we advised the *Sonderbeauftragter* to contact the licensed manufacturer and order a formula without the additive."

"And you said the additive was what exactly?"

"I did not say exactly, but it was an irritant – a lachrymatory substance, something like methyl bromoacetate or chloropicrin – to act as a warning component."

"To prevent users from accidentally exposing themselves to a dangerous dose."

"Indeed. It was quite common with pesticides, before this marvellous invention, of course."

The two of them had strolled towards the open front of the awning, from which a stream of sorry-looking German civilians emerged in clouds of DDT powder. Inside, three British Tommies were wielding the dusting guns, three others yelling and pulling at the shaken adults and terrified children.

"Bare your head... Open your coat... Hold out your skirt..."

On Sicily, in similar circumstances, the locals had shouted extravagant insults in return. Here the most they did was mutter under their breath.

"And this 'Special Representative' was SS-Standartenführer Konrad Pfeffer?"

"Just so. He told me that the Reichsführer had selected him personally to be in charge of pest control in the eastern territories because he knew him from the Lebensborn, before the war. There were some financial irregularities in that foundation for which he was held accountable, but he claimed – and Himmler believed him – that he was blameless."

"But Stransky didn't know about any of that."

"He had no reason to be interested and I did not tell him. To Stransky, Pfeffer was Himmler's pest control specialist. And anyway, we told him we couldn't be of service."

Bradley looked the man in the eyes as he ground out his cigarette. *So far, Stransky's story checks out,* he thought. *But I wonder how far yours does, Herr Doktor.*

As he replaced the lighter in his coat pocket, his thoughts turned to Mila. Having had to flee Nazi-occupied Czechoslovakia without her baby son, she had volunteered to return as an agent with only one secret mission in mind. But in her absence the boy's father had approached Stransky for help with offloading his unwanted burden. Stransky had given Gustel Lamprecht's name to Professor Lossner, instead of Pfeffer's, simply because he hadn't known that his pest control contact had gone on to develop a third career within RuSHA, the SS Race and Settlement Main Office: that of abducting and fostering German-looking children from Belorussia, Poland and Czechoslovakia. Which was why Lossner had next approached Lamprecht, among others, and why Stransky had ended up sending Mila on that wild goose chase in Silesia. Except it hadn't quite been a wild goose chase. Having worked their magic and figured out the connection for themselves, they'd come back to grill Stransky about Pfeffer, but even then, and in fear for his life, he had been unable to say anything about the man's subsequent activities or whereabouts. All he'd been able to give her was a list of names of the other people who had met Pfeffer at the munitions manufacturing plant he'd managed, formerly the Brünn Agrochemie Fabrik.

One such name being Dr. Christian Schlosser.

"You told Pfeffer that B.A.F. couldn't be of service. But then you made a trip, didn't you, Doctor, in the summer of '42?"

Schlosser's face, the face of an ageing Lothario, went as white as his phony physician's coat. He would have realised, of course, that Bradley's information came from speaking to Stransky, but he hadn't reckoned on Hoffman's ability to fill in the gaps.

"I took an extended motoring holiday from Moravia, yes. With a friend."

"With one of your many lady friends. This one being the young cousin of a 'Brown Sister' who was collecting for the Nazis' *Winterhilfe* appeal at B.A.F."

"Herr Fisher, it was wartime. We are both men of the world."

"Sure. Only I never brought a date to a place like that."

"A place like what, please?"

Bradley looked at him with purposeful contempt. It wasn't hard to muster.

"A place like Auschwitz."

He led the man away from the tents and around the side of the rubble mound. The southern gate of the Elbbrücke towered over them, a mock-Medieval castle of shrapnel-scarred brick and sandstone. Beyond the portal, the great steel switchback of the suspension bridge appeared more or less undamaged, unlike most other bridges across this branch – or any other branch – of the Elbe, and very definitely unlike the city on its far side.

They stepped back to allow a couple of Canadian Chevies to bypass the *cordon sanitaire*. Lean, toothless Tommy faces leered from the tailgates.

"That's one of those place names tends to stand out on the *Fragebogen*," Bradley said. "But then I guess you didn't feel it was relevant to your responsibilities in public health."

Schlosser regarded him suspiciously. Bradley had identified himself to the German chemist in his U.S. Government observer's persona and he could sense the man wondering to what extent he was being investigated as an individual of interest as opposed to quizzed in general, perhaps in order to formulate policy. Bradley saw his jaw set and guessed he was going to try to brazen it out.

"You know we are struggling to protect the inhabitants of Hamburg from a possible typhus epidemic. The colder the weather, the less fuel for heating water and so the more lice. I have been hired by the British authorities precisely *because* of my experiences in the east."

"In the camps."

"Yes, although I was only there a short time, to see and learn."

"To suck up to Himmler's favourite."

Schlosser shook his head.

"You would not understand. They were fighting typhus and malaria – delousing clothing, fumigating spaces. They were trying to save lives."

"With this brand-name pesticide, what was it?"

"I don't recall..."

"...from which Pfeffer was attempting to remove the warning component. Why would they want to do that, wouldn't that endanger the men carrying out these tasks?"

"I don't know. As I say..."

"You were only there a short time."

"Precisely."

"Well, Stransky clearly thought you'd done enough brown-nosing out there to be the kind of guy who might know what became of Pfeffer." Bradley forced himself to smile. "That's what he told me, anyhow. And what he told the girl, the second

84

time she visited him. Question is: what did you tell her?"

"Wie bitte?"

Before the man could even flinch, he seized Schlosser's jaw, turning it this way and that. The swelling had gone down but the bruises were still there. He thought he could make out the finger-marks.

"The girl who's looking for Pfeffer. You gave her something, or someone. Not Pfeffer himself, I reckon. You gave it up too easy to be him. Plus you're still alive for now, just in case."

From the look on Schlosser's face, so far that thought had not occurred to him, but from now on it would be a hard one to dismiss.

"Where did you send her, Doctor?"

*   *   *

He spent the rest of that short winter's day at the Atlantic on the *Außenalster*, trying to put a call through to Hoffman in Munich. The hotel was full of British brass who regarded his Brooks Brothers get-up with evident mistrust, but Bradley had learned by now that posing as a lieutenant was worse. In uniform, there was always an officer who was senior to you and therefore wouldn't cooperate on principle, whereas the same sticklers were more than happy to give assistance to a civilian 'expert'.

By the time he got through on the telephone, one or two of the questions that Schlosser had left nagging at the back of his mind had started to crystallise.

"Did he corroborate Stransky's story?" Hoffman wanted to know first. "Did he give you anyone?"

"He gave me someone," Bradley said. "His driver on that grand tour you dug the dirt on. A guy named Georg Düttmann, from a place down near Hanover called the 'Free State of Schaumburg-Lippe'. Yeah, no kidding. Reading between the lines, he was Pfeffer's man all along."

"Who? The driver – or Schlosser?"

"I'd say both. Or let's say Pfeffer lent Schlosser his driver, his car too, probably, and from that point he was hooked."

"What about his female companion on the road trip? Lamprecht's cousin."

"That's what's bugging me. According to Stransky, the MERCURY team came storming back from Silesia claiming Lamprecht had let slip that he knew Pfeffer. They'd linked it all through Lamprecht being a 'Brown Sister' who ended up working on the *Sonderkommando Aktion*. They also bought into it when Stransky maintained he knew nothing about it. And when he suggested that his buddy Schlosser might.'

"So?"

"I don't know, but now I've met him I get the feeling Schlosser's up to his neck in it. And if Pfeffer already knew Gustel Lamprecht from his early days with the Lebensborn, maybe they were using her cousin as another bit of bait to reel him in. So maybe MERCURY has got on the tail of the right guy despite making the wrong assumption – or maybe they're not on the right track at all..."

"And what is it you think Schlosser's up to his neck in? The kid-stealing?"

"I don't know. Something people are still keen to cover up, that's for sure. He also told me about this pesticide they were trying to modify..."

"We're hearing more and more about that. Sounds like the stuff the Russians found at Auschwitz and Majdanek. The Brits up where you are have been investigating what happened at the Neuengamme camps also, and specifically the involvement of a Hamburg company known as 'Testa', short for Tesch & Stabenow. That's the company Schlosser trained at before he moved to Moravia."

Bradley thought he could hear a new buzzing on the line. Then, like an electric arc about to overload into flame, he realised that the note of dread was in his head. Deep down and without acknowledging it, he had known it would be something like this.

"You mean the cyanide? For the gas chambers?"

"Tesch & Stabenow distributed it under the brand name 'Zyklon B'."

"Jesus, they were trying to remove the component that warns people they're being exposed..."

"Yeah."

"And they asked Stransky to help. Schlosser claims he didn't oblige them, but Schlosser's a goddamn liar. Is there a way to put Stransky on the line now – if you still got him on ice?"

Silence, except for the static. For a moment he thought the connection had been lost. Then he heard Hoffman curse under his breath.

"What is it?"

"We got him on ice for real now. He was found hanged at the safe house the day before yesterday. Looks like he did it himself."

Bradley couldn't help but picture those deep-set eyes. Like gun muzzles nestling in a pillbox, the girl had called them. He tried to imagine them bulging out and couldn't.

"Bullshit. That guy was about self-preservation, at all costs."

"She'd driven him half crazy. Who knows what was going through his head? And I've got to tell you, a CIC safe house ain't for the faint at heart."

Bradley surveyed the gilded splendour of the Atlantic lobby and nodded.

"I need to get moving," he said.

"You're heading down Hanover way. You'll need transport."

"I've bummed a ride with a couple of UNRRA types. I can still speak their lingo. But first I'm going to see Schlosser again. I might stick my pistol in his face while I'm at it. I don't think he told us the whole story – or her."

*   *   *

As soon as he'd left the lakeshore behind, darkness had descended over Hamburg. With the power so capricious and the remaining streetlamps few and far between, shadows crept out of alleys and doorways and the shells of buildings turned to Jack-o'-Lanterns. Women and boys called to him but he set a steady pace and kept walking.

The chemist lived just north of the Elbbrücken on the fringes of the devastated Hammerbrook district. For ease of access to the cordon at the bridges, he'd been billeted in one of several old railroad freight cars that were positioned semi-permanently against the wall they'd built to close off the no-go zone in '43. There had been a serious lack of accommodation in Hamburg since the night the world had learned a new term: firestorm. In places like Hammerbrook, that had translated to a serious lack of people too and the ruins had become a forbidden city. But with the influx of ethnic Germans expelled from the east, now those barricades were being opened up again. Through the breaches and the watching crowds, running parallel with the first of the endless ranks of gutted facades, Bradley saw sappers under floodlights installing a long street of corrugated iron Quonset huts.

Veiled in the resulting shadows, the freight car he was heading for had no wheel-set but still required visitors to mount a little rubble platform. No light came from the narrow barred windows either side of the door. He shooed a couple of moochers from the steps and pulled out his flashlight.

"Schlosser?"

There was a drop bar arrangement to shut the door from either side, but it lifted so easily he doubted it had even been latched. With the darkness and the silence inside, that set his senses tingling. It didn't look the kind of neighbourhood where you'd go out and leave your property unlocked.

The car had been partitioned off into separate compartments. The one to the left, marked A, was Schlosser's. The communal area was taken up by a stove and flue around which clothes horses and washing lines were clustered. Sanitary arrangements, it seemed, were limited to a curtain and a covered bucket at the rear.

He pushed open the door to compartment A.

It wasn't much of a way to live, although Bradley had been in barracks that were worse. A straw palliasse and heap of blankets on the floor. A couple of crates for furniture, one a table, the other a wardrobe, of sorts. There was also an ornate wooden armchair. On a shelf sat an oil lamp, unlit. In the chair sat Doctor Schlosser.

Bradley hadn't really intended to draw his side arm. Now he did.

With his other hand he played the flashlight over the slumped head and arms. Not tied up.

So why in God's name hadn't he taken off the mask?

It was the mask that had killed him, Bradley was sure of it. He could smell it. It had escaped into the room and out through the window grilles, probably some time ago, yet even now there was a pungent, bleachy odour in the air and his eyes and nose were stinging as though he'd been slicing onions. But he knew instantly that the source of the fumes was the gas mask itself. It was evident from the reeking residue of chemicals that had bubbled up and formed oily stains around the seal of the big silver filter unit on the front. And from the burns on the exposed skin around the throat and ears.

And of course from the bloody eyes through the yellowed lenses, staring up from the fires of hell.

An irritant, he recalled Schlosser's description. A lachrymatory substance, like methyl bromoacetate or chloropicrin, to act as a warning component. But those were also the kind of chemicals the Germans had developed to use as weapons in the Great War. In sufficient concentration... such as brewed up in a gas mask filter...

A guilt-ridden chemist's final experiment, perhaps.

But if not why, then how. How had he not clawed off the mask when the burning started?

Bradley forced open the window grille before lighting the oil lamp to take a better look.

He had no intention of taking off the mask.

89

No ligature marks visible on the wrists. Schlosser didn't appear to have been tied up and untied post mortem. Yet the fingernails were bent and broken, and the arms of the chair deeply scored, presumably at the same time. So it seemed likely he'd been fully conscious at the start of it. What would make a man sit and take his torture like that?

What, or who?

He searched the room, finding only medical textbooks and the expected ration cards and passes. Tucked inside one of the books were a few personal mementoes. Love letters, they looked like, and snapshots of half a dozen women, one of whom may or may not have been Lamprecht's cousin. Struggling with the German handwriting, he shoved it all into his coat pocket and moved on. Beneath a scrap of mirror, an enamel bowl held toothbrush, tooth powder, razor and strop, plus a couple of bars of medical-issue soap, one of the perks of a job in public health.

Nothing to show who he had really been.

Bradley became aware of the clang and clatter from the other side of the stone barricade. His thundering heart and anxious breathing had been drowning out the general din but now the sappers and their SEPs must have moved on to a noisier phase of the construction process. If the low-pitched engine note wasn't the sound of a diesel generator running the floodlights, perhaps they had brought up a truck and started dropping off the next batch of heavy steel members. Or had the vibration a moment ago, which at first had barely registered, been caused by something else?

Such as movement on the rubble platform outside the wagon, or in the next compartment?

He turned down the wick and went to the door. There was the faintest trace of a glow under the door of the neighbouring unit.

"Ist da jemand?" he called out.

Aiming the .45 through the thin wood, he tried the handle and felt it give. Warm light spilled around the edges of the door. Then the light trembled.

That was the moment he knew the danger was past. He lowered his gun as he pushed his way in, the door snagging on a mess of blankets, rags and knick-knacks. Sure enough, the candlelit faces on the bundle that passed for a bed were those of two small, frightened children – a boy and a girl – and a smaller, wide-eyed kitten.

He crouched down, forcing himself to smile for the second time that day.

"*Was ist passiert?*" He couldn't remember the German for 'next door' and resorted to a jab with his thumb and: "*Dort.*"

But whatever they had seen or heard (and he didn't want to think about what they had heard), they were not going to tell him, not like this.

Probably they had seen nothing anyhow. Assuming the bums on the front steps had deliberately hidden their faces from him when he'd arrived, and supposing that had been the hit team's rear-guard hanging back to see who showed, they would hardly have been so sloppy as to leave these kids as witnesses.

He sniffed the funk in the compartment and decided that the gas had dissipated. Enough to leave them there, anyway, while he found a policeman to tip off.

The three pairs of eyes watched silently as he kicked aside the rags he had disturbed.

How many more would be watching him when he took to the streets?

Like many of the guys in his old unit, Bradley had cut back his holster flap so it would tuck out of the way when necessary. Now he slid the .45 in beneath his coat, ready for a quick draw. No way he was going out like Schlosser. No way at all.

He gave the kids a wink and closed the door.

CHAPTER EIGHT

The Education Branch of the Internal Affairs & Communication Division occupied several properties on one of the more prosperous streets of Bünde that had been requisitioned en bloc and cordoned off by the British element of the Control Commission for Germany. The Records and Registry sections were distributed between a pair of former private houses, although it was impossible to determine how long ago these had been taken over and laid out – poorly, in Marjorie's considered opinion – as offices and archives. Military institutions the world over shared a talent for making everything drearily utilitarian yet in the same breath barely serviceable.

She walked in through the open hallway and pretended to study the noticeboard while she stamped slush and grit from her galoshes. Her heart pounded as the door to the front room swung open, but it was only Tony Valance, a fellow volunteer, on his perennial search for a fresh brew.

"Morning, Marjorie. I see you're still resisting the lure of the Grenadiers!"

He meant her continued insistence on wearing mufti, which she had decided was essential if she was to relate to the local women's leaders on equal terms. Like most of the Civilian Mil.Gov Officers, Valance wore the shapeless plain battledress of the C.C.G., also known as 'Complete Chaos Guaranteed' or 'Charlie Chaplin's Grenadiers'.

"I'm only here on a flying visit," she said, affecting a breezy manner. "Just popped in to run a check on one of my 'ringleaders'."

"If she's a trades union type I'd be surprised she had anything to do with the Nazis. Surprised they left her alive, to tell the truth."

"I thought it couldn't hurt to dig out her *Fragebogen* before we accept any further help from her. D.C. thought so too, given the coming change-over."

Valance's eyebrows arched high above his pebble-thick spectacles. If their boss, the great Donald Riddy, had given her his blessing, that was good enough for him.

"Yes, quite. Set a precedent, for when we bring in the Germans to run denazification for themselves. Well, don't let me keep you. TTFN."

"Ta-ta for now."

Marjorie hurried through to the rear of the building and let herself into the windowless room marked 'I.A.&C. – E.B. (Westphalia-Lippe-Lower Saxony)'. Breathing a sigh of relief to find the lights off, she eased shut the door and flicked the switch.

Two rows of tall oak cabinets ran the length of the narrow room. If it had been the Nazis who'd first converted these dwellings, as she now rather suspected, Marjorie shuddered to think what information they had once cross-referenced from here. She pulled out the SCH drawer for Schneider – her pretext, albeit not one that 'D.C.' knew anything about – before tiptoeing to the far end of the aisle and the Zs.

Helmut Ziegler had indeed applied to return to academic life. She found his file almost immediately. When she extracted the *Fragebogen* and saw the man's answer to Question 11, present address, she let out a nervous chuckle.

Of course, she thought. How could it be anywhere else?

There was no question of sneaking out the *Fragebogen* and leaving the file all but empty, yet a quick scan of the six pages confirmed Mila's suspicion that Ziegler had answered few of their 131 questions honestly. How could he have? Even so, the surveyors had seen fit to deface the forms and their accompanying *Anlagen* with multiple underlines, exclamation marks and queries. She copied down the address in her little notebook and went to dig out Frau Schneider.

After another excruciating exchange with the ever-vigilant Tony, and the meeting of Miss Gemmel's committee for which she had come to town, Marjorie found herself approaching the cordon sentries on leaden feet. The inevitable pairing of British redcap and *Feldgendarmerie* bulldog, chatting away like old buddies. As usual, the German's coalscuttle helmet and chest-slung machine pistol gave her the willies, but this time she felt as nervous of the redcap.

Pull yourself together, she thought. These fine fellows are here to check German staff's passes and keep grumpy German civilians out. They're not going to search or question you. The only spies they're interested in are the four Soviets at the military liaison mission, and the only things *they're* sneaking back and forth are Scotch and nylons.

Sure enough, she was waved through with barely a glance. The benefits of being a victor, even one dressed more like the vanquished. At a judicious distance along the road, buttoned up against the weather, Jacob's man was waiting for her in the jeep.

She raised a triumphant hand.

*   *   *

Mila watched Staff Sergeant Carter drag one of the tail fins of the broken-up night fighter across the waste ground and prop it against an empty engine cowling forty yards away. His face wore a raffish grin as he sauntered back over and accepted the strange-looking weapon from his subordinate.

"Looks sorta like a sawn-off, don't it? But ain't no need to put yer fingers in yer ears for this one."

He cocked the rifle's action, took aim and squeezed the trigger.

The only sound was a Ping! from the swastika on the tail fin. It looked like he'd pierced it dead centre.

Carter cackled.

"'S'basically a No.4 service rifle, chambered for .45 – see, the magazine's from a Yank automatic pistol. The whole barrel section's a bloody great suppressor. Loudest thing you'll 'ear is your target's 'ead cracking open. Cop a load of that..."

Mila took the gun and felt its weight. With the pistol grip and folding stock, you could wear this over your shoulder, under your coat. A useful accessory.

"'S'experimental..." Carter was saying. "Secret ops, yeah? These ones specially. The three crates we've come by are all there is. Go on, try it out."

She raised the silenced carbine and put another hole somewhere near Carter's. It was tempting to re-cock with the weapon still levelled, using thumb and forefinger on the rubberised bolt handle and her middle finger on the trigger, as she'd been trained, but something about the shortened action felt tighter than a normal Enfield and, anyway, that wasn't what she was trying to prove. She resisted the urge.

"Very nice." She offered the weapon back to the staff sergeant and his man.

"Keep it, as a sign of good faith."

"Alright."

"I'm shipping the rest home pronto, before they start wondering what happened to their test pieces. These will go like hot cakes in some parts of London."

At that, Mila gestured for Stas and 'Uncle' Ludvík to bring the leather doctor's bag from the jeep. It took the two of them to carry it between them.

"And what about these?" she said as they let it fall to the bare earth with a thud.

While Carter crouched down, Mila caught Ludvík's eye and nodded. They were dangerously exposed now. The waste ground, spread across a barren expanse of sandy heathland surrounded by low hills and patchy forest, was part disused airfield and part rubbish tip. The piles of torn-up wings and fuselages offered scant cover, yet plenty of opportunity for their host to hide many more stooges than the three scruffy REME-mechanic-types they had already seen. It was the same with the other vehicles: Carter's soft-skinned 15-cwt cargo truck and the 3-tonner crane that had dismantled the aircraft before the local work gangs took over with their hammers and chisels. The only substantial structure – and it didn't look that solid – was the long, low, twin-chimney smelting mill. Save the furnace itself, even that seemed thrown together from rusty lattice girders and corrugated iron.

From down below came Carter's sarcastic version of an appreciative whistle.

"Oh I am impressed!" When he stood up he was weighing the coil of copper-clad cable in one hand, a pair of heavy-duty pipes in the other, and wearing a nasty sneer. "This little lot, plus the brass gears and other stuff in there... I'll give you five bob for everything. An' another shilling to sling yer 'ook and stop wasting my time."

"I'm sorry...?"

"No offence, darling, but you're in the wrong game, ain't you – I'm only letting you off without a solid thrashing 'cause Marjorie vouched for your Polish arses, the silly cow, but you ain't even proper Polski. And gimme me bloody shooter back!"

Mila put on her best look of polite incomprehension. In the corner of her eye she could see Stas trying to restrain Ludvík without making it obvious.

"You mean... you want to pay me for the samples?"

It was the moment she'd been waiting for, the one she'd engineered, the one she needed. Carter frowned and his head rocked back. Just for an instant, he had lost his balance.

"Do what?"

"The samples – of the supplies we secured from the Hamburg and Kiel shipyards when we were up that way recently. Five thousand metres of that unused Pyro. Two hundred and fifty ten-kilogramme spools of winding wire for U-Boat motors. As much tubing as you want, of course. We're only limited by the transport requirements..."

He wasn't going to smile. He had too much face to save for that.

"Got any bronze?"

"Bronze?"

"Bronzes. Statues. A bunch of them got whisked away and shoved in a warehouse somewhere. The Jerries probably pretended they was melting them down for Messerschmitts, like we done with our Spitfire Fund. You find me that warehouse, don't keep it to yourself."

"I wouldn't dream of it."

"Alright then. Looks like we got the makings of a deal. What is it you need?"

Mila deliberated. A moment ago she had lured him on and unsettled him, quite deliberately. It had been important to show him she was no soft touch. There would come another moment when this message would need to be emphasised, but in the meantime it might be best to wind her neck in, as Carter would probably say.

"Well, the transport, like I said. Our contact can give us access, but we can't move it without muscle. And at least a couple of lorries. Army lorries."

"That's what we're here for. What else?"

"Something to open doors," she said.

And now he did smile.

"Like a sort of jemmy, you mean?"

He beckoned them over to the stacks in front of the smelter. These weren't the roughly trimmed pieces of aircraft that were about to go in. These, neatly arranged on layers of planks, were what had been coming out.

Shiny silver ingots of freshly recovered aluminium, destined to be the pots, pans and other harmless implements of the new, forward-looking Europe.

"Try one for size," Carter said.

Mila selected an ingot from the top layer and picked it up. It was heavy, but manageable.

"Now try one from under there."

She set down the ingot and put her fingers around an identical example from the layer below. This time, she could barely move it, let alone lift it with one hand. Her thumbnail picked at a hardened drip of silver paint at its bottom edge, revealing the colour beneath.

"That the sort of door-opener you're talking about?"

"That's the sort."

Carter scratched his chin. It looked odd, a British NCO with his collar unfastened. He hadn't even shaved.

"Them bars is a bit out of your league, and they tend to attract too much attention, if you know what I mean."

With a practised twist of the wrist he picked up a different ingot and passed it to her, grinning when she had to take the weight in two hands. She turned it over but could find no signs of silver paint on this one.

"You get us all that copper – specially the refined stuff – and I'll give you a couple of these. Think you can make it a regular supply run?"

She turned to Stas. He was playing the man with the shipping contacts here, although the actual tip-off had come from an over-obliging Schlosser. The only trick would be keeping Carter's men from discovering that it was simply a finite stockpile in a semi-derelict storeroom, but that was child's play for a master of theatrical illusion. Savouring his moment in the limelight, the old ham brought his lips together in an expression of confident approval.

"I imagine we can come to some arrangement," she translated.

In the quest to bribe, bully and cheat out more information about Konrad Pfeffer and his vanished organisation, Carter would prove a useful contact, as Mrs Jessop had suggested, and he scored over Stas's Hanseatic equivalents in two important respects. Firstly, he was real, not fictional, and secondly, he was one of the victors, not the vanquished. Yet she couldn't shake off the impression that there was something very wrong about this British soldier, and that far from being just another example of the occupying army engaging in a bit of private enterprise, his schemes were considerably more ambitious and he was no more a member of that army than she, Stas, Ludvík, Marek or Miro were.

But if it was a con, it went further than fake uniforms and stolen vehicles. This was a British-sanctioned clean-up operation, on the edges of the British-controlled proving grounds. Over the next rise, they were testing the Panthers they'd put together at the Hanover works out of the unfinished hulls and turrets left behind at the war's end. It was inconceivable that Staff Sergeant Carter and his men would be here without some kind of official blessing.

The logical assumption was that the unit had an equally crooked commanding officer. Carter had been stationed here to melt down the steady influx of German loot into untraceable bullion, and to disguise it all as aluminium for regeneration projects. It was a clever stunt. As well as orders, he probably had a licence from the Control Commission to do it. Then there was the man's fixation with copper. She wasn't sure what that signified but clearly he, or his C.O., had an eager buyer. The problem was his unshaven chin and open collar, plus the general unmilitary air. She and her crew were better at playing soldiers than this bunch. So who were they? And who was in charge?

Just play along, she remembered someone telling her: another mystery-man in a uniform that didn't match his purpose. Just play along and something will turn up.

"Pleasure doing business with you," Staff Sergeant Carter spat into his hand and proffered it, his dark features splitting into a broad grin when she reciprocated without batting an eyelid. Then his grip tightened. "Now, give us a lift in your nice Polish jeep and we'll all go meet Marjorie, eh?"

*   *   *

Reichsstraße 1 had been the trade and military route

connecting Aachen in the west with Magdeburg, Berlin and the lost province of East Prussia. It was the *Via Regia* from the days of the Holy Roman Empire and the *Hellweg* of Charlemagne. Yet here, in the wake of Hitler's autobahns and Hitler's war, limping tiredly across the winter fallow between the fragments and outcrops of the old Teutoburg Forest, it was little more than a byway.

And now, again, it was the site of an ambush. But this time there would be no Augustus to butt his head against his palace walls and cry 'Give me back my legions'.

Marjorie summoned the last of her diminishing resolve and met the vindictive stare of the leader of the German bandits, the modern-day Arminius, her captor.

"I am not your enemy," she said in emphatic German. "I am not from the army."

The bandit leaned in through the open side of the jeep and seized Craftsman Tate by his bloodstained tunic. The dead man, eyes rolled back, fell forwards on the wheel.

"This is an English soldier."

"He was driving me home."

"Home? This is not your home."

"Right. But I am here to help."

The man heaved Tate out of the jeep and leaned in further. She could smell the drink and tobacco on his breath and, behind them, the smoke and damp of rough living.

"No. You're here to pay."

Marjorie shrieked as another set of filthy paws took hold of her from behind, pulling her out of the passenger seat into the gathering mist and an even fouler miasma of odours. She turned around to see a toothless giant right out of Grimm's Tales.

When they had first emerged from the fields, like scarecrows, she had thought they might be *Ostarbeiter*, those former slave labourers from the east who had taken to the hills hereabouts, or DPs seeking vengeance on the German population, or perhaps the liberated Russian POWs who'd shown no great yearning to return to their motherland. But with the first shout, sadly disregarded by her driver, she had understood that these were natives. Deserters or absconders – among their rags and blankets they wore the remnants of uniforms, but then so many did nowadays – or simply starving locals who had formed a band to raid the surviving estates and any other likely source of food. Clearly, from the sporting rifles and shotguns the six men carried, the raids had been successful.

They held her at gunpoint while they searched the jeep and her bag, finding nothing of interest besides Tate's cigarettes, side arm and leather jerkin. A thin, wet snow was falling again and Marjorie thought about asking permission of the bandits to put something over Tate's upturned face on the roadside, but she decided this was not the time to show any sign of weakness or sentiment. What she dreaded, more than anything else, was being taken away from the jeep. Then no one would ever find her.

The leader made her remove her coat and went through its pockets. After a cursory examination, the little black notebook joined Tate in the mud and slush.

"Now that," the beast said.

When she did not respond, his underling the giant grabbed a fistful of her skirt, pulling it down over her hips, where it snagged.

You're used to violating younger women, she thought.

The four scarecrows were still spaced out in the field behind. Marjorie was struggling to unfasten her waistband when, bizarrely, she noticed the furthest of the men sink to his knees and pitch forward out of sight.

No one had seen or heard anything.

She let the skirt slip down and kicked it aside.

"And those," the leader's unspecific gesture indicated her scarf, jacket, cardigan or blouse. Probably, she realised, all of them at once.

"Please don't hurt me," she said, staring bleakly over his

shoulder and seeing the next scarecrow's head fly back in a spray of moisture.

This time, when the rigid body toppled like a falling tree, they heard its impact with the frozen ground. Scarecrows three and four spun around and scarecrow three continued spinning, yelling out and groaning as he did. Now the bandit leader and the giant were distracted too and Marjorie took the opportunity to scramble back inside the jeep.

She heard a loud blast and a quick-fire exchange of shots, shouts and screams. Footsteps thundered on the road surface and something heavy fell against the jeep.

One of the voices, she thought, had been Jacob's.

When she raised her head to peer through the gap where the canvas hood met the cut-away side, the first person she saw was Mila Suková. The young Czech woman, wearing a long raincoat over her Polish uniform, was striding purposefully towards them from the direction of a second jeep a hundred yards back down the road. Marjorie nearly fainted when her view was suddenly obscured by the bulk of the bandit leader, who had evidently gone to ground next to the jeep and was standing up again.

His had been the first voice to shout. He shouted again as he raised his shotgun.

"Stop where you are!"

Without breaking stride, Mila raised something long and tubular from under her coat. There was a tiny flash and a puff of smoke.

Marjorie had ducked. When she looked again the bandit leader was no longer there. Instead, there was someone else at the side of the jeep, weighing it down and leaning in. She curled into a ball and let out a squeal of fright before she realised that it was Jacob.

"Marge, love. Are you alright? I'm so sorry..."

"Sorry?" She accepted his hand, and the coat that someone was holding out to her. Mila was holding it out. It was Mila's coat, the one beneath which she'd concealed the weapon.

"He thinks he let you down because his pistol jammed after he'd killed *him* and wounded *him*." Mila was looking at the road beside the jeep and Marjorie realised she didn't need to ask who she meant. She saw Mila tip Jacob something that looked pretty much like a cheeky wink as she added: "I reckon he did well enough, for an amateur..."

Jacob gave a grudging nod and looked away while Mila helped her dress properly in her own clothes. Her skirt was a little mucky, but it might have been worse.

It might have been so much worse.

Now she was standing, she felt able to take a few steps. She saw the second jeep draw up and two Polish soldiers get out, one middle-aged, the other seemingly ancient. She recognised both from Christmas Eve in Hanover: Mila's designer of false identities and her rock.

"I took care of the first two with this," Mila said, patting the peculiar tube-gun. "Stas and 'Uncle' Ludvík got the next two from back there, and your knight in shining armour charged in to settle matters."

Jacob shook his head, at least partly in wonderment.

"You settled matters."

"We were lucky. Lucky we arrived when we did. Lucky they were unprepared."

"Lucky I gave you that," Jacob said.

"Yes. But in my experience, that means our luck's due to run out. We need to clean up, quickly."

"Then it's also lucky I've got a furnace and enough coal to start a proper riot."

Marjorie read the concern on Mila's face but in that moment she could not read Jacob's.

"Are you sure? Your man here..."

"Tate," Marjorie said.

"...he was a British soldier."

Jacob shrugged, but not lightly. Just for a moment, it seemed he had the weight of the world on his shoulders. The world and everything strange in it, including honesty.

103

"Arthur weren't really a soldier. Least not since me and him had it away from basic training in '39. He wouldn't have minded anyhow and he ain't gonna bitch about it now."

Marjorie did what she had been avoiding doing. She looked down. Mila, or one of Mila's crew, had laid the raincoat over Tate's head and torso. The other two, Arminius and the giant, lay crumpled face down in puddles of slush and mud and blood.

It was then that she spotted her notebook. Quickly she picked it up and flicked through the waterlogged pages. Ziegler's address was still legible.

Was this the right moment to tell Mila? Would she be buoyed by the knowledge or burdened by it? What was best when you had just murdered three people like that – reflection, or distraction?

How could anyone possibly understand what she was feeling?

Marjorie turned from the bodies in the field to the empty, decaying stretch of imperial road. A little way further along, she noticed for the first time the signpost that named the next major town, 20 kilometres northeast up the Reichsstraße.

Where else, in this land of twisted fairy tales, would you seek out a man whose trade had changed in the blink of an eye from serving all the townsfolk to stealing all their children?

CHAPTER NINE

Stefan Düttmann leaned across and grabbed the loop of worn leather to pull shut the driver's door. As he straightened up, he caught the keen eyes of his latest fare in the rear view mirror. Was that a flash of understanding and sympathy, or another sort of vigilance entirely?

"Where to, mister?"

"*Bring mich nach Hause.*"

Terrible pronunciation. Stefan persevered with his equally terrible English.

"Your house? I not know where..."

"No." The look was fierce and piercing, like the pistol muzzle Stefan knew would also be present in the rear cabin, possibly already trained on his spine. "Not my home. Yours."

Stefan shrugged. His hand moved toward the ignition, which was also the direction of the passenger-side alcove where he knew that Georg had hidden their father's police pistol beneath a bundle of oily rags.

"Another who wants to ask about my brother," he muttered.

"No," the American in the back repeated. Less emphatically this time. Almost tenderly. "I want to talk to both of you – about your sister."

Stefan twisted the key and put the Olympia into gear with an uncharacteristic clunk. When his hand returned to the steering wheel, it was shaking.

"Don't you know that no one in Germany talks about his sister any more?"

Just the watchful gaze. Stefan suspected that his English wasn't up to communicating such a message. Or perhaps the American wasn't up to hearing it.

By today's standards, the morning train from Osnabrück had been more or less punctual. Georg would not yet have gone out to his *Doppelkopf* game. If Stefan could cover the twelve or thirteen kilometres to Bückeburg without encountering any roadblocks or convoys, they could call 'mealtime' and listen to what this official had to say about Anna. Whatever nonsense it was, whatever questions they wanted answering, none of it would bring her back. But Stefan remembered from the initial surge of occupation that the Americans were much more generous than their British counterparts, who were almost as stony broke as the local populace. There might be money to be made somehow.

He looked out over Minden's grim expanse of railway sidings, bridges and basins, most of it bust-up and flooded-over. Although they had demolished the town with their bombers, the Allied Powers claimed that the great aqueduct where the Mittelland Canal once crossed the River Weser had been blown up by the Wehrmacht during the last retreat. But then they would say that.

"OK mister, you're the boss."

*   *   *

Following the one-armed taxi driver up the steps to Holzgasse 18, Bradley had a funny feeling that he had been here before. At first he assumed it was because of the railroad car in Hamburg, and his dread of what he might find in there. Then he realised it was because of her. He was treading in her footsteps again.

Not that the apprehension wasn't real enough. It didn't take a genius to see a pattern in the deaths of Stransky and Schlosser, nor to extrapolate two distinctly possible and possibly related explanations. Either he'd stumbled on an operation to hush up whatever it was the doctors had been working on, or he was the one leading the assassins to their targets.

And whichever way you looked at it, Georg Düttmann might be next.

He had done what he could to cover his tracks. He had switched back to his butterbars for the drive from Hamburg and helped the UNRRA guys unload medical supplies at D.P. assembly centres all the way down to their zonal administration in Spenge, near Bünde. Then it was on to their gigantic central warehouse facility in Herford, where he took the opportunity to enter Civvy Street again, before hitching another ride to British Army headquarters at the spa town of Bad Oeynhausen. From there, having put through another call to Hoffman and gotten the dope on the brothers Düttmann, it had simply been a matter of ensuring he was on the train that Stefan met with his taxi each morning. And keeping his eyes peeled all the way back to Bückeburg.

Except nothing was ever really simple – and after what he had found in that freight car, he wished he hadn't thought about peeling eyes.

His hand was on his pistol as Stefan unlocked the front door.

The similarities with Schlosser's last resting place continued inside. Furniture and fixtures had all been burned for heat or sold for food. Even the panelling and floorboards had been stripped back to the bare minimum. Georg sat at the single remaining table in the kitchen, finishing a bottle of schnapps for breakfast. The big man with the military buzz-cut and the bandaged neck gave his brother an accusing look but did not get up.

Wise-ass cover stories would be wasted on these guys. Bradley pulled out his Special Agent's gold badge and flashed it like he imagined the Gestapo might have done.

"Doctor Schlosser gave you up," he said to Georg in the German he had practised.

"That does not surprise me."

"He gave me something else..."

Bradley delved in his coat pocket for the photographs and letters he had found in Schlosser's medical book. Even with his eager *Abwehr* helpers, Hoffman had only been able to fill in some of the blanks over the phone. It seemed that after Lamprecht's cousin, Schlosser had become less discriminating. He passed the photographs one by one to Georg and Stefan until they froze.

"Anke," The word snagged in Georg's injured throat.

"Yes," Bradley said. "And there was this."

He unfolded the letter, seeing the brothers stare in dismay at the pale blue paper and cramped handwriting. He had to remind himself of their military records, especially Georg's, or what little was known of it.

"I had these translated for me," he went on. "But my German is poor, so perhaps you would read it out..."

Stefan seized the page, examined the date, and found the passage he had marked.

"'*Dearest Christian, I beg you please do not insist I go to work for that man again! For you, anything, my love. But the things he makes me do — if you knew, you would not ask that of me. I pray you will receive this before he comes again...*'"

When Stefan's hand, crumpling the letter, fell onto the table, Georg enfolded both in one huge fist. Their heads leaned together like cattle and Stefan said in a small, tearful voice: "That was two weeks before she killed herself."

Wrapping both arms around his brother, Georg fixed Bradley with a savage glare and spoke in guttural English.

"Where is Doctor Schlosser now?"

"Dead."

"You?"

"No."

"The woman – the Polish woman?"

Polish? It was close enough and Bradley could not imagine who else he might mean.

"I don't think so. Whoever killed him came after that."

"A pity. She can make a man suffer, that one."

"I assure you, Doctor Schlosser suffered."

Bradley could tell that Georg had read it in his face. Georg had seen such memories written on faces before.

"You want to know who this other man is. The one that Anna..."

"I already know who he is," Bradley cut in. "What I want to know is where you told the woman she could find him."

"You think I told her?"

"I think you came off very lightly if you didn't."

That was beyond him. It took all three of them and a mixture of broken English and German to make him understand. At length, he let his features split into a humourless smile.

"I told her nothing. I gave her the name of someone who would never know where to find the Standartenführer. I chose this person for a joke."

"What joke is that?"

"If you're looking for her, you'll find out."

Stefan was staring at his older brother not with affection but with horror.

"Why would you cover for this man now, after what Anke wrote? Is that what you did in this unit of yours, share your sisters around? Is that what it means, 'my honour is loyalty'?"

Georg had Stefan's hand in his fist again. Bradley's was back on his pistol. He suspected that this was the first time Stefan had ever admitted he knew his brother had been in the SS, possibly the first time he'd admitted it to himself. The knuckles of Georg's hand were turning yellow-white when he let go.

"Say that again, you'll have nothing left to wipe your arse with. And I won't be the one to do it for you." He seized the bottle and stood up, knocking over the table with thighs like tree trunks. "I'm late for my *Doko* game."

"I can't let you leave," Bradley said. Georg cast a dismissive look at the hand that was brushing back his coat to clear the quick-draw holster.

"Tom Mix, *ne*? 'The Ringo Kid'."

"That was John Wayne," Bradley said.

"You can't stop me. Not if you want to find him. Or her."

He left the threat, and perhaps the accusation, hanging in the air. The front door slammed. Bradley sat down next to Stefan, who was slumped forward, clamping his hand between his legs to soothe it. Probably he was also trying to hide his tears.

"Where's he going?"

"A bar in town. The only one that's too poor for the British."

"How's he get there? Your car?"

Stefan reached into his hip pocket and pulled out the car keys.

"He takes the back way. He borrows Old Norbert's bicycle."

"Whose?"

"Our neighbour here."

Bradley levered himself back to his feet, massaging his knee in anticipation of his next thankless task. On an impulse he laid a hand on Stefan's withered shoulder and gave it a compassionate squeeze.

"Has Old Norbert got any other bicycles?"

*   *   *

Holzgasse skirted a hillside on the edge of town and the 'back way' was a dank, twisting track that cut through patches of denuded forest, lumberyards and workshops. Bradley's progress was slowed several times by clumps of bundled-up civilians out foraging in the woods, many pushing old prams or carts for their pickings. For a stretch, a trio of skinny kids ran alongside him, greatly amused by his laboured pedalling.

He first caught sight of his quarry when the track opened out into the back end of a minor avenue. Passing the well spaced out dwellings up ahead, which were mostly villas and some still standing, he recognised the disproportionate figure atop the better of Old Norbert's bicycles. Georg was weaving excessively around the muddy bomb craters and rusted red skeletons of cars and Bradley realised that he was gaining on him.

If his knee only held out, he would catch him somewhere between the next cross street and the one after. But then what was he going to do?

In an instant, the question became immaterial. As Georg reached the cross street an army truck appeared from nowhere and barrelled into him at sickening speed. It didn't seem to have braked at all, or even sounded its horn. The only thing Bradley heard was a violent thud that his mind judged far too deep and concussive to have been caused by four tons of steel hitting a human being. But it had.

By the time he arrived, the truck had halted sixty yards along the cross street. The remains of Old Norbert's bicycle were crumpled beneath one set of its double rear wheels.

Georg had come to rest against a garden wall, which he had cracked into several separate pieces. He was still alive, although his blood-soaked forehead and temple looked the wrong shape. Scattered about him were his playing cards – on his chest a turbaned knave and crownless queen.

One eye focused on Bradley.

"It was a bad joke," he gasped.

From the blood and bubbles he was spewing, it was obvious that his lungs had been punctured by the shrapnel of his bones. Probably his other internal organs too. He didn't have long.

"What was, Georg?"

"Hameln. I sent her to Hameln. *Der Rattenfänger...*"

"The rat-catcher. The Pied Piper, who led away the children when they wouldn't pay his bill?"

Blood sprayed across the knave of clubs as he let out a last, stuttering laugh.

"We were the real *Rattenfänger.*"

"What about Pfeffer?"

Georg's abdomen heaved. His voice was fading now.

"...couldn't let you get to him first... I had to find him, for Anke... but now you must finish it for me."

Bradley was aware of the kind of sound that stood your hairs on end. Something was telling him he was in danger now himself. He needed to look around, but first...

"Where is he?"

"He deals in stolen art... in Bremen..."

That was to the north, in the American enclave that linked up with their port of embarkation at Bremerhaven. If she was looking in Hamelin, in the British Zone, she would never find him there.

Bradley was about to take Georg's hand, to help him over the edge, when his instincts got the better of him. The alarming sound, he realised belatedly, was the whine of the army truck reversing back towards them, mixed in with the clatter of the mangled bicycle trapped between its wheels. He turned to look over his shoulder just in time to see it bearing down on them. As he leapt aside, he heard and felt the rear fender bar impact the wall. If it made a sound as it flattened Georg, this time he did not notice.

The truck lurched forward again, pitching and twisting to free itself from the remnants of the wall and the second bicycle. Bradley came up on his skinned hands and knees. He was about to reach for his side arm when he spotted it several yards away along the unpaved road surface.

And that, he imagined his old supply sergeant drawling with undisguised delight, is why we don't cut and fold away any part of our holsters...

As the truck moved past he spotted an unfamiliar stencil on its bloodstained bumper. TTG. And a slogan crudely chalked on the tailgate in mockery of an old Nazi motto *Kein Volk! Kein Reich! Kein Führer!*

No people, no empire, no leader.

And a pair of smirking British soldiers in the back, one covering him with a Sten gun in case he thought about retrieving his pistol, the other delivering an ironic version of an American salute.

Once the truck had driven on and turned the corner, people began emerging from nearby houses. One after another, outraged voices were raised. Dogs barked. A horse and buggy was flagged down. Another German on a bicycle diverted his route to come and look at Georg.

Bradley picked up his pistol and set off walking.

He had heard the stories, of course, same as the local residents must have heard them: how trucks and armoured vehicles in the British, American and French zones of occupation, especially the French, would swerve off the road every now and then and take out a bunch of pedestrians, for kicks. Temporarily unsighted, they would claim with impunity, especially the tank drivers. But this was different. That sustained salute made it different. They must have known who he and Georg Düttmann were.

So what was the story behind this TTG unit? Were they the ones who had done for Schlosser? It seemed likely. What better cover, that night in Hammerbrook, than British support troops in another US- or Canadian-built truck? He had even heard a heavy vehicle dropping something off or picking up, right after finding the doctor. And although Stransky in the Munich safe house might have required more guile, from the knowing looks as they rumbled away, these guys had it in spades.

He checked behind him. The Germans didn't seem to be following, but they weren't the only ones that concerned him. There was little doubt now that somebody was tipping off these assassins about his movements, and there was only one person who had known he was going to see Schlosser and Düttmann. The same person who'd had Stransky under lock and key.

Bradley recalled Hoffman's reaction to the Czech gendarmes, the expression on his face and the finger on the trigger of his grease gun when he'd accused them of helping the Nazis with their roundups.

Or was it whoever Hoffman reported back to, which the man himself had hinted might be Doyle and his phantom residue of British Security Coordination? Right from the start there had been something odd about their motives for hunting MERCURY down. Doyle had said it was to avoid a confrontation with Moscow, yet he'd also claimed the British Intelligence community was getting too close to the Soviets anyhow.

There were other things that didn't add up. How come, after all Doyle's careful preparations, he had been picked out and followed from the moment he'd arrived in Lisbon? The couple on the 'Main-Seiner' hadn't been any kind of freelancing British soldiers.

And how come Doyle had known anything about what had transpired at the NKVD Tyurma-lager? Was Bradley supposed to believe that the Reds had been so embarrassed by the con she'd worked that they'd given the Brits the squalid details?

Despite the pain in his knee, he found he was picking up his pace as he headed into town. He didn't know the answers to any of those questions, but he knew that he was getting closer to his true objective. And now he had something to bring to the table.

Pfeffer's unit had operated throughout Eastern Europe. Georg would not have mistaken a Czech for a Pole without good reason: such as MERCURY carrying Polish I.D. or wearing Polish uniforms. So the next thing to do was to ask around in Hamelin for any Free Polish units, one of which would presumably be pursuing the false lead Georg had fed them.

He was going to have to be very careful, of course. He could no longer trust Hoffman and he'd be back to watching every street corner and every shadow. If he located MERCURY and blundered in regardless, that might be what the opposition were waiting for, whoever they were and whatever game they had going.

But if he played his cards right – and there was another

image he'd have to live with now, another memory to be read on his face for ever more – he might be able to set her back on the right track. That was worth a hundred ugly images, because it was the antithesis of and the antidote to those images.

He passed a burned-out house. It was a blackened shell, yet someone had hung old coal sacks at the ground floor windows to keep out the cold. As he looked, a corner folded back and a grimy face peered out.

Lost children. If only all of them still had their mothers searching for them.

CHAPTER TEN

The first indication that she had reached her destination came when a pair of gateposts loomed out of the thick winter fog. Each was overgrown with ivy, barbed wire and a plethora of overlapping and displaced signs, chief among these EINTRITT VERBOTEN, OFFICERS' CLUB and 29th INFANTRY DIVISION – '29 LET'S GO'. Despite these warnings, the iron gates had been forced open and a heavy vehicle had recently ploughed the neglected crust of mouldered leaves and frozen mud.

Mila nudged Stas. With an uncertain grunt, he turned their jeep into the ruts that ran along the drive. On either side, rhododendron trees wore a heavy blossom of ice. The road ahead vanished in impenetrable whiteness.

All the while, thrust deep in her coat pocket against the cold, her fingers fussed with the familiar shape and weight of the little gold cigarette lighter.

Richard had given her that lighter. On the eve of her first mission into Nazi-occupied Czechoslovakia, surely knowing, as she did, that it would also be her last, he had arranged to remove the incriminating English inscription *For a pilgrim soul*. Whether through shame, carelessness or, intuitively, as a kind of breadcrumb trail, she had left the lighter with another of the war's despairing wanderers. And now, somehow, it had returned to her.

She replayed the events in her mind. Leaving the obnoxious but clueless Helmut Ziegler to his grievances and his bruises. Telling the rest of the gang that she needed some time alone to clear her head. (Wishing she had not been so hard on Stas about his *Babička*, so that he might have had a spare bottle to hand.)

Crossing one of Hamelin's many temporary pontoons to the Werder island and gazing back at the old city's demolished girder bridges, water mills and weirs.

Looking upstream to the *Zuchthaus*, where the British had hanged the men and women from the Bergen-Belsen trial and would no doubt soon be hanging many more.

Like those bridges, like every bridge in Germany, it had all seemed a dead end.

And then the children running pell-mell across the pontoon. Hearing them coming on the freshening air, feeling their footfalls through the chesses, here of all places. Thinking in that moment that her heart would burst.

And feeling too, instead of the fatal stab of that invisible stiletto or the irresistible urge to fling herself into the Weser, the subtle brush-past, the hand in her pocket...

"Hey!"

Catching the boy by a thin, grimy wrist.

"Nice try..."

Turning over his hand and forcing it open to reveal – nothing.

Letting go, beginning to formulate some kind of apology and then, on an impulse, checking her coat pocket.

Finding the impossible lighter and the simple note wrapped around it.

NOT IN SEASON IN HAMELIN. TRY THE BREMEN ART MARKET.

The boy rubbing his wrist and scowling, but not running off after his six or seven friends: having proved a messenger not a thief, he'd been waiting for a reward.

Mila had studied him closely, looking at the many-layered, much-patched and oversized clothes, looking beneath the patina of grime. Eleven or twelve, possibly a little older. At least three years too old, in other words, even though a part of her had leapt blindly toward the thought.

"Who gave you this?"

"Cost you. Pack of smokes."

"Done." The kid wasn't fool enough to smoke them anyway. They were currency.

"A man. An Ami. Over there..."

Back towards the west bank where the land rose to the *Klütturm*. Mila had seen no one watching them, nor had she expected to.

"He told you to slip this into my coat?"

"*The young Polish army lady, you can't miss her...* You weren't supposed to notice until later." A chagrined shake of his head. "Who'd have thought I'd get caught twice!"

"Wait – you mean you tried to pick his pocket first?"

"And he nabbed me, same as you did. Just my luck!"

But of course it hadn't been luck.

She had lit a cigarette then, not offering one to the boy. (After all, he had his own.)

Not luck. Training. But whose?

An Ami, the boy had said. And a hand-printed message, in English. Ten words. And that cheeky code: seasoning to represent Pepper. A sense of humour. And caution.

"Wait a minute," she had called out as the boy, bored now, made to leave. "What's your name? Where are you going now?"

"People call me *die Ratte*."

"That's no kind of name."

"It means they'll never catch me."

"In *Hamelin*?"

"What about it?"

"I'm sorry, you probably had no one to tell you the story."

"What story?"

"Never mind. But *I* caught you. *He* caught you."

"Yeah." A rueful head-scratch. An almost adult squint to the heavens. "Maybe it's time to move on."

"Where to? Home?"

And he had looked her in the eye – a look a thousand years old – and laughed.

"Maybe Hanover again," he'd said eventually, with a shrug.

Mila had folded the note and buttoned it away in her battledress pocket. She had been about to return the lighter to the Rat, for luck, but instead she pocketed it and pulled out the bribe they had grudgingly prepared for Ziegler. Whatever a pound of silver might be worth these days, it was more than a rolled gold lighter.

"This might help you get there."

Now, so close to her own objective, she clasped the lighter and hoped that it had.

Having clung on to the little talisman, almost on a whim, she had been amazed how everything else had fallen into place. After the ambush on the Reichsstraße, and the successful delivery of what he imagined to be the first instalment of *Kriegsmarine* copper, Staff Sergeant Carter had been eager to volunteer his services. He had made inquiries, as he put it, about the Bremen enclave and its trade in stolen art. By his account the Yanks were taking 'liberties' with the sheer amount of loot they were acquiring and smuggling out through the port of embarkation at Bremerhaven, *which we only handed over to them so's they'd have a way to ship their boys back home.*

Soon enough, his contacts had put him onto the local dealers in Nazi plunder. Mostly these were middlemen, keeping their hands as clean as they could in this blackest of black markets. But one name stood out among them. Gottlieb von Salzen, purveyor of antique *objets* and rarities.

Salzen for Pfeffer. If she had not already seen how these people considered themselves beyond justice in post-war Germany, Mila would not have dared to hope that a man known as Pepper possessed the nerve to change his name to that. As it was, her prayers were all but answered. Staff Sergeant Carter reported that he had met the man in person, that he was a Southern German or Austrian of the appropriate age and height, and that his left pupil was significantly more dilated than his right, giving each eye an apparently different hue. (Dr Schlosser had called the condition anisocoria and claimed that it was a result of exposure to toxic chemicals.)

Von Salzen also knew, Carter said, where to pick up some extremely valuable bronzes, which was what today's meeting at the Herrenhaus would be about.

That had been the clincher. Because it hadn't taken silver to get the tight-lipped locals talking. The merest promise of Carter's synthetic butter had lubricated tales of how, before the now-departed 29th Division had turned the place into a combined casino and rest camp, the British and the Americans had stumbled on a Nazi secret there. A great reporter from LIFE magazine had even filed a completely inaccurate story about it. A former groundsman had a copy, and his widowed neighbour a photo album from those days. Not hers, of course, but worth a little something, no?

The manor house at Gut Hohehorst, tucked away in the ironically named 'Bremen Switzerland' north of the flatland city, had been one of the Lebensborn homes: Heim Friesland.

Little wonder that the man named 'Salt' knew where its treasures lay.

At last the driveway looped out of the trees and, like those suspicious English neighbours lurking behind their voile curtains, the building peeked from the mist.

There were no curtains visible anywhere on the Herrenhaus. Beneath the steep-pitched roof with its single, ghostly turret, the mansion had been symmetrically laid out with a modern classicism that in these parts would be termed an 'English' style yet bore no relation to anything she had seen across the Channel. Here, whether surmounted by triangles or arches – or, as in the case of the many dormers, alternating between the two – the windows were resolutely shuttered in European fashion.

Three vehicles were parked between the enveloping wings of the portico. Mila recognised Carter's REME lorry. There was also a jeep like theirs and a streamlined DKW limousine in tarnished grey and black that could only be Pfeffer's.

All at once the tightness in her chest was the same as on the pontoon in Hamelin, the same as when she had swung her legs over the edge of the howling 'Joe Hole' in the belly of the Halifax, the same as on the station platform at Bratislava as the last train for Vienna whistled impatiently and her erstwhile lover and their child did not come.

He was here, the man who had taken Pavel from Theodor five years later.

The man who knew what had happened to her son.

"Miss Nightingale…"

Stas's hand was on her leg, not so much to attract her attention, she thought, as to be ready to pin her down should she leap precipitately from the jeep. She followed the direction of his gaze and saw the figures on the rise beyond the arches of what had once been a rose garden. Three men, shadows in the fog. A nude woman with a spear or staff. Flanking her, two deer, the stag with antlers lowered, the doe's head raised in alarm.

Staff Sergeant Carter saw her looking. He lifted a hand in greeting, then did a little dance beside the Diana and slipped his arm around the statue's waist. He had his precious bronzes at last.

Sure enough, the other man in British uniform was beckoning something out of the fog and firs. The sound of its engine echoed around the estate as Carter's cabless crane-lorry reversed gingerly along the ridge toward the statues' plinth.

That left the other man, the one in the long overcoat. Was it him? Striding through the withered rose garden, Mila was conscious of the silenced carbine hanging under her own coat. If necessary she could go to ground in the disused fountain and take them all out from here. But of course that was the worst possible outcome.

As she drew closer, her spirits sank. Konrad Pfeffer was reported to be of medium height and build but this civilian accompanying Carter was tall and thin. Pfeffer would be forty-three, but this man was in his mid-fifties at least.

She thought of 'Uncle' Ludvík and his hard war. It was true that people aged rapidly nowadays, and most had been on a crash diet. It was also true that Carter was no professional and might have got the wrong man. She gave him a smile nonetheless.

"Good morning, Staff Sergeant."

"Corporal Zielińska. Let me introduce you to our fellow art-lovers." He was putting on airs and graces, and not just for the civilian, she thought. There was a degree of deference to the way Carter ushered forward the REME officer who had been directing the crane.

"This is Captain Prentice. He's from Head Office, so to speak."

The man looked every inch the English gentleman, until he opened the side of his mouth in what was almost a canine snarl and uttered a gravelly *Aw-right?* Another Londoner, and no more a serving soldier than Carter. But he was neither the crooked C.O. she had first imagined nor the big boss from the firm back home. Another middleman.

The other man stepped forward, clicked his heels and inclined his head. Put your bloody chin up, Mila wanted to scream at him. Let me see your eyes!

"And this is Herr Becker. He's here as a representative of the current owners. They're taking this opportunity to *liquidate* some of their more portable assets, before the Americans come back."

A pair of perfectly matching, perfectly cold, grey eyes.

"I had understood von Salzen would be here to oversee that," she said.

It was not her imagination. The trio exchanged furtive glances. They were cooking something up that might well include Pfeffer but evidently didn't include her.

"I am authorised to advance Herr Carter your share of the finder's fee," Becker said.

If you lie down with dogs, she thought.

"Then I'll leave you to it." For Carter's benefit, she added: "Those arches in the rose garden are bronze as well."

"I'd spotted that," he beamed.

Before she could drag him away, Stas had blurted out: "They ought to fetch thirty pieces at least."

"Come again?"

Mila ignored Carter and addressed Herr Becker.

"If you don't mind, I'll take a look around the house before we go."

What could he say? She could tell he had spotted the gun under her coat.

"By all means, *gnädiges Fräulein*. I don't think the Americans have left very much but you are welcome to see for yourself."

"Wait for me in the jeep," she snapped at Stas as they passed the 29th's long-abandoned Christmas tree in the centre of the frozen lawn. At the steps up to the four-columned portico, she paused to look back across the gardens. On the crest of the rise, swathed in mist, Diana the huntress swung from the crane like so much prey.

She pulled out the pages from LIFE and unfolded the photo-spread.

"SUPER BABIES" — *these Nazi bastards in a German chateau have no father or mother but the now-defunct Nazi state... This nurse replaces both parents in raising this illegitimate SS child. They willingly gave up all claims to him.*

How avidly, in spite of herself, she had scanned those oblivious faces, knowing all the while that they were too young and that the Americans, seeking salacious stories of Nazi breeding centres, had jumped to the wrong conclusions: that in fact those blond super-babies they'd found at 'Heim Friesland' had turned out to be a last evacuation of unfortunate Norwegian children, born to girls who'd had their lives ruined by the German occupiers, and that there was another, darker tale this place had to tell.

A picture from the widow's album showed the main hall here in Nazi times. She clutched it in her fist as she tried the front doors of the Herrenhaus.

Locked. But the glass panes were no match for the butt of her carbine.

Inside the vestibule, it became clear that the hunting theme would continue. Mounted antlers lined the walls of the transverse corridors, reminders of when the manor had been summer retreat, model farm and *Jagdgebiet* for a family of Bremen industrialists. Mila went through a second set of arched glass doors into the main hall.

Despite the subdued daylight through the shuttered windows, the architect's clever use of aligned fanlights in the doorways and stairwell spared her the fool's errand of trying the power supply. She studied the photograph and compared the exposed beams and the shape of the fireplace. Everything matched. Here, in this now-empty decorative niche above the mantelpiece, the bust of Hitler had stood, with the black altar cloth of the SS spread beneath it. On either side, you could still see the marks where they had hung their embroidered slogans:

ONE BLOOD DEMANDS ONE REICH.

FOUNDATION OF THE FUTURE RACE.

Whatever black magic they had performed in their rituals here, it was far more insidious than the American reporter had imagined. Mila wanted to be sick. And she wanted to run outside and fetch Stas as well, because here was one of his paradoxes, perhaps the ultimate paradox that had lain at the heart of the Nazis' death cult, greater even than the unstoppable force and immovable object.

Blood and race, she thought. How one denies the other. And how those who build their dreams on the past are building, like this refuge on the horst, on sand.

At the foot of the grand staircase, the ornate banisters and extravagant hunting scenes clashed with a different sort of carving in darker, glossier mahogany. An antique church pulpit almost the height of the first flight of stairs had been installed as a feature in the corner of the hall, presumably in counterpoint to all the modern woodwork. Near life-size figures seemed to be approaching her from out of the gloom. A man flanked by a woman and an angel. The man had his face in his hands.

It was a fine example, undoubtedly worth more than all of Carter's haul combined, but she had seen such things before and knew that it depicted Adam and Eve, expelled from Paradise. What was striking was how appropriate Adam's shame appeared in this setting.

And it was even more horrifying to imagine what the children who had passed through here must have thought of the man who looked a lot like Jesus. Why had he hidden his face behind his hands? Why could he not bear to look at them?

A voice rang out behind her.

"This is where the naming ceremonies were conducted. It was important to change their names."

In the doorway by which she had entered stood another German civilian, a well-dressed man in his forties, of average height and build. Two bigger, bulkier men fanned out to either side. All three wore fedoras that cast their faces into shadow and had at least one hand in their coat pockets.

The man who had spoken made a gesture with his gloved hand that Mila took to refer to the photograph in her own.

"You seemed interested in the history of this place," he said, as though this explained his portentous declamation. After the *Plattdeutsch* dialect she had grown accustomed to lately, his German sounded more like the kind she had learned in Bohemia. She suspected that he had suppressed his Austrian accent.

"Herr von Salzen?"

"At your service, Corporal...?"

"Zielińska."

"Ah, yes," he said, as though her being Polish meant something to him. Perhaps it did. "Well, I was simply recounting what I have heard about the foundation that operated here..."

The black glove made an almost musical gesture toward the

doorway at the foot of the staircase. Carved into the wood above it, rather more crudely than the surrounding motifs, was the *Reichsadler*. The Americans had chiselled off the swastika but left the eagle itself, with the runic emblems of the Lebensborn either side.

"Before adoption, all Aryanised children were renamed, to bury their old identities and welcome them as lifelong members of the race. While some were simply Germanized, those names with religious or regional associations were to be altered unrecognisably. Little Bogdan's foster family would be told his birth parents were martyred heroes of the Reich, and all assuming that his cries for *Mamusia* had been beaten out of him, they would never even need to know his origins."

During this speech, wearing a sympathetic smile that looked like he had sliced it off another man's face, he had been advancing steadily towards her. She forced herself to meet his stony gaze. In the dim light, both pupils were dilated. She could detect no discrepancy between them.

She affected an air of casual interest that wouldn't have fooled the local idiot.

"How sad. So one would need the records to trace a child's true parentage..."

He was studying her eyes now, even more closely than she had studied his.

"Alas, there were no records kept. You see, Corporal, that was the whole point."

He had made the connection, of course he had. A woman, ostensibly Polish, enquiring about the fate of the abducted children, a large proportion of whom had come from Poland. Trying to keep the tension from her face, Mila wondered where Stas was, and how this brazen group had bypassed him, and if they had. Stas was wearing Polish army uniform too. Perhaps they had dealt with him first.

The carbine was slung from a single swivel over her right shoulder, under her coat. The photograph and folded pages were in her right hand. She took a short step back, making it seem as though she was simply clearing space between them to pluck open her left coat front with her left hand and return the items to an inside pocket with her right. Except there was no inside pocket. As the photo and papers fell through her coat, her left arm extended vigorously, pushing von Salzen away from her, while her right arm swept back to clear her coat and seize the carbine's pistol grip. In the same movement, sensing that one of the henchmen was behind her and reaching out to grab her, she was falling sideways out of his clutches.

The two men's grunts of surprise and exertion convinced her she had chosen the right moment. It was the other one who worried her. As she hit the floor and poised to roll away, she spotted him, still at the door, in the act of drawing his pistol.

You had your hand on it anyway, she thought as she flicked off the safety and put her first silent bullet in his chest. Why waste time getting it out of your pocket?

She came up on one knee and used thumb and forefinger on the rubberised bolt handle. Her middle finger curled around the trigger.

Von Salzen was backing away, employing his bodyguard as cover. The bodyguard had his revolver out and pointed at her head. The other henchman sat down heavily and let out a low groan, but there had been no sound loud enough to warn the men in the gardens, or Stas in the jeep out front, if he was still there.

For a moment, Mila wondered who was more afraid of alerting the others. Given their secret business together, there was every chance that the men in the gardens would side with von Salzen, even Carter, she acknowledged. If that was so, the silence of these Germans suggested that they had not yet disposed of Stas. Or had they already slit Stas' throat as an overture to killing everybody, perhaps because von Salzen surmised that his identity had been revealed and this meeting was not a transaction but a trap?

Given the peculiar angle of his shoulders, she suspected that he too had a pistol drawn, behind the other man's back. That was a shame. Her next bullet had a fair chance of preventing the bodyguard's brain from transmitting the signal to pull the trigger, but there was no hope of re-cocking and getting off another shot in time. If he was Pfeffer, von Salzen was an SS officer. He would have had plenty of practice shooting people at close range.

So, stalemate. Possibly. And possibly time to try something else.

"Standartenführer Pfeffer?" she said. "I believe you knew my husband."

She and Pavel's father had never actually been married, but she knew that Theodor's colleagues had continued to assume they were, even after she had fled for England.

"Excuse me?"

"Professor Lossner. He sought you out in late '44, in Prague. The Professor asked you to arrange for our son to be adopted through the Lebensborn with the other eastern children. He would have been six years old, nearly seven. His name was Pavel."

"You're not Polish?"

"I am Czech. My son's name was Pavel. Pavel Lossner. You will have treated him as a special case."

Nothing changed in von Salzen's demeanour. He continued to look both aloof and perplexed. The bodyguard, listening to his comrade's diminishing splutters yet unable to react in any way, never shifted his wide-eyed stare. The change was in her, prompted by the sound of the bland, bureaucratic German on her lips – treatment, special case – and by something else – *religious names to be altered unrecognisably...*

She pulled the trigger and drilled a hole between the bodyguard's staring eyes. As the man fell, von Salzen froze. Sure enough, he had drawn a pocket pistol but he dropped it now to raise his hands in surrender.

Rising from a crouch, bracing it properly so as not to require another lucky shot, she very slowly and pointedly re-cocked

128

the stockless carbine. It was to show him that through inexperience if not plain cowardice he had misjudged her ability to fire a repeating shot and therefore thrown away a golden chance to shoot her first. It was to underscore the fact that, even with a single shot against two guns, she had achieved psychological dominance by virtue of not caring in that instant whether she lived or died. And of course it was to make him think she was about to shoot him too.

"One chance," she said. "Start talking."

But despite her best efforts, his wits were functioning again.

"If you kill me, you will never find him."

Mila heard herself laugh.

"You're not the first to try that tack, but this time the circumstances are different." She lowered the carbine until it was directed at the front of his trousers. "Before I'm finished, you'll beg me to send you to Hell with an overdose of morphine."

"He was here, the boy from Prague," von Salzen said.

"His name was Pavel. His name *is* Pavel."

"I don't remember."

"What happened to him?"

"I don't remember that either, only that he was brought here."

"Show me."

"Show you what? There's nothing left."

"Start by showing me where he would have slept. It will be best for you to begin jogging your memory."

"I wasn't the administrator here. I just delivered him, as a favour."

"But you *were* the administrator weren't you, before the war? So show me."

Von Salzen – or Pfeffer – regarded his men, both of whom looked dead, then pointed to the staircase.

"Up here."

Mila kept just out of reach behind him. This was his terrain and she didn't want him making a break for it. Although she had not yet had time to process everything, his words kept coming back to her.

There were no records kept, that was the whole point... There's nothing left...

This man and his memories were all she had to believe in now.

After the first, intermediate landing, the stairs opened out onto a broader landing space that gave onto the balcony above the colonnade at the rear. The French doors here were as shut and shuttered as all the other windows had been, but an internal arrangement of arched windows brought daylight from the stair well into the centre of the building, where two galleries ran the length of the first floor and another lightwell served the corridor at ground level. Matching blind arches lined the walls, each filled either with a gorgeous inlaid door or a set of mounted antlers. Although the dim illumination along the gallery expired every few yards in a pool of darkness, it seemed any other ornamentation – lamps, pictures, rugs – had disappeared with the Americans.

The German led her to a door near the end of the gallery.

"In my time, there was a dormitory in here..."

"You first," she said.

It was not a big space in comparison to the rest of the house, but in place of the mullioned windows of the larger rooms it had an unshuttered bullseye, which let in plenty of light. The kind of room you'd choose as a nursery, Mila thought, biting back a gasp.

Certainly the Americans had not bothered with it. It still contained a row of little iron beds, a stack of wooden cots and a heap of white-painted bassinets. Since it looked like the cots and baskets had been thrown in here during a clear-out of the other wards, it followed that this room, and one of these beds, might have been Pavel's.

Mila had to grab the nearest bedstead to keep her balance. Somehow, the simple fact that none of the children would have been able to reach that round window to gaze out of it cut her more deeply than anything else. It was all so white and sterile. Without a view of the trees, without a glimpse of the gardens or the driveway, how would they know where they were? How might they sit and dream of that magical day when their mothers would come to rescue them? How could they even remember...

"They cried a lot at night," von Salzen said. "Sometimes all night."

"What did you just say?"

"Comforting them was discouraged among the sisterhood. Bedwetting, in particular, was fiercely punished." Here, now, in this bright white room, his eyes were different colours, one blue, one an olive green. Beneath their level gaze, and utterly dissociated from it, the smile was apologetic, almost. It was also nearly his last.

But, of course, that was what he was counting on. He needed her angry enough to get up close to him. It was his only chance of preventing her from using her gun.

"You're very well informed, Herr Pfeffer," she said.

"I received regular reports. The Reichsführer always maintained an interest in the project."

"Yet you kept no paperwork?"

"Oh, we maintained detailed records, just not of the subjects' original identities."

"So there'd be a list of foster parents – of adoptions."

He nodded. Very good, his eyes said. The children's names would be their new names not their old ones, but there would be dates to match up, and German couples, with addresses, to investigate. It was something. If it was true.

"Perhaps in the office..."

He moved so quickly for the door that she knew he was bluffing. Yet what else could she do but follow him?

The brightness of the dormitory had spoiled her vision for the low light in the gallery and she hoped that with his condition it would take Pfeffer even longer to readjust. She stumbled after him as he bounced from wall to wall, heading for the reception area at the top of the staircase. Suddenly he lurched into an unseen alcove. As she overran him she saw too late that he had torn down a set of stag's antlers from the wall.

Clutching the wooden mount between gloved hands, baring his teeth, he lunged at her with the vicious points. The arm she raised to protect herself was the one that held the carbine's pistol grip. There was a clash, a painful stab and the front-heavy tube spun from her grasp to clatter on the parquet floor.

"Damned sow!" He swung the horns at her and she leaped back, colliding with an unseen obstacle. Both of them lost their balance. In horror, she saw him release his grip on his unwieldy weapon and grab for something else in the shadows. Her gun.

There was no special trick to it; it was based on a common bolt-action rifle and she'd had it cocked and locked with a round in the chamber. She was still on the floor, fresh out of ideas, when he raised the fat tube of the barrel and pointed it at her. Although he was little more than a silhouette, she could see that he was gasping for air.

"I was lying – there are no records left – they burned them all on Himmler's orders. Your son is lost forever. He will never even know he had a different mother – or how she died."

He squeezed the trigger with no result. She'd had the safety catch on, but he knew how to click that off.

Nothing for it now. It was completely hopeless but she was damned indeed if she was going to be slaughtered on her knees by any man, especially a Nazi, especially this one. She got a foot planted for leverage and launched herself at him.

And as she did, so did something else. A shadowy figure, taller and broader than Stas, sprang out of the darkness with a roar. It must have been creeping up on them, using the alcoves, or perhaps it had slipped down the side stairs from the second floor. When it wrapped itself around Pfeffer and wrestled him along the gallery into the half-light of the internal windows, she saw that it was Sam Bradley.

"No!" she cried out as Pfeffer crashed through the glass to the floor below.

CHAPTER ELEVEN

Anguished voices, echoing from bare wood and walls. One of the voices hers, endlessly pleading *ne, ne, ne, ne...* Another groaning in agony. And another.

Thunderous footsteps that felt like a mess hall at chow time. Flickers of a flashlight. A blade of daylight unsheathed.

A boot turning him over, slowly – yet with the impact of a mule kick.

At first he thought he must have fallen with the fellow he'd manhandled through the window. What else could have laid him flat out with his head ringing fit to burst and every nerve raw? Then he realised that charging Mila's attacker and hoisting him like a sack of flour had thrown his shoulder out again. He had fallen, but only to the boards at his feet. As for the two voices that had been grunting and groaning so, he guessed one belonged to the man he'd bundled out and down to the ground floor. The other must have been his own.

Ne, ne, ne, ne... The incredulous sobbing chilled him. He had only heard her so distressed once before, and then it had been tempered by anger and resolve. The Mila he knew had never given up, yet this voice seemed to have no fight left. It was coming from below, in the corridor or the lobby, through the broken windows. Had she fallen too? Impossible. He had saved her. And the first time she'd cried out 'No!' it had been from up here in the gallery. She must have peered through the hole and then run downstairs.

He recalled hearing another voice, a man's, also Czech, conferring with her in frantic tones. It was all mixed up with his own groans and those of his latest victim, but Bradley thought the exchange equated to something like *Lift him, lift him!*

And her second, horrified cry, trailing off into the *no, no, no...*

By then the chow call must have sounded, because the running boots were everywhere, one of them kicking him over with that burst of stupefying light.

The pounding in his head took up the beat of the barracks bugle.

Soupy, soupy, soupy, without a single bean...

And the strange-sounding voices above him.

"So 'oo the bloomin' 'eck's this?"

"Dunno. But he ain't 'alf put the kibosh on everything!"

Every*fing*. Like a child and a bruiser combined.

"Least yer got yer shooter back, 'ere..."

"Bloody dented, innit. Typical! What's 'e gibbering?"

"Not sure, boss. Sounded like *Coffee, coffee, coffee, without a speck of cream.*"

"A Yank! I'll give him blasted coffee! Come on, let's schlep the big bugger downstairs an' all."

Three or four men in shitsack battledress, looking rough around the edges, even for the Brits. When they lifted him, the pain slipped into overdrive. Bradley muttered in protest and felt blood drool from his mouth where he had bitten his lips or his tongue.

"What's that? *Porky, porky, porky...?* Oh, not on your nelly, me old china. You're gonna tell us the gospel truth!"

...without a streak of lean.

Step by step – blow by blow – the imaginary bugle faded, his heartbeat steadied and its rhythm formed a guide sheet to keep his thoughts in line. He was going to be interrogated, obviously. But what was the truth he was going to tell? That he had snuck into the house via the basement areaway while they were all at their meeting in the rose garden – and had been halfway up the spiral staircase in the loft to use the turret as an OP when he heard the fight begin? That he had followed her

134

jeep out here from Bremen and left his commandeered BMW in the woods? That he had been chasing her, off and on, for nine months now and this was only the second time he'd gotten close? That he wasn't about to let her slip through his fingers again?

Funny, the realisations you came to when you were knocked half silly by pain. And when your situation was putting rather more pressing concerns in front of you.

Down by the main staircase. Thrown down by the strange pulpit. All the doors open, all the way to the front.

A religious group of sorts: a man's body cradled by others. Blood on the inlay.

"Still a pulse... get him to Bremen... lift him, lift him... he's our only 'ope now."

Another body, unattended.

Into the lobby, but not following the others out of the front door. Frogmarched along the corridor instead.

The girl slumped on the floor, also cradled, by her compatriot from the jeep. Impossible not to see this, too, as a perverted tableau of Mary and Jesus.

The rough voices of the men supporting him, resounding in the empty lightwell.

"An' what the bloomin' 'eck we gonna do about *that*?"

On the wall facing Mila, above drips of blood and shards of glass, beneath the broken gallery window, Standartenführer Konrad Pfeffer hung impaled on a set of mounted antlers, his eyes raised to the heavens.

Woman, behold thy son... behold thy mother.

Gospel truths indeed.

And Mila looking up suddenly to meet his blurry gaze. The despair in her eyes. And something else. The hatred.

*   *   *

Jack Penny squinted at the I.D.s like hole cards. He discarded the Polish passes and paybooks. Forgeries, they looked like, as he'd expected. That left the U.S. Treasury Department I.D.

and the CIC Special Agent's badge from the geezer's secret inside pocket. As far as he could tell these were either kosher or near-as-makes-no-difference.

Although he might have spotted something hooky if Gerry hadn't insisted on conducting the interrogation in the bloody wine cellar, where it was dark as a schvartzer's coal hole!

He shone his torch in the American's face.

"Why are you over here?"

"Huh?"

"What's your job here?"

"Hunting Nazis."

"To kill?"

A bitter chuckle. A shake of the tender head.

"To recruit – to the cause of freedom."

Penny snorted.

"You've fucked up there then."

The American glanced at the woman on the chair beside him.

"Don't I know it!"

Penny threw the Charles S. Fisher I.D. at him.

"This is your cover story, bluebottle. What's your real name?"

There was resignation in his eyes. He'd have shrugged if his arms weren't tied behind the chairback. And if he hadn't done his shoulder, which he plainly had.

"Bradley."

Gerry had decided it was his turn. Putting on his Captain Prentice act, the hooligan paced back and forth between the vaulted arches.

"Well, Mr Bradley, you have done more than rob us of a valuable informer. You have jabbertised an important operation."

Give me strength, Penny thought, trying not to laugh. He met Bradley's suspicious stare.

"'S'an engineering term. Means we're back to jabber-jabber-jabbering what to do."

"Yeah," 'Captain Prentice' nodded enthusiastically. "'Cause von Salzen had the plans in his head, and if his minder don't know them, or don't pull through..."

It was then that the so-called-Polish woman spoke, using English that seemed less accented than before, not to mention a good thirty degrees colder.

"That was not all he had in his head."

At which, oblivious to the true intended recipient of those words, and probably chuffed at how well his Captain Prentice act was going, Jimmy the Shiv's surprisingly trim kid brother let out a knowing oink.

"Nah, 'e 'ad a deer 'orn through 'is me-doolah oglomb-garter!"

Penny had straddled another of the surviving upright chairs, arms crossed on the backrest. He rubbed the stubble on his jaw across his bare forearms and although he knew that he hadn't been the intended recipient either, he fixed her with a steady gaze.

"What was it? I know he was SS, so I'm guessing something to do with your family."

"My son."

"But not revenge, eh, 'cause I'd never have gone along with you if I'd thought you was just going to top him – not someone as valuable as that. Your son's alive?"

"As far as I know."

"And von Salzen – Pfeffer – knew where he was."

"I don't know. But it was my last chance."

"Till Bradley here took that away from you... Not quite the knight in shining armour, eh?" Penny remembered what she'd called him, for Marjorie, that day on the Reichsstraße. But then his thoughts were overtaken by an image of the red-haired Lancelot outside Gardiner's. That was what you got for trying to save people.

He exchanged a glance with Gerry Lonsdale.

"I didn't want to cheat you, neither, Mila. Not after all we done together. But once you'd put me onto Pfeffer it was out of my hands. The swine had too many juicy connections. So nothing personal, but I got to ask you now where your other men are."

She looked at her driver, tied up on her other side. He shook his head, but she was past caring.

"Outside," she said. "Somewhere in the grounds. With rifles."

"That's what I thought."

He raised a finger and swung it between the captives bracketing her, as if deliberating. *Eeny, meeny, miny, moe...*

Gerry had other ideas.

"We don't need none of them. We just drive away and her lot can come in and find these three after."

"Dead..."

"They've seen us, ain't they?"

"And when your man and that schmuck Becker get on the blower to say the minder's snuffed it – 'cause he's going to, Gerry, before Becker's tame quack has even got his strides on – where does that leave us? Jimmy's not going to be happy."

"He'll get over it. We got the bronzes, and we'll strip this effin' place before we leave. Plus, moving into Bremen has come up trumps, even without von... Pfeffer. Becker will help us set up the local branch of the Commandos. And he says he knows a Yank who can siphon off half the cigs coming into their Post Exchange."

"And what about your buyers? What about their order?"

Mention of his clients set a dark cloud over Gerry's features, much like the one that Penny felt cross his own, each and every time he thought about Jimmy. Some people you didn't want to disappoint.

"I ain't happy about it neither, Jack, but we'll fob them off with something. Perhaps Becker's Yank can siphon off the weapons dumps and all. They'd go for that."

Penny got up and started pacing too. It wasn't just to draw the confabulations away from where the prisoners could earwig any more about the score that von Salzen had dumped in their laps – however jeopardised, jabbertised or otherwise. He was trying to pin down his own thoughts as well as Gerry's. In disbelief he realised that he had gone from thinking about Jimmy to thinking about Marjorie. She wouldn't like it either.

"Sod that," he said. "We ain't going into business with the Yanks. The reason Jimmy bit Pfeffer's hand off on this job is it's a chance to get one over on the flash bastards!"

"Was a chance, Jack. You said it yourself. It died with Pfeffer."

Marjorie, he was thinking. And Mila. And the wink she'd tipped him on the road to Hamelin. I reckon you did well enough, for an amateur, she had said.

"You're wrong, Gerry. I was wrong. Alright, alright, it was Pfeffer's caper. He come up with it without us asking. He had the inside knowledge and the contacts. But we've sussed out the target and its location. You got the buyers lined up. All we need is a crew."

He looked back at the trussed-up threesome beyond the arches, where they were half-lit by one of the cellar's stained glass portholes, like votive offerings.

When Gerry grinned, Penny couldn't help but shudder. He remembered what Gerry had been doing the last time he'd seen that leer.

"Take your point. A ready-made crew. Nice one, Jack."

"We'd have had a hard time putting one together anyhow, what with the risks involved."

"And that was when we had the Jerries working with us." The leer – sick enough to start with – had begun to sour. "This is pretty much suicide now."

"But no skin off our schnozzes," Penny said.

Gerry nodded pensively, for him.

"Jimmy will know we done our best. That might even count for something with the buyers too."

"Exactly."

"Alright then. Let's go explain to them how Jimmy does business. They step on our toes, they got to pay a forfeit. This is their forfeit. Pull this off for us and the slate's wiped clean."

Yeah, Penny thought. But I know you and I know Jimmy and I know her. I know the way he loads his forfeits too. If she gets away with it, against the odds they'll be facing, and you welch on that part of the deal, it will be Hamelin all over again, for all of us. The Pied Piper's got nothing on her.

*   *   *

The fog had thinned around the Herrenhaus and in its place fell the wet, dispiriting snow that had characterised this part of northern Germany this winter. Dispiriting it might be, but its relative mildness had likely saved hundreds of lives. In Berlin, whole families were being dug out, frozen.

With the British staff sergeant's silenced carbine pressing into the small of his back, Bradley stepped through the rear windows into the whiteness of the terrace.

"You first," the man had said with an apologetic smirk. "They'll be pretty edgy by now and frankly, me old china, you ain't no other use to us."

Statues on plinths – hunters, animals. A stylish bronze balustrade. Colonnades ran off either side, topping fans of stone steps that swept down to the misty flowerbeds and the ghosts of trees. Courtesy of the army and its many ways of trampling on memories, Bradley had visited a good dozen of these forsaken manor houses over the past years, yet what this vista invoked, more than anything, was the ruined sanatorium in the mountains of Czechoslovakia. Winter mist for summer cloud, shrouded gardens for half-glimpsed valleys, but the sense of peril was the same, and the uncertainty. The first time he had found her, somehow both a guest and a prisoner in that Nazi hideout at the war's end, he had been desperate for her to trust him and terrified that she would not. Now he was afraid she would never look at him or speak to him again.

Not that it seemed that would matter for much longer.

The British came out after him, pushing the two Czechs ahead of them. Although their captors numbered only five, it was plain that they meant business. The staff sergeant in particular, Bradley thought, and that evil-looking bastard who's no more an officer than I am: even if he's never guarded Surrendered Enemy Personnel, much less gotten them to surrender in the first place, you can tell that holding folks hostage comes as natural to him as breathing.

Four marble figures lined the curved bow of the terrace. The British took cover behind these, positioning their captives, with hands bound, in the spaces between: Mila in the middle, her driver on her left and Bradley on her right. Only the swarthy, thickset staff sergeant left himself exposed, making a bulky target for any hidden snipers in his ill-fitting battledress and jerkin. He rested the fat tube of the carbine on his shoulder, flaunting it.

"How many, did you say?" he asked Mila.

"I didn't."

"We have twenty, surrounding you," the driver blurted out. "And if you do not release us..."

"You got three out there, maximum, Stas."

The staff sergeant threw Bradley a wink and mouthed the word again. *Free.*

"They forget I seen their mob before." He took his gun in both hands and cocked it. "Let's get this sorted out before we all freeze our knackers off. You, Mila, are going to call on your men to show themselves and surrender – or I'm going to put a bullet in one of these two."

Her voice sounded far away.

"What makes you think they'll do as I say?"

"Oh, I know they will."

"What makes you think I care?"

Out of the corner of his eye, Bradley could see the staff sergeant watching her. He watched her too, as well as he was able. Surely she would have worked her hands free by now. It was only rope, and simple knots. Had it not been for his dislocated shoulder, he was confident he'd have had that asshole's gun out of his grasp and under his nose before his comrades could react. As it was, he could barely move his fingers.

And it looked like she had given up.

"Mila..." Ignoring their captors, he spoke to her directly for the first time since the mountaintop. "We'll still find him, I promise you."

She didn't turn her head, didn't even shift her sightless gaze.

"All those things I did to get to him... All those people I hurt... Lamprecht, Stransky, Schlosser, Düttmann, Ziegler..."

It was clear that by *him* she meant Pfeffer and had lost the will to look beyond that. If he could not appeal to hope or purpose, perhaps he could stir her sense of intrigue, even indignation.

"You may have given them a few bruises but someone else has killed them now. The last one, Ziegler, was found floating in the Weser yesterday."

Again no reaction, from her. The staff sergeant was lapping it all up of course.

"I killed them," she said at last. "Just as surely as I killed Pfeffer's man in there – and the men in the field."

Bradley didn't know who they were, but if they had been anything like the guys protecting Pfeffer, their pistols drawn, it had been more than justified.

"How, Mila – how did you kill them?"

"I led someone to them. Or you did."

"Yeah, but don't you want to know who?"

A pause. A long, white puff of breath. A sigh.

"I know who followed me here to kill Pfeffer."

He recoiled at the accusation. Was it because of her English, which on occasions revealed itself to be less than perfect? Didn't she mean followed me here *and* killed Pfeffer? She couldn't think...?

"I followed you, sure. Been following you for ages. But you must know that was never my intention. I was trying to save you."

"And of course no one asked you to do this..."

Her toneless scorn, the way she wouldn't look at him, killed him too. He couldn't help but remember another time, soon after the revelation that had so inflamed her, the revelation that had exposed Professor Lossner's lies about her son's fate. It was just before Bradley's solo breakout from the mountains, when she had pressed her burning cheek against his and whispered *I'm going to be counting on you.*

"I was only trying to help," he said.

"Then thank you, Sergeant Bradley. I release you from all further obligations."

At which point, the phony captain had clearly heard enough. "Get on with it, Jack."

"Right you are." The staff sergeant – Jack – stepped back out of sight. "Well, Mila darlin', we all love a natter but this is crunch time. Call them out now or the next thing you'll hear is your man's head going pop."

Bradley bit back on the pain and tensed himself for action as best he could. If she did not comply, Mila would have to try something. He did not believe for a moment that even cowed, even crumbling, she would give up the life of one of her closest associates without a fight. The moment Jack put his gun to Stas's head it would all kick off. Literally, most likely. Their wrists were tied but no one had thought to hobble them.

Mila would go for Jack, of course. She'd either knock him out or send his weapon over the edge. The others had service revolvers. Harder to aim a kick at and quicker to move out of the way if you did. But they weren't gunslingers. If he could fell the phony captain and wrap his legs around him, maybe that could force a standoff and buy her the time and the targets that she and her marksmen needed. All assuming he hadn't passed out first.

He blinked in surprise as the cold, hard muzzle of the silenced carbine pressed against the back of his skull.

*   *   *

From the derelict outbuildings of the grange, the dispersing mist and wintering vegetation granted a line of sight across the park and through the avenue of chestnuts that ran along this side of the gardens' pleasure ground. Even from the low angle, and behind his camouflage of icy evergreens, the watcher with the field glasses could identify the figures among the statues on the terrace.

He had also spotted the three so-called Polish snipers in their own hides, with their own coatings of twigs and mulch, their own wrapped-up rifles. The cover they had chosen was not sufficiently deep or carefully ventilated. Their breath gave them away.

The watcher had not drawn a bead on the terrace, nor on those who had. His weapon was strictly for self-defence, should he be discovered, and he had taken every precaution to ensure that this would not happen. His mission, this time, was to observe.

And so he had observed. He had observed the so-called British soldiers arriving earlier that morning, and the Germans in their fancy four-door *Schwebeklasse*. He had observed the two arrivals of the jeep full of so-called Poles. He had observed the arrival also, from his BMW in the woods, of the so-called American civilian. And the departures of course: the trucks with their treasures, the limousine on its mercy dash with the wounded German. He had observed and he had listened. He had heard the shots and the shouts, not long before that mercy dash. Then nothing, save the grumbling of the so-called Poles. And now this. The deadlock on the terrace.

We were all so-called Poles, once, the watcher mused, extending and flexing his muscles to generate warmth in his stiff leg; in between being so-called Lithuanians and so-called Russians. Better to be united under a common cause and a supranational identity. A so-called supranational identity.

I don't know if you're all ethnically Czechs like your leader, he found himself thinking, despite his political education, but I know you're not from my part of the world. You would be able to spend all day frozen without complaining if you had ever been ice fishing below Karmazinai. You'd know how to keep your trigger fingers warm.

Assuming they still had sufficient blood in their fingertips, and assuming they decided to do so, he wondered what he would do if they opened fire. Nothing, he supposed. That would be the correct action, if one could call such a response an action. His job was to observe, to identify, to join up every dot and to report, so that someone else, someone less attuned to ice fishing, could follow up on that. Whoever she or the American had killed in the Herrenhaus – he had his suspicions, but that wasn't his job either – it made no difference to this task. They would all be dead soon enough anyway, like all the others. For the moment the only thing was to watch the ice.

CHAPTER TWELVE

Although the billiard room occupied a part of the basement that drew ample light from the areaway below the terrace, they had strung two Tilley lamps from the chandelier above the table to illuminate the maps and photographs that were spread across the baize.

Jack Penny stood up at the centre as though proposing a toast.

"Couple of months' time, couple of Jerry nobs is getting hitched. Princess Sophie of Greece – whose first husband was the prince who put the 'SS' in Hesse – is tying the knot with her cousin, George William Lardy-Dardy of Hanover. It's big news in royal circles, what with all of them being related – invites to go out sharpish, proper old knees-up to be organised... So, couple of weeks ago the servants go to dig up the Crown Jewels of the House of Hesse, what they'd buried in the family castle of Kronberg in case the first wave of Yanks into Frankfurt took a fancy to them..."

He looked for Bradley and saw him chance his mended shoulder with a cagey shrug.

"...only they ain't there no more, 'cause the second wave – the ones who ran the officers' club like in this place – have had them away. The word from our acquaintances across the Pond is that the silly sods are trying to fence them in Wisconsin."

At his side, of course, Gerry Lonsdale had to stick his oar in, if only by parroting what his brother had said on the radio relay.

"All they'll get for them is Conduct Unbecoming and a

stretch in the glasshouse, on account of how the effin' things are hot as mustard! Which is one reason why..."

"We'll come back to that," Penny interrupted, as forcefully yet sweetly as he could. "What matters is they've gone. And poor old Sophie can hardly have a lend of her future hubby's Hanoverian tomfoolery – the reason being Queen Victoria half-inched that a hundred years ago!"

He surveyed the group gathered around the billiard table, conscious that the home-grown gen wouldn't mean much to anyone except his own men, who weren't all that big on history and wouldn't be going on the caper anyway. Five of the group, Mila and her gang, were Czechoslovaks or something close to it. Bradley was a Yank and Becker, their fixer, a local. That left only one audience member who might appreciate the background detail, and she had helped him come up with half of it herself.

He cleared his throat.

"We ain't concerned with none of them, except to say that me and Jimmy is of the opinion it's time the Yanks stopped getting away with this sort of outrage and we bloody started! Problem is, like I say, in the British Zone the best German tom was snapped up years ago by our own royals. But not quite all of it. There was a Royal Commission what ordered young Queen Vic to stop being such a greedy bint and hand some pieces back – and all kinds of people have had their beady eyes on them ever since. Which brings us to the father of the groom: Ernest Augustus, former Duke of Brunswick, still head of the House of Hanover, and an old mucker of our dear departed King Edward VIII, not to mention *his* old mucker, Adolf Hitler..."

He tapped the newspaper file photo of the fierce-eyed baldy with the moustache. It was lying on the army map of the target region, which he was coming to next.

"Ernie here spends the war hobnobbing with his Nazi chums at Schloss Blankenburg in the Harz mountains. And then with the Yanks and the Brits when we take over. Only the officers, mind. Scrambled eggs all round. But a few months ago the Russkis get their knickers in a twist about this British... what's it called?"

"Exclave," Marjorie said.

"...exclave — meaning this odd bulge in the border what pokes into their territory like a frotter on the 'ampstead Tube. So they start blocking our supplies from getting through, we start eyeing up land for swapsies, and after a bit of ducking and diving it's announced that the town of Blankenburg and its district will shortly become part of the Soviet Zone."

He shook his head in feigned wonder and snuck Marjorie a look before continuing.

"This don't half put the wind up Ernie! He gets a message to the King, God bless 'im, saying Help, Cuz! Bygones be bygones and all that... And quick as a flash, the first convoy the Reds let through is fifty empty British Army lorries with orders from on high to shift the Duke and his possessions to his other castle, near Hanover."

"A shocking disgrace!" Marjorie burst out.

"You ain't lying, girl." Penny's finger bent nearly double on the map when he heard Gerry snigger.

"You're saying the remaining treasures of the House of Hanover are back in the British Zone..." That was Mila, coming out of her mood to indulge in a bit of wishful thinking.

"No, I ain't, and even if I was, they got Marienburg Castle buttoned up so tight you couldn't sneak out a fart. What I'm saying is the opposite. One of them British Army Bedfords come back empty too."

"That's what Pfeffer was involved in?"

"Bingo. Pfeffer was in cahoots with a chamberlain from Schloss Blankenburg who'd got hold of some of the cargo: literally off the back of a lorry. Knew what to grab, I suppose... Seems the bloke has set himself up as a receiver, maybe even a banker, for all these renegade Nazis who are looking to buy their way out of schtuck. We only know him by his business name, Elster, and we don't know where he's stashed the loot, but thanks to Pfeffer, Herr Becker and Mrs Jessop here, we've worked out what he's got, and why the buyers are prepared to pay so handsomely for it."

"Which is?"

Penny had wanted to hold her in suspense. All of them, but especially Mila. The trouble was, Gerry didn't know the meaning of the word. Nor many others neither.

"It's a crown, innit – Queen Victoria's crown!"

"Queen Victoria's *nuptial* crown," Penny corrected, flicking through the papers to find the page he'd torn from the art book. "Or, more accurate, Queen Charlotte's small nuptial crown, what Queen Vic borrowed for herself and never wanted to give back. Eventually she had a near-copy made, for our own Crown Jewels, but this is the one she kvetched about returning – and the Royal Family have had the hump about it ever since."

Mila studied the portrait of George III's consort, Charlotte of Mecklenburg-Strelitz, and the mass of diamonds and jewels upon which her left hand rested.

"So it's somewhere in the vicinity of Blankenburg Castle, which is now occupied by the Russians? And the only thing we know for sure is that the bearer goes by 'Magpie'?"

"You got it."

"Who are the buyers and why do they want it so much?"

Penny turned his eyes from Mila to Marjorie, who gave an encouraging nod, and then to Gerry, who most definitely didn't.

"You don't need to know that."

This time it was the American who emitted the snotty laugh. Cheeky blighter! He oughtn't to have been here at all, much less acting like he was too good for it. It was a far cry from the twitch of surprise when he'd felt the shooter at the back of his nut: he hadn't expected to be singled out like that. But it hadn't taken a C.C.G. Professor to clock there was something between him and Mila – and sure enough she'd called out her men straight after that. Since then Penny had watched them

149

closely, those two. It didn't seem like an act, the hostility, the resentment, but nor did she appear to want rid of him. It was her who got her men to stretch him out and put his arm back in, and it was her who'd started making noises about him being a part of the crew, whatever the job might be. And that was against the recommendations of her own men, as well as Gerry's. Somewhere inside, in spite of herself, she knew she needed him.

She had been poring over the map. Now she glanced left-right, at Stas and the old boy, before straightening up and giving a little nod.

"OK," she said.

Gerry – or rather 'Captain Prentice' – missed the whole point, of course.

"That's very magna-minous of you, seeing as you got no alternative!"

But Mila ignored him and so did Penny. Instead he caught her eye and held it. He knew she hadn't meant OK, I'll do it, she had meant OK, the job was doable. The nod hadn't meant I'll try, it had meant I'll get it.

And this look now, between them. He knew what that meant and all.

*   *   *

Later that afternoon, Marjorie found Mila on the side terrace overlooking the rose garden. The younger woman was absorbed in a sheaf of papers and photographs.

"Hello again. Going over the plans?"

Even as she said it, Marjorie saw that the uppermost photo, torn from a magazine, featured not European crown jewellery, nor baroque castles on a hill, but seven, small, blonde children seated around a circular table, attended by brawny women in shirtsleeves and aprons. Mila had been comparing the flagstones, railings and louvred doors, which showed beyond doubt that the picture had been taken on this spot.

"*Supper on the sun deck,*" she recited, without needing to look.

"Grown pig-fat, each tow-headed Nazi bastard licks his platter clean like a little super man."

Marjorie did not know how to respond to that. What she wanted to say, what she always wanted to say, was *at least he's alive!* But then she would have to talk about Peter, and his father before him. Peter had been on her mind all day. Not that he wasn't normally, but today especially, with all the talk of blessed royals, she had heard him calling out for her, almost as clearly as she had heard him that cold night in May 1940, when the venerated Lord Mountbatten, cousin to Princess Elizabeth, had left him behind to die at Namsos Fjord.

Instead, she resorted to the convention of a sympathetic face and was relieved to see Mila pull one in return.

"How are you, Marjorie?" Meaning, of course, *how are you bearing up?* Or in other words – for otherwise there should be no need to descend to such fulsome intimacy – *how are you coping with having very nearly been raped at the roadside?*

"Oh, can't complain," she said.

"No," Mila gave a sheepish smile that was also an apology, although she had nothing to apologise for. "No, that wouldn't do at all!"

"Is there anything I can get you – anything you need?" *Besides your son, or the miraculous resurrection of the only lead to his whereabouts.*

"I don't suppose you want to tell me who the buyers are?"

"I do actually," Marjorie said. "But I don't suppose I ought to."

Mila nodded, putting away the papers and producing a packet of cigarettes with a little gold lighter that Marjorie hadn't seen before.

"Operational Security. Makes sense, for if we're captured." Having lit Marjorie's cigarette, she lowered her gaze to light her own, adding: "Or in case we decide to go free lance."

"I wasn't thinking that."

"No." As they rounded the corner of the terrace and moved back under the cover of the colonnade, the ice blue eyes

---

scanned the shuttered windows. "But they are."

Marjorie thrust her spare hand back inside her coat and shivered. Here at the rear, as the light went and the temperature dropped, a fresh flurry of snow swirled around the Herrenhaus. But it wasn't that.

They. The hint of accusation in the word. Or was she adding the interpretation herself? Two formulaic expressions had got mixed up in her head lately: *strange bedfellows* and to *fall among thieves*. Each seemed to obfuscate as much as it encapsulated. Or was it that she was trying to propagate a figurative meaning from the two, where none might exist. Didn't she really mean that she had *fallen*?

That was another word that was open to interpretation.

"Jacob – Jack – said that Helmut Ziegler was dead. Drowned in the Weser."

"So the American claims."

"Did he kill him?" When Mila responded only with a shrug, Marjorie ventured: "Did *we*?"

Shutting her eyes, she tried to picture the plunge from the embankment in Hamelin, like the rats in the story, or the vanished children in some versions of it. Instead she saw a scarecrow sink to its knees and crumple into a pile of limbs. Like a puppet.

And then the other heaps, the other puppets of skin and bone.

"I know you must think I've sold my soul to the Devil..." she began, but the words dried.

Mila wasn't listening. She was staring out across the darkening gardens, through a veil of snow that just then seemed more suggestive of churned-up ash or lime.

"I thought I saw something – through the tree line, towards the grange."

"An animal perhaps." Marjorie pulled a face. "Life goes on, doesn't it?"

"Mmm..." She could tell that Mila had decided not to alarm her. "Yes, I'm sure that's what it was."

"We should go in anyway. I ought to help you set up for the evening briefing."

Mila gave an affirmative grunt and flicked her cigarette out over the balustrade. It was an extravagant, even reckless, gesture nowadays, when doing such a thing would more often than not cause a scramble of scavengers, like carrion birds. Perhaps a part of her relished the isolation and with it, as Marjorie did, the sense of abandon. As she was going through the side door into the hall, Mila turned back and her face brightened.

Her eyes lifted to the bronze lamp fitting above them and she pursed her lips to whistle six lilting notes.

Underneath the lantern...

Then the smile was gone.

*   *   *

In the twin pools of light on the billiard table, and with the general gloom beyond, it was getting hard to distinguish between cigarette smoke and the condensation on everyone's breath. To Mila they were a shadowy cluster of livestock, steaming in their winter coats.

"Go take another butcher's at the heating controls," Penny told one of his men, his teeth chattering. "The Yanks might have left some juice in the system."

"But, guv, it's like an effin' ocean liner back there..."

"Yeah, and you're all supposed to be effin' engineers!"

Mila stepped forward into the light.

"I think I'd better start. I shan't be long anyway."

She tapped the smaller-scale military road map upon which was drawn the demarcation line between the British and Soviet Zones of Occupation. It was largely for show, since they had so little firm intelligence and would have to conduct rapid reconnaissance on the move, but she knew that her job now was also to provide reassurance. They were moving into unfamiliar territory in more ways than one.

"Here. Bad Harzburg, the northern gateway to the Harz —

well south of the control point at Helmstedt-Marienborn. That's where we'll cross. There'll be plenty of Army traffic around the camps at Goslar. UNRRA too. I'm sure many vehicles blunder back and forth across the line. The border guards must be used to it. Their main concern is policing the flow of refugees anyway."

"And then?" asked Jack Penny. She knew who he was now.

"Down this road, skirting the high ground."

"Straight to Blankenburg?"

She shook her head and gestured impatiently for Herr Becker to hand her the bloodstained notebook. It was the only personal effect that had come back from the tame doctor's surgery in Bremen: the well-used if largely indecipherable notebook that had been found in the coat pocket of Pfeffer's henchman, recently deceased, and most likely the obstruction that had caused the delay in drawing his pistol.

"No," she said, wiping such trivialities from her mind. "Not all the way. When we see these ruins here, at Heimburg, we turn south for this location."

"And what's there?"

She gave the stocky Londoner a thin smile.

"Your precious crown, with a bit of luck. Look here, among the sketches of possible route-markers, Pfeffer's man or one of their contacts has doodled and annotated a cluster of derelict religious structures, including what we gather is a former Cistercian abbey and the monks' oil mill that once served Blankenburg castle. Even leaving aside the issue of why else Pfeffer would have made such drawings on his tour of the region, I'd say Elster, as a castle official, would be familiar with this place, as well as certain other sites in the immediate vicinity."

"Which are?"

"Caves, here and here. A hermitage and chapel carved out of the rock. From the notes it looks like the Nazis fortified them and used them as a sub-camp of the Mittelbau-Dora concentration camp at Nordhausen – no doubt scaring the locals away in the process."

"The magpie's nest, eh?"

"I can't think of a better one."

"And if you're wrong?"

"If we go in softly, no harm done. We carry on to Blankenburg and find another way."

Throughout the discussion so far, Gerry Lonsdale had been lurking in the background. Now he made his way through to the table.

"He'll have someone he cares about. A wife. A daughter. Yeah, Jack?"

Mila didn't look at him. Instead, she focused on Penny, trying to judge the degree of aversion in his face. Penny was smart, smarter than Lonsdale, and he paid attention to people. He knew how she'd react to the suggestion of seizing someone's child. From the look of him, he felt the same way. But she read something else in his expression too. A warning. Tread carefully.

"I'm not doing that," she said. "But yes, it's the right sort of thinking. If we don't find the loot at the monastery site, our goal should be to grab Elster and get him to talk."

"He'll be protected," Gerry scoffed, unconvinced. "Left you a draw-ring of the defences, did he? Got a note in there about how many guards?"

She smiled broadly this time.

"I know what I'm doing."

"You and who's army, eh?" That was Penny, jovial again, and eager to move things along.

"Exactly," she said. "That's the next decision to make."

"We can't remain Free Polish," Stas said. "The Russians will eat us for breakfast. So do we go as British, like before – get lost on the road to Berlin?"

"That's a long way to stray off course without noticing," Marek grumbled. He was still sore at her for letting that amateur in Hamelin off so easily. By his professional standards, a failed pickpocket did not deserve any reward, let alone one so generous. "And they watch that road closer than any other."

"As Russians then?" Miro was probably already thinking about how to acquire and recreate the documents.

This time it was the American who butted in.

"I wouldn't. They'll be looking out for that, after Silesia."

Mila saw her team react with surprise and anger. How could he know about that?

'Uncle' Ludvík pushed through and prodded him on the shoulder, choosing the one they had only just put back in place. Bradley winced.

"I met you before, didn't I, matey? You came snooping round Prague Old Town Square, searching for her. Always sticking your nose in."

Ludvík had no English and had spoken in Czech. Bradley caught her eye.

"He says he wouldn't come to you for advice about a cover identity either, and I agree," she told him. "You're compromised."

"So what's the play?" Penny said.

She threw Bradley a dismissive look.

"Americans, of course." Returning her finger to the map, she indicated where the redrawn Soviet Zone bulged westwards north of U.S.-occupied Hessen. "It seems to me that green troops, in bad weather, might accidentally cut across the line of demarcation on their way south from Bremerhaven to Eschwege, say. And I think I overheard Captain Prentice mention Herr Becker's contact here who can get American supplies from their Post Exchange. We'd need new uniforms, and perhaps a truck..."

Although he looked as though he'd rather spit on her shoes, Becker gave a grudging nod.

Penny was laughing properly now.

"That's why you wanted Bradley in on this! I thought you was soft on him, but you just needed a Yank as a front man."

"There's more than that," she said. "He's our insurance policy. Whatever his people are up to, they won't want him embarrassing them with the Soviets, so if they find out about this, they'll have to give us assistance – as long as we get the operation underway before they can stop it."

"A proper shady shickster you are! My mum warned me 'bout girls like you!"

As the welcome mirth subsided, Gerry Lonsdale stood up tall again, this time noticeably flanked by a couple of his burliest men. The habitual smirk that tugged at his upper lip changed its shape and with it his whole demeanour. He flared his nostrils and tightened his cheek muscles. Although she had only an inkling of who he was, Mila was struck by the impression of a man both aroused and repelled by his own taste and odour.

"Since we're talking about insurance policies, Jimmy has asked me to take one out on all of you. Sorry, Jack."

She saw Penny freeze. Only his eyes, narrowing, gave any sign of life as they swept back and forth across the half dozen men in REME uniform. None of the craftsmen would look back at him. Four, it seemed, were Gerry's now and the other two suddenly undecided. His mouth fell open.

"Where's Marjorie?"

"Don't think of it as another forfeit," Gerry said. "This is more like a security you've fronted, yeah? Like bail or something you've pawned."

"I haven't fuckin' pawned Marjorie!"

"'course not, Jack. Only Jimmy reckons this will help you keep your eye on the ball – remember who's the boss, that sort of thing."

He took ahold of one of the Tilley lamps and raised it up, as though to give them all a clearer view of the expression on his face, which was not so much a grin as a wanton extension of that snarling sneer.

"Same goes for you and your crew, Miss Nightingale, or whatever your name is – I seen the two of you chumming up out there. Do the job and the slate's wiped clean. Do us wrong and Mrs Jessop has another little accident on the road."

CHAPTER THIRTEEN

Up in the attic that ran the length of the Herrenhaus, between industrial-scale heating pipes and the white Gothic arches formed by the converging chimney breasts, the American had been drilling his ersatz compatriots into a superficially convincing squad.

Squad, remember, not section.

He had disarranged their brand new fatigues and corrected their overly formal posture. He had taught the Brits to turn their palms the other way when saluting, and the so-called Poles to stop using two fingers. He had briefed them on how and where to sit in the deuce-and-a-half they had borrowed and when to flash the I.D. cards and paybooks that Miro had produced.

Most importantly, he had handed out the Wrigley's.

Now he regarded the six of them – Stas, Ludvík, Miro, Marek and the two men Penny had sent for from his smelting operation on the Sennelager ranges – and he shook his head in apparent despair.

"Not much use doing this if they ain't here. Where's Mila? Where's Jack Penny?"

"Miss Slavík," Stas countered, in a passable American accent. "Has more important business to attend to."

"Yeah," Craftsman Keeffe added with a similar snarky emphasis, albeit no attempt to change his normal voice. "An' so does Staff Sergeant Carter."

Bradley shrugged.

"Then *take five*, fellas. *Smoke 'em if you got 'em.*"

And with that he pulled out his own cigs, offering none around. It seemed that he could speak pointedly too.

The Czechs withdrew to huddle with their secrets, while Keeffe and Davies, being British, went off in search of tea.

When she appeared, it was not up the staff stairwell but down from the spiral staircase at the centre point of the attic. She had been in the turret, alone with her thoughts. Her sour scowl matched the downturned curve of the scar on her cheek.

"Mila, listen…"

She raised a hand.

"I heard. And I don't need slouching lessons, thank you. I'll be hidden in the back of the lorry anyway, since your army isn't in the habit of integrating women, nor any other disadvantaged groups."

"That's not what I wanted to talk about."

"I don't have anything to talk about with you, Sergeant Bradley."

He looked around to check if anyone was listening, which might at least explain her coldness, but saw nobody.

"Mila, please…"

"What?"

"Did you, er, did you get the lighter?"

"You know I did, since it led me here to witness you demolish the last proper hope I had of finding my son. Surely you aren't asking for my gratitude?"

"Not that, dammit. Just some acknowledgment…"

"Of what?"

"Of what it means, that lighter. How you and Colonel Smith had the inscription removed. How you left it with Karel Sec as… what, a clue, for anybody tracking you?"

"Not a clue," she said, more to herself than to him. "As an offering. A penance."

"Well, however it was intended, it became the clue that led me to you, even if it did take a bit of sleight-of-hand from SMERSh…"

"I told you, it means nothing." Interrupting his jumpy

narrative, which was all too obviously a desperate attempt to engage her in reminiscences, she took the little gold object from her pocket and tossed it without even looking at it. "Here, have it."

It wasn't a very good throw and Bradley these past few days was like a man adrift. The lighter thudded to the bare boards. Penny, who had been watching and listening closely, chose that moment to emerge from the archway in the chimney.

"SMERSh, eh? Who are they when they're at home?"

Mila's cold gaze warmed fractionally, he reckoned. By half a degree, perhaps.

"You may be a few hours from finding out for yourself. Why would you change your mind and decide to come with us?"

"Why do you think?"

"You won't save Marjorie if you get captured with the rest of us, Mr Penny."

"You never know, I might help keep you out of chokey. And I reckon we're close enough now for you to call me Jack."

He bent to pick up the lighter, turning it over and over, testing it.

"What I want to know…" he winked at Bradley and pressed the lighter on him. "Since we're all pals now… is why you, Mila, haven't just cut and run. You're not in the game, this ain't your manor, so why do you care if Gerry or Jimmy Effin' Lonsdale imposes a forfeit on you? If you escaped the clutches of SMERSh, and I reckon I can guess who they are, you could have it away from that pair of wankers."

"That's why you decided to come – to keep tabs on us?"

"Hardly, bluebottle," he responded to Bradley with a sneer. "I ain't stupid enough to imagine me and my boys could stop her mob if they decided to do a disappearing act."

Mila stepped between them to defuse the tension.

"I'm playing along, Jack, because I *am* in the game, just now. Even if it's a long shot, I'm going to need free run of the British zone to try all the available channels for tracing adoptions from this place. And there's another thing now…"

Before he knew it, she had laid a hand on his arm and was giving it a reassuring squeeze.

"What?"

"I'm going to need Marjorie safely back in her job at Bünde."

He placed a big hand on top of hers, feeling suddenly what…? Paternal?

No, more like she was his old mum and was going to make everything all right.

"You and me both, girl. You and me both."

*   *   *

Outside, in the frosty driveway of the Herrenhaus, Bradley set aside his concerns about the girl and decided to concentrate on his concerns about the mission.

There was plenty to be going on with.

Among Gerry Lonsdale's REME vehicles and their crews, which were completing the stripping and removal of the remaining fixtures, sat the U.S. Army truck that Becker had acquired from his contact at the Bremerhaven PX. Ironically, given their recent indenture to the absent Lonsdale brother, it was a GMC 2½ ton 6x6 of the type known as a 'Jimmy'. This one had a hooped canvas cargo cover and a hard two-man cab with the hatch above the co-driver but no machine gun mount. They had dressed it with external stowage that subtly obscured the bogus unit markings, but the days of draping military vehicles with any old junk were gone and today's MPs – of all nations – were on the look-out for anomalies. That was worrying enough. More so was the suspicion that their papers wouldn't pass close inspection either. All they could hope for was that the Brits would wave them through as far as Goslar, with the same lack of care that had allowed the 'TTG' truck to roam around creating so much mayhem – and that the Reds, if and when they ran into them, might be less able to spot a phony American.

He watched them now as they loaded the supplies. The plain ODs and steel helmets helped, of course, but even so, Mila and Ludvík would need to join the cargo in the back of the truck and pray that the shadows masked their features. Bradley had no idea if real replacements arriving at the Bremerhaven staging area would have rifles on their person nowadays, but having opted for the helmets instead of the more revealing soft covers, he judged it prudent to let them all appear unarmed. The weapons they were taking would be hidden among the kitbags with everything else.

Riding in the cab, carrying Miro's prized motor vehicle operator's permits and movement orders, he and Stas alone would wear sidearms. This was perfectly reasonable, for even on this side of the demarcation line, occupied Germany was far from safe for a lone vehicle, especially when one took to the backroads as they'd be doing. What was less confidence-boosting was that they had made it clear only Stas's pistol would be loaded. Since Stas would be doing the driving and as little talking as possible, Bradley had reluctantly pinned on the butterbars of Lieutenant Limpdick again.

And speaking of phony soldiers, Jack Penny, now demoted in order to ride with his heavies in back and handle any checkpoint guards who might stick their noses in there, came crunching across the icy gravel to the vehicles with his version of a G.I. salute. It was a humorous and even conciliatory gesture, yet there was no mistaking the suppressed fury in the man.

"All set?"

"Just waiting for her," Bradley said.

Penny looked almost sympathetic.

"I reckon you'll have a long wait there, mate."

Bradley nodded. Then he indicated the two men handing up boxes.

"How do you know Gerry hasn't got to Keeffe and Davies too?"

Penny shrugged.

"I don't. But brains are brains and muscle is muscle."

"Meaning you don't trust them?"

"Meaning I wouldn't trust Gerry to come up with something so fiendish neither. But yeah, we'll have to keep an eye on them." He gave that distinctive pouting nod that looked like he was trying to convince himself. "They're not exactly the only suspicious characters in this little venture."

"Now don't start again…"

"I didn't mean you."

"Then who?"

"Well, take your pick. Did you notice Herr Becker has found somewhere else to be, even though he's supposed to be the one finalising this salvage operation on behalf of the owners?"

"You think he's setting us up?"

"Come through nice and sharpish with them sketches, didn't he? And helped us identify the abbey buildings, despite protesting he'd never been to that part of the country. But hey…" Penny gave a half-assed grin. "You're the sodding Special Agent, you tell me!"

They both looked up at the sound of the main entrance door and the glass that Mila had broken on her arrival a little over a week ago. This time it was Gerry Lonsdale in full Captain Prentice regalia, wearing his Sam Browne belt and service revolver, plus a big proprietary grin on his face. At Bradley's side, Jack Penny muttered an obscenity.

"Hadn't you better be on your way?" Gerry boomed as he descended the steps. "It's a good 'undred an' forty mile to Goslar – could take you the rest of the day."

"We figured on hitting the border a little before nightfall," Bradley said. "That way we can check out the situation and decide whether to cross in the dark or lie up and go early in the morning, just before they change the watch."

"Okey-dokey…" A curl of the lip that put one in mind of a hyena baring its teeth in warning – before he turned it into a cheeky wink. He was having fun. "Oh, and Jack, don't you worry none 'bout Marjorie. We'll look after her."

Bradley could sense Penny counting to ten and reaching maybe five.

"That's Mrs Jessop to you."

"Alright, alright, she's your old lady, lover-boy." Gerry sniggered, as if a thought had just occurred to him. "What is she, fifty? I suppose they're grateful at that age..."

He was a head taller than Jack Penny, with the lean frame of a Billy Conn and the unpredictability to match. Penny, by contrast, was short in the legs, playful by nature and carrying a fair few extra pounds. But one look at the Jewish streetfighter and Bradley knew who he'd put his money on.

The problem was, if it came to it, he wouldn't just be betting money. And while Penny was unarmed, 'Captain Prentice' was not.

The empty .45 had never felt so light on his hip as it did now.

"Say that again, Gerry." Jack Penny jutted his jaw and cocked his head, as though presenting an ear to catch something he might genuinely have missed the first time. But he hadn't missed it, as illustrated by the way he had also widened his stance and angled his left side toward his opponent.

Something like fire lit behind Gerry's eyes.

"What I was getting at, Jack, is that it's probably for the best – you being another dog that's had its day."

Penny's breath, condensed on the bitter air, was like a bull's.

"Just tell us where she is," he growled. "Tell Bradley here where you've got her, here in Germany or back in the Smoke, then you and me can go for it."

"Oh, I'd like that, Jack. But Jimmy might have something to say about it."

"Fuck Jimmy. And fuck you."

"Enough!" The girl's voice sliced the atmosphere between them. Everyone turned to look at her. Carrying her helmet in one hand and her kitbag in the other, she was wearing the same bulky fatigues as the rest of them, which only served to emphasise the slightness of her neck and wrists and shoulders. Her eyes were bright and moist, her nose and cheeks red, her expression fierce yet tormented. She had been weeping.

"My God! How much have you already invested in this 'caper' of yours – and you're going to waste everything on a schoolyard fight? If this is how professional criminals behave, no wonder so much is left for the amateurs!" She met Penny's eye, then Bradley's, then turned to the rest of the crew. "Get in the lorry, now. Let's get out of here."

As he turned back to his own men and their activities, Gerry Lonsdale chuckled, mirthlessly.

"Too right. Clock's ticking. For all of you."

*   *   *

As an honorary New Yorker, Doyle knew the joint from driving past on Houston Street (and he knew how to pronounce Houston also), but the truth was he had never dared venture inside. Although its neon sign stood proud amid the competing jumble of barrels and awnings, the plethora of Eastern European names and wares in this part of the Lower East Side – and the preponderance of beards, sidelocks and headscarves on the overflowing sidewalks – left him convinced he would stick out like a sore thumb.

Sensing his hesitation, his companion gave him a shove through the doors and pulled out his handkerchief to wipe the steam from his horn-rim eyeglasses. With the clatter of turnstiles, trays, dishes and knives, plus a hundred shouted conversations in a dozen languages, the cacophony inside the cramped delicatessen was deafening.

"Take the meal ticket he's handing you," Berman gave a grimace of combined exasperation and apology to the aproned bruiser whom Doyle had incorrectly assumed to be trying to take his hat and coat. "Let's go! We want to eat sometime this year…"

The ensuring process, if it could be called that, made the

increasingly bewildered Doyle wonder if this was what demobilisation was like. He followed Berman blindly as he shouldered through to join a series of lines at different counters, each time handing over his ticket in return for an incomprehensible exchange, a demand for a tip or bribe, and another plate of food that looked enough to feed the neighbourhood. Finally, they took their trays over to the close-packed tables in the centre, where Berman appeared to bully a young couple to vacate their seats.

"Sit. Eat," he said.

"What am I eating?"

"You know what this is: the city's finest pastrami and rye, with Russian dressing and sauerkraut. These knishes? Well, just try one. This? Matzo ball soup."

"And no one's joining us…?"

He meant it as a joke, but Berman chose to answer literally.

"Who would you wish to invite? Another of Hoover's men? They couldn't blend in here. Not that they can blend in anywhere, of course."

"Incidentally, the one you launched off the roof survived. Seems there's a setback under there after all. I gather he's spent the past three months learning to eat through a straw."

Berman just looked at him.

"This is not a game," he said. "The people I represent…"

Letting his discomfort and frustration get the better of him, Doyle couldn't help it: he looked around and faked a compassionate smile.

"Truly God's chosen!"

"I will assume," Berman said icily. "That was my admonishment for the FBI man and not an outward expression of your antisemitic soul."

Doyle contrived to look sheepish.

"Hadn't you heard? We don't have souls at BSC."

"I thought you said you were on the side of the angels."

"That was for Mr Bradley. As *you* said, he is one of Nature's innocents."

166

"And as you told him, BSC does not exist anymore."

"Not in so many words… or so few letters."

Berman took a huge bite of his huge sandwich and chewed purposefully. Doyle, on the verge of using his knife and fork, set them down and attempted the same. Berman laughed.

"My problem is not so different to yours. The people I represent are not a concentrated force but a loose amalgamation of causes. On the one hand we have… let us call it the 'escape'…"

"From Europe. To Palestine."

"Precisely. And, of course, connected to this is what we can call the 'defence'."

"Of Jews in Palestine?"

"And of the right of Jews to be in Palestine."

"That's a broad interpretation of defence. Not to mention the fact that it rather brings you into conflict with the local Arab population, and the British who are running the place."

"Just so. And then, you see, there is a third imperative."

"Which is?"

"Vengeance." Berman said.

"Of course."

"So, you will see how these different strands of thinking both complement and contradict one another…"

"I do see that, Berman. I mean, that was the whole reason for sending Bradley in."

"Yes. But my point is that when you have three different masters – at least – then matters can become many times more critical. Things can get out of control, fast."

"And I would argue that they've come pretty bloody close to doing just that. Your people wreaking vengeance have been so hot on my man's heels they've nearly taken him out in the same breath. Twice."

"I understood that he took MERCURY's target out himself."

"So we believe, although we've lost our direct contact with Bradley." Doyle, cursing Hoffman's lack of discretion and wondering where the other man was getting his information, gave a rueful shrug before continuing: "But Berman, no one has yet taken out *our* target. It would be a crying shame if someone did before Bradley and the girl can work their magic. Especially as it would likely mean that they are walking into a lethal trap."

"This is why I have warned you about things becoming critical."

"And it's why I'm telling you now to get your house in order. The people *I* represent – a thoroughly godless bunch looking after long-term British interests in the Middle East – are very closely aligned with both American interests and yours, in a way that official British policy may never be. But as I said to you before, there have to be limits, especially when it comes to that rather generous definition of defence that you've advanced."

Off came the horn-rims again. Handkerchief. Steam. Weary eyes.

"I will see what can be done. But you must understand that these are brutal, dangerous men, the hardest we have ever known. They do not respond to appeals to common humanity. They no longer believe in humanity."

"Then you must give them something else to believe in, before my people stop believing in you."

Berman nodded.

"I understand, my friend. It's good to clear the air."

Finding himself unable to prevent a tangy burp, Doyle covered his mouth apologetically. Apologetically – and by definition too late, of course. He hoped that such lateness wasn't a new trait he was developing.

"Fresh air sounds pretty good to me right now."

"Fresh air? What are you, a farmer? I know exactly what you need. Chocolate *babka*, washed down with an egg cream soda..." As he levered himself to his feet, Berman grinned and snatched Doyle's ticket from him. "My treat. What do you say?"

CHAPTER FOURTEEN

It was unwelcome, but not unusual, for unannounced visitors to come knocking at all hours. Refugees and other vagrants roamed the countryside and would often resort to begging for food or work. Yet although this was a place from which alms had once been dispensed, lately any vagabonds were more likely to be seen off with a dose of birdshot.

So when, as darkness fell that evening, the gatehouse keeper unbolted his front door and raised his lantern, he was no doubt expecting to have to threaten some ragged band with a few choice expletives that would cross the language barrier from Ostfalian to the Slavonic tongues. Instead, he was surprised by a smartly dressed lady of uncertain age who had a dramatic streak of grey woven through the wave of dark hair at the front of her headscarf.

"Please help," she said, in a fluster, and in German. "I was being moved by Mister Lonsdale and Mister Becker's men, but there's been a terrible smash-up on the road and they are hurt!"

The gatehouse keeper, a beefy, moustachioed fellow wearing only his undershirt with a thrown-on shooting jacket, regarded her curiously. He moved his light to show the gun in the crook of his arm.

"What cock-and-bull is this? Are you drunk, Madam? Be off home – don't you know what time it is?"

"I was with Herr Lonsdale, and Herr Becker..." She was sobbing now, yet kept repeating the names.

"I know of no such gentlemen. This is a private establishment. You've come to the wrong place."

Good enough.

"Oh well," Mila said. "It was worth taking precautions."

She pulled her hand from her coat pocket and put the big American pistol to his head. Her other hand reached for the shotgun.

"I'll take that, if you don't mind."

If the people at the entrance to the abbey complex had been in on it – working with Becker or somehow forewarned by Gerry Lonsdale, for whatever purpose – they would have been expecting a soft approach, quite possibly from a harmless-looking woman. More pertinently, they would have been expecting a particular woman, a woman versed in the art of disguise and subterfuge. So the appearance of any woman would have aroused their suspicions and put them on their guard: unless it was a woman they thought they knew. Giving them someone who looked and sounded like a second-hand account of Marjorie was a chance to get in close without a fuss, and potentially to expose any double-dealing.

As it had turned out, the ruse appeared to have been unnecessary. The gatehouse keeper was presumably one of Elster's men but not, it seemed, Becker's or Lonsdale's.

While she came to this conclusion, Ludvík and Miro had gone in past the pair of them, fast and hard. By the time she shepherded her captive down the passage and into the kitchen, which was the only room illuminated, they had a rosy-cheeked woman at gunpoint, the gatehouse keeper's wife. They had seen her going about chores around the compound throughout the day, breaking ice on the well to draw water, feeding the chickens, taking steaming pots and cloth-covered baskets into the quad. Now she had been caught arming herself not with another plausibly rustic shotgun but a German army-issue machine pistol.

Behind this public face of the abbey's security, it was evidently a para-military base.

Stas came in behind her to report, with Bradley trailing sheepishly in his wake.

"The four sentries are where the American pinpointed them. The others are watching them."

"And the watch changed half an hour ago as he predicted? Are you happy with his assessment?"

A nod from Stas, more embarrassed than grudging. It was Bradley who had spotted the fourth sentry after all, the one they had missed. And yet she was speaking as though he wasn't even present.

"Still armed the same?"

"All MP 40s, like this one."

"Very organised. Elster probably has quite an arsenal here as well as a treasury…"

Taking off the headscarf with its wave of paint-daubed hair still affixed – and digging into her cheeks to remove the cloth pads that had altered the shape of her face – she unbuttoned her coat to unstrap the extra padding around her chest and waist. This was her American uniform, which she pulled on again.

"They wouldn't carry guns like that cocked, but even so we can't risk an itchy trigger finger raising the alarm. We'll take the sentries all at once if we can." When Stas ran his own finger across his throat she shook her head. "Not if we can help it. If we tie these two up, that gives us two men per sentry. Enough to use the chloroform, if we give it time to work."

"And you?"

Mila picked up the wife's MP 40 and checked the 32-round magazine. She shrugged into the wife's shabby coat and woolly hat and went over to the stove, where a casserole that smelled like rabbit stew was bubbling and another pot stood ready.

"Let's assume this is for the men who've come off sentry duty half-frozen. If not, it will be a nice surprise. I'll walk into the quad with it and stay in the shadows to give you all a good five minutes with the sentries. But if something goes wrong and anyone sticks their head out of any of the buildings, I'll make sure they pull it back again."

When Bradley butted in, he sounded more anxious than at

any other stage of the preparations.

"You don't know how many of them are in there..."

Mila's reply was almost contemptuous.

"We have a good idea. Four tired sentries chilled to the bone. Four more to take the next watch, most likely resting now. Plus Elster and his inner circle, we guess. We counted two or three women who went to the outhouses during the day... wives, whores, ex-*Aufseherinnen* from the camps... these are Nazis after all. But no way he's got an army in there."

"We could cut the power – disorient them."

Those shadows she would be using as cover were cast not by the moon, for it had yet to rise, but by the exterior lights that were dotted around the abbey complex. The location was not on the local power grid, which was itself barely functioning. They could hear the hum of the generator behind the outhouses from here. It was a valid suggestion the American had made, but again she treated it dismissively.

"I don't think we'll gain anything by getting them jumpy. Now, all being well, once you've dealt with the sentries and we're back to strength, we'll take each side of the quad one at a time: that's two men watching for anyone sneaking out the back, four men going in through the cloisters, and two of us – that's me and Jack Penny – watching the other sides and running the show from the middle."

"Where am I?" Bradley asked. "Leading the assault team?"

Mila did not even look at him.

"You're here at the entrance, ready to handle any unexpected visitors, or to make sure no one comes sniffing around where we've hidden the lorry, or to deal with anyone who tries to get away."

"Get Penny to do that. You need me in there."

And now she did look at him, without a shred of sympathy.

"I don't need you at all, Mister Bradley. I thought I had made that clear. But if a local busybody or, God forbid, a Soviet patrol comes down the road, I want our genuine American on the spot to spin our story about getting lost, breaking down and encamping here for the night. That's your only value now."

They had arrived at the location two days ago, after an uneventful journey on snow-choked back roads that had seen them cross the demarcation line before even recognising that they had done so: a perfect endorsement of their cover story. She had split the team and reconnoitred the two sites on the first day: the abbey complex and, half a kilometre further into the hills beyond the derelict oil mill and farm buildings, the caves. They had decided that the latter, apparently watched over by a single caretaker-cum-poacher, had been abandoned as a stronghold. So, for the bulk of the first night and second day they had concentrated their surveillance on the abbey itself.

At the heart of the complex was a largely intact structure built around four Romanesque rib-vaulted cloisters, a facing pair of which appeared to have been filled in with crude brickwork since the days of the white monks and their contemplative walkways. Behind the cloisters would be the original cells, chapels and chapter facilities. The half-timbered upper floors and steeply pitched roofs were heavily weathered and full of holes, and the general state of filth and degradation suggested lengthy use by agricultural workers and their livestock, but the integrity of the quadrangle was unbroken, save for the arched gateway.

Three of the sentries had been stationed among the outlying buildings, enabling them to cover all four sides. The fourth had a kind of improvised shelter in the cloister facing the entrance. He was the one that the others had missed and only Bradley, on his scouting mission, had spotted. But by the time Mila had counted zero plus five and carried her stockpot and machine pistol into the quad, he was lying flat out in the shadows of a prominent buttress, being ministered to by Stas and Penny.

Faint lights showed behind the shutters in the two walled-up cloisters. When the others arrived from trussing up the exterior sentries, Mila sent the assault team of Stas, Ludvík,

173

Miro and Marek to check inside the other cloisters. Sure enough, they came back reporting no signs of life: empty rooms behind the one on the left; a pair of locked dormitories or refectories behind the one on the right, but barred and padlocked from the outside. The upper storeys were all lightless, with missing shutters. Excepting the lookouts they had silenced, Elster's entire gang must be accommodated within the two closed cloisters.

"Change of plan," she communicated, in a mixture of Czech and English, whispers and hand signals. "We hit both sides simultaneously. Miro and Marek, take the rifles and go seal up the backs, now. Shoot to wound anyone who tries to get out that way. Stas, you, Penny and Davies take this side with the gate. I'll hit the other one with Keeffe and Ludvík. Same drill as planned."

With that, she pulled open the bag at her chest.

There were two windows either side of the door in the middle of the cloister, all crudely formed with stone and mortar out of the remnants of the arches, and each blocked with much-repaired shutters. At the signal of Stas' dropped arm from across the quad, she hissed "Now!".

The brawny Keeffe used the butt of his rifle to break the window beside the door with two blows. Even before they heard voices raised in panic, Mila had flung a heavy object like a lightbulb inside and scurried to the corresponding window on the other side of the door, which Ludvík had forced open by now. Again she threw in a German chemical grenade, angling it downwards to the flagstones, and was relieved to see and hear the two-part flask explode with a flash and a burst of white smoke as the titanium tetrachloride and aqueous calcium chloride mixed violently.

She stepped back, pulled the American gasmask up over her face and cocked the MP 40.

Cries of alarm. Coughing and choking. A feminine shriek. Then the thudding echo of a rifle shot and another scream, masculine this time but no less high pitched.

They had found the back way blocked and knew that they were caught in a trap. The non-lethal smoke grenade was designed to work in the confines of bunkers and armoured vehicles, but Mila doubted that the rooms in the cloisters were much bigger, or better ventilated. Surely it was a matter of seconds before they had to come out into the quad.

To dissuade them from considering an armed breakout, she put a burst of fire into the door above head height.

"Out, now! One at a time. Hands up!"

It took all her concentration to focus on the door through the haze of smoke and the blurry lenses, but she was dimly aware of the shouting behind her from Stas' cloister. So far, she had not heard a shot from them.

The door creaked open and a cloud of white smoke escaped. From the thinning vapour protruded a broom handle with a table cloth attached: the best white flag they could find under the circumstances, which surely included near-blindness.

"We're coming out. Don't shoot!"

Instinctively, Keeffe and Ludvík had used the nearest cover to protect themselves and steady their rifles: a large stone planter, a heavy wooden bench. Only Mila remained in the open with her machine pistol. Satisfied that she would not have to go in for the moment, she raised the mask to ensure she could be heard clearly.

"Three paces out into the quad then down on your bellies with your hands on top of your heads."

Ludvík, ever loyal but ever the traditionalist, saw fit to call out in German: "Do as the lady says or you're dead!"

Mila rolled her eyes.

* * *

Ninety minutes had passed, during which they had cleared the smoke-filled accommodation blocks and located the keys to the strongrooms. These had turned out to be full of junk. Empty boxes predominated. If it had been here, the treasure had gone.

The prisoners were still gathered in the centre of the quad, now mostly kneeling in the snow or squatting with their hands bound behind them. The exceptions were the four sentries, who were still unable to hold themselves upright without fainting or vomiting, and the man who had been shot in the leg. He at least was grateful for the anaesthetic. All told, that made twenty men and five women, including the couple from the gatehouse. Some were spotty teenagers who must have spent all but the last months of the war in the Hitler Youth. Others had the prematurely aged faces and posture of defeated troops. Many, and this included the four younger women, wore that particular look of misplaced victimhood that always astonished Mila when she encountered it: the look of people who had somehow contrived to find the war a minor inconvenience and were outraged at how they had been treated since it had ended.

Nazis or Nazi-sympathisers all. But there was no one who had identified himself, or who might be identified by anyone else, as Elster.

The moment it became obvious that the promised treasury or armoury was not materialising, Penny and his men had gone deeper into the woods to check the caves. Now they had returned with a twenty-sixth prisoner, the caretaker-poacher, and more bad news.

"Sweet F.A.," Penny said. "Nuffink in the 'ermitage. Nuffink in the bit the sods had turned into a work-camp. So where is he then? And where's all the bloody *gelt?*"

Mila was steeling herself to begin aggressive interrogations when a voice sounded from the shadows of the gateway and the missing member of her team trudged in behind two trussed-up captives of his own.

"This might answer both of those questions."

Bradley gave each man a shove and they staggered forward into the light. One was a large man in a superbly tailored leather coat and double-breasted striped suit. He had a loose-jowled face and a well-oiled pompadour of overly black hair.

Although this was presently somewhat disarranged, he would not have looked out of place in the garb of a senior castle functionary.

The other man was a Soviet officer.

Bradley put away his .45. Mila wasn't about to let on to the Germans or the Russian that it was unloaded.

"That's Elster?" she said.

Bradley nodded.

"Getting his buddies to give him a lift home from his other job."

"Which is?"

"What do you think? Playing both sides. Taking Nazis' loot, selling them out to the Reds. Keeping some of the loot in return, I guess, and maybe safe passage for a select few, himself included."

"And our target?"

"We've been having a bit of a chat about that," Bradley said. He gave Elster a kick. "Go on, tell her."

The former chamberlain looked down his nose at her. Of course he did. And because he assumed she was as American as her uniform, he did it in impeccable, clipped English.

"The small nuptial crown of Queen Charlotte of Mecklenburg-Strelitz is back where it always ought to have been, in the Treasury at Schloss Blankenburg."

She switched her gaze to the Russian captain. It seemed he had been following the conversation.

"I'll bet that bought some goodwill. Death to the bourgeoisie and its lapdogs, eh, Comrade – or not quite all of them?"

Bradley coughed.

"There's another couple of these guys tied up in their car at the front," he said. "Blue-topped caps like the NKVD boys used to wear, but brand-new versions of the old shield-and-dagger badges. 'MGB' it says now, if my Cyrillic hasn't let me down again. I suppose we'd better bring them in before they freeze to death out there."

She gave him a stony look.

"There was no other way?"

"They were set on coming in for supper."

"Then this mess is not strictly your fault…"

Jack Penny almost exploded.

"Leave orf, love! He just captured 'alf the Red Army with an empty pistol!"

The Russian's eyes widened. Then, perhaps sensing that his life was not as threatened as he had feared, he set his feet apart as best he could and addressed them all in heavily accented English.

"You are trespassing on Soviet territory. I insist you hand your prisoners over to my authority and return to your own zone."

"Flippin' Bolshies," Jack Penny scoffed. "Always livin' in cloud cuckoo land!"

"Slečna Slavík…" Stas was at her side. He at least had had a fruitful search. She could smell the drink on his breath as it clouded around her. "It is not a bad proposal. We cannot hold these people here. And the crown is securely locked away."

She laughed, inwardly.

"The immovable object," she said. Then, to Penny: "Ideas?"

He threw up his hands.

"Well, we can't storm the effin' castle. It's where these Bolshie bastards are headquartered and we left our siege catapults behind… Plus Stas is right, no chance of holding onto all our prisoners – 'specially this bugger – while we snoop around for a way to go in sneaky, if there even is one…"

Elster scoffed.

"There is not."

"I dunno where you get off so hoity-toity," Penny said. "One word to the next bunch of Nazi renegades through these parts and you'll need more than this Bolshie's blessing to keep that pretty head on your shoulders, bodyguards or no bodyguards…"

Mila wasn't paying attention. She was looking at Bradley.

"And what do you think?"

"I think you've already made up your mind and you're not going to listen to me."

They regarded each other for several seconds in a mixture of apparent distrust and regret. Then Mila saw Bradley give a little nod.

She faced the others.

"We're not turning back now. We have the momentum. We should keep going."

"How?" Penny wanted to know.

Mila approached Elster, much shorter than he, yet matching his supercilious gaze. She began to study his face, first from one side then the other, as though deciding if it would make a good mask.

"I'll bet it's still crated up for its trip to the British zone, isn't it? These Russians are hardly going to make a show of it... And you can identify the crate, even though, of course, you'd never deign to help carry it yourself... What's so funny about that...? Why can't my people just carry it out of there?"

Elster broke the stare and raised his eyes to the rising moon, worried that he had revealed something. Mila's laugh was audible this time, if no more humorous.

"You were right, Jack. We own this creature now. So he's going to walk us into the castle and lead us straight to the crown. And the captain here is going to wave us through – unless he thinks his masters will approve of profiteering with the fascists."

The MGB officer went white. Elster was already a pale shade, not only because of the plummeting temperature but by virtue of the foundation he used.

"My activities are sanctioned at the highest levels," the Russian said.

"Oh, I'm sure they are. But I'm not so sure they'll be queuing up to admit to it."

"Bloody hell, girl!" Penny let out a visible gasp, a mixture of admiration and trepidation. "That's a hell of a risk."

"No," she heard Stas mutter with resignation. "It's the irresistible force."

"What is?"

Her mind was busy racing through a thousand possibilities. People. Clothes. Boxes. Documents. Vehicles. Timetables. Road layouts. Borders. Customers. The plan that was forming already had as many blind alleys and other lethal pitfalls as they'd be likely to find in the castle itself. The more it came into focus, the more problems she envisioned and it was tempting to let any one of them overwhelm her. Then, perhaps because of the way the shadows shifted and the light changed, she became conscious of the others stepping back, even Penny, even Elster, and her whole team forming up beside her.

Stas. Ludvík. Miro. Marek. Bradley.

And Stas' answer to Penny, his voice less slurred, more confident now.

"She is. The irresistible force. You're looking at it."

CHAPTER FIFTEEN

Captain Grigoryan offered around his cigarettes while they waited outside the locked door that led, so Elster had claimed, to the treasury in the depths of the castle. They were the characteristic Russian *papirosi* consisting of a cardboard tube with a small amount of very strong tobacco in the end. Bradley did not recognise the brand and his Cyrillic was not up to transliterating, but having wised up the hard way about Belomors and Kazbeks, he was surprised when the MGB officer made a show of pinching the cardboard shut to create a mouthpiece. Every other Russian he'd smoked with had thought it the funniest joke to watch a first-timer go green and cough his lungs out.

So it looked like the guy was making an effort, which was encouraging.

Having held it long enough to uphold the honour of the United States Strategic Services bureau, if that was what it was called and assuming it had any honour left, Bradley exhaled gratefully. At his side, Stas and Jack Penny followed suit.

"Flippin' 'eck!" Penny coughed. "You Bolshies start embalming yourselves a bit previous! Trying to catch up with Comrade Lenin?"

They were in a dingy, vaulted corridor that tapered to the heavy oak door. Penny gave Bradley a conspiratorial wink and walked him several steps back towards the bisecting corridor, leaving Stas in stilted conversation with Grigoryan. Like most of the other parts of the castle that they had seen since pulling up in the Russians' car in the courtyard, this area had been stripped of ornamentation and was already showing signs of the universal military desecration he had witnessed at the Herrenhaus and elsewhere. Earlier there had been a thin traffic of staff paper-pushers hurrying by with files or flimsies, flashing nervous salutes at the MGB captain as they passed and running uncritical eyes over the others in their purloined MGB uniforms, but now this section appeared deserted. That was a relief, given that the uniforms they had stripped from Grigoryan's two men – plus his sheepskin coat and a helmet they'd found – could only go so far to clothe three imposters.

Penny spat out a flake of tobacco and grimaced.

"Only thing more poisonous lately is the way she's treating you."

Bradley shrugged.

"I'm not her favourite person, it's true."

"No, there's more than that, mate. She's using you – and I don't just mean as the Yank frontman for the original caper. We're into a whole new house of hell now and she's setting you up to take the fall."

"How so?"

"You said yourself how you was supposed to smooth things over after the last time she conned the Russians like this – but you're going to get saddled with the blame for doing it again. Maybe me too. Why else do you think she said we had to wait out here while she and Elster went in? I'll wager you something…"

Bradley looked over Penny's shoulder. Stas and Grigoryan had run out of things to say and instead they were passing a hipflask between them. From the wincing that accompanied each swig, even the Russian's, it looked as potent as the *papirosi*.

"Why do I think I'm going to lose my shirt…?"

"A gentleman's bet then, just to prove a point."

"Alright."

Penny turned him to face the others and the door.

"When she and Elster come out of there they'll be schlepping more than one crate. And you can definitely bet on her mob being the only ones who'll be told which one is kosher."

"That's crazy! How can you know that?"

"Because I've been in her position, thieving stuff to someone else's orders. First thing you do in that situation is find a way to keep schtoom about half the loot you found. She can't hide a crate from the rest of us, so she'll come out with at least two."

"With Elster's connivance?"

"She'll have to cut him in. You saw her sizing him up. Maybe if he was still a full-on Nazi she'd have balked at it, but with him turning out to be a part-time Nazi hunter like you…"

Morally compromised. Bradley heard the insinuation. And the inference: we're all cut from the same cloth.

"OK, say you're right. What's her plan?"

"How's she going to do the dirty on me and the Lonsdales? No idea, but I reckon somewhere between here and home she'll pull a switcheroo, and you'll be left holding the baby. Meaning the blame – and the Almighty Wrath of Jimmy the Shiv, not to mention all the Bolshies we're in the process of pissing off something rotten."

Bradley shook his head.

"She doesn't know your clients. The crown's nothing to her without that information."

"She's worked it out. Or silly bloody Marjorie told her. Or she's guessed who else will pay 'andsomely for it."

"She said she wanted to help you get Marjorie back."

"They say a lot of things, birds like her. I dunno, mate, maybe she's planning on selling it back to Gerry in return for Marjorie, in case Gerry goes back on his word, which wouldn't be a first. All I know is that *this*…" he tapped the side of his nose. "…don't lie. She's working something with Elster and her people to cut one or both of us out of it. But here's a funny thing – I got me own little secret from *them*."

Before Bradley could ask, there came the sound of heavy bolts being shot and the door creaked open. Mila and Elster had manoeuvred two wooden ammunition boxes along the passage and Mila was beckoning for help. Each box was about 20 inches square, stencilled OBEN. NICHT WERFEN! (for THIS SIDE UP. DO NOT THROW!, as Stas informed Bradley) and nailed shut. One had the numeral 3 daubed on it, the other a continental 7 with a line crossing the upright. Both were equipped with canvas straps and were heavy enough to require two men to carry comfortably.

Bradley caught Penny giving him a triumphant look. He nodded in return.

"Two crowns?" Stas said.

Mila fixed Grigoryan with a fierce glare and raised a finger to silence anything he might have been about to say.

"Just a bit more insurance."

Unlike the others, she had made no attempt to pass as a Soviet official. Having availed herself of the store of stock costumes her team had hidden in the back of the 'Jimmy', she wore a long faux sable coat and suiter hat complete with a veil. The impression, even if it would not stand up to closer inspection, fell somewhere between Elster's glamorous assistant and a lady of the castle, come back to make trouble for any humble *soldat* unlucky enough not to get out of her way.

While he and Penny carried box 7 and Stas and Elster box 3, Bradley watched her striding ahead with Grigoryan. The two of them were engaged in conversation. Was she plotting another turnabout?

"So, what was your secret?" he grunted to Penny.

"Wouldn't be a secret if I told you…"

He had to laugh.

"Fair enough. You got me."

"Tell you who the buyers are though, if you like. I mean, I ain't going to trot out their names and addresses but I'll give you the general picture, sort of thing."

Was Penny being serious? From his abruptly earnest face, which seemed itself a challenge or a test, it was impossible to tell. Bradley turned to the front again. The others had disappeared around a corner in the passage, but were they out of earshot?

"OK, who are they?"

"Jews, Mister Bradley. My people. That's right – the 'front wheel skids'. Despite the best efforts of the fuckers round 'ere, enough of us is left alive to make sure it ain't never going to happen to us again. And the best way of doing that is to be armed and ready to defend ourselves."

"In... the Holy Land?"

"Over there. Over here. Everywhere."

"But what's the crown for?"

"That's the good bit...."

They had rounded the corner. Mila and Grigoryan appeared to have been waylaid by a pair of off-duty Soviet army officers and the others had set down their box so that Elster could join the discussion. It seemed convivial enough, but Bradley noticed the way that Mila's hand was held behind her back, the thumb and two fingers extended in a signal to Stas. Whatever that indicated, Stas had reached inside the unbuttoned front of his tunic and now his hand came out holding the hipflask.

Penny set the box down and sat on it.

"I notice you use the expression the 'oly Land, which is very sympathetic and American of you. Us British are too busy being unbiased. Far as we're concerned, it's been Mandatory Palestine ever since us and the Arabs kicked the Turks out. You got any fags?"

"Er, fags, yeah…" Bradley pulled out his Luckies.

"Mmm…" Penny took the lighter from him with a ghost of a smile. "That's better… Them Bolshie fags was effin' rank, weren't they?"

"Rank," Bradley agreed. "But Jack, I know most of this…"

"I know you do. I just like the sound of me own voice sometimes, 'specially when I'm behind Russian lines in the middle of *free* different swindles all at once... So yeah, the point is that even though they started it, the British see themselves as juggling a delicate situation, with Arabs revolting on one side, local Zionists on the other and a League of Nations mandate to keep the peace. The last thing they want is to let all the Jews who survived Hitler turn up and ruin the precious balance."

"I read the papers. They've been stopping ships and interning illegal immigrants in Cyprus..."

"In *camps*, mate." Having raised his voice, Penny checked to make sure that the others were still calmly chatting. He pulled a face. "Sorry about that."

"No problem. And the crown?"

"Yeah, the crown. Well, let me ask you this: what is the one thing what would prevent a Royal Navy gunboat from turning around or boarding a merchant vessel what might or might not be smuggling illegal weapons to the Zionists in Palestine? Say if someone was out in the bows of the merchant ship, threatening to drop it in the Med?"

"Something the royals want?"

"Bingo. And what might just happen if before they got their hands on it, another 'alf dozen ships turned up in the next few days?"

"The floodgates would open."

Penny exhaled luxuriantly and nodded.

"Bob's yer uncle."

"So, your clients have contracted you to provide... the arms... and the means of getting them past the British blockade?"

"Yeah. Like I says, I ain't going to tell you how to find them, though."

"I think I might have met them. Some of them anyway."

"Then frankly, mate, you're lucky you're still breathing. The thing about these people – it's like Gerry says, and her – you need insurance. Gerry and Jimmy have agreed to provide them with weapons. You seen some of them, like my silenced Enfield, and there's a load of Czech-made MG 34s we got our hands on. But that's Gerry and Jimmy. What if they decide to

186

stiff the buyers and flog the crown back to... well, the Crown?"

"You need your own insurance."

"I need my own insurance – and so do you now, 'cause it's our arses hanging out in the wind."

Bradley waited. He wasn't sure why, but he knew that Penny was going to tell him the rest.

"So here's another little tale to pass the time... This one's about a couple of brothers, Löb and Moses Simson, putting all their money into a steelhammer works in Sühl. They build bicycles, racing cars, perambulators and, among other things, Lugers for the Kaiser's army in the Great War. Then Adolf sends them packing, 'alf-inches their company and renames it after some antisemitic weatherman, Gustloff, who's just got himself assassinated, by a Jew I'm very pleased to say. So now it makes weapons for the Nazis. And as they start losing the war it makes worse and worse weapons, cheaper and cheaper, out of worse and worse materials, until it ends up with an 'orrible rifle designed to equip the old men and boys of the *Volkssturm*. Now... as we know, that didn't work out so well, since by then everyone was rather partial to surrendering. But Gustloff produced the rifles anyway. And I just found a whole bunch of them in Elster's caves. Think of it – a new Jewish army, equipped with rifles built for them by a Jewish company, paid for by the Nazis!"

"Horrible rifles, you said..."

"Yeah, they are. 'orrible. Couldn't hit anything you aimed at beyond a hundred yards. But they're self-loading rifles with 30-round magazines so you don't need to be Annie Oakley. And it's a sight better than a slingshot for anyone who ain't called David."

"And how many is a 'whole bunch'?"

"A hundred boxes. Ten in a box."

"A thousand rifles? Jesus! How are you planning on getting them back?"

"That's where you come in. Reckon your Yank 2½ tonner

can carry twice that?"

"On pavement, sure. I wouldn't even think about going off-road. But you're forgetting the rest of the load. Mila and her people."

"Like I say, that's where you come in…" Before Bradley could react, Penny gave him a cautious nudge. "Aye, aye…"

Stas stood over them. He gave a stooping courtier's bow and hand-flourish.

"Miss Slavík wonders if either of you has a sturdy knife about your person."

"Does she now…?" Penny said.

"…or something else to prise open one of the boxes."

"That's a turn-up!" Catching Bradley's eye, Penny bent forwards to fumble under his coat at the back of his belt. With a grin he produced a claw hammer.

"Old habits," he said.

"Which box?" Bradley asked.

"Either, I think," Stas said, but when Penny handed him the hammer he turned back to Mila, Elster and the Russians, weaving slightly as he went.

"Either!" Penny scoffed and sat down again on box 7.

"Not coming?"

"I can see from here."

By the time he joined the others, Bradley saw that Elster had already worked the claw beneath the lid of box 3 and was levering it free. Mila and Grigoryan were still swapping whispered remarks, apparently unconcerned, while the two off-duty Soviet officers, in loose shirts and riding breeches, squatted like Cossack dancers, eager to catch sight of the contents.

Bradley tugged at Stas' sleeve, but he just gave a meaningless shrug and muttered something. Bradley realised it was a translation.

"Here you are, gentlemen, as promised…" Speaking fluent Russian, Elster wrenched off the lid and lifted a straw-wrapped object in reverential hands. "…and as once prized above all else in St. Petersburg – my apologies – in Leningrad…"

"*Klikoskoïe!*" one of the officers slapped his thighs in delight.

Bradley watched, bemused, as Elster handed out six bottles of Veuve Clicquot champagne.

Penny's voice echoed along the passageway.

"Same in this one, eh? A case for them and a case for us – seems only fair – or should we swap, do you think, before we get on our way?"

Bradley saw Mila's eyes flash, once, as in place of a reply she exhaled a long, dismissive jet of smoke. In the half-light, in her fur coat, with the saucy cockeyed hat and that vampish veil, she looked completely alien to him now.

*   *   *

If it had ever been a proper fastness befitting its imposing situation above the town, Schloss Blankenburg had been extensively remodelled over the ages into a Baroque residence; but if you were sitting in a stolen car in the shadows of the clocktower, with that trapezium of many-storeyed wings enclosing you and what seemed like a dozen helmeted, greatcoated figures guarding the only exit, it looked unassailable enough.

Grigoryan's car was a Soviet copy of a Ford. There was no trunk or rumble seat but with the front seats pushed forward they had found room for the six of them: Grigoryan driving, Elster beside him, with Penny, Bradley and Stas squeezed into the back seat and Mila sitting sideways on box 7 in front of their legs. Although the windows were soon steamed up and in need of frequent wiping, the arrangement in theory allowed her to see out between Grigoryan and Elster, and to cover each of them with her pistol. On either side of Bradley, albeit unsighted, Stas and Penny cradled a pair of MP 40s.

Bradley was tempted to close his eyes. He was powerless to do anything and none of their arrangements would matter a damn should they be challenged at the courtyard gate, or at the main gate in the surviving section of curtain wall. They had no papers, only Grigoryan. He had played along when they had been coming the opposite way but at that stage they were putting their heads in the lion's jaws not withdrawing them. Was he now awaiting his chance to turn them in? If so, this would be it.

But then they were through and descending the snowploughed S-bends into the sleeping town. Now he could worry about the next problem instead.

What Jack Penny had meant by *that's where you come in.*

Try as he might to find other interpretations, there was only one conclusion to be drawn. Penny and his men needed the truck to haul their rifles, which left no room for Mila and her crew. He was cutting her out anyway, partly because he seemed to be cutting out the Lonsdales to make his own deal with the buyers, and partly because he believed that she was about to work a double-cross of her own. And he had told Bradley because it was clear that when it happened, there would be no place for him on Mila's side. Penny wanted Bradley on his side instead, ready to help him move against the others.

As their headlights illuminated the turning to the monastery complex, Bradley called for Grigoryan to stop. The camouflaged shape of their truck had vanished and there were fresh tracks in the snow at the entrance.

"They prob'ly just moved it in. Nuffink to get excited about."

Bradley shuffled around to squint at Penny. His face gave 'nuffink' away either, but his leg knocked against Bradley's as... what? A go-signal? A warning?

"Let me out here," Bradley said.

"If he wants to walk, let him," Mila scoffed. Stas got out to permit Bradley to clamber past.

As the car scrabbled and fishtailed into the compound, he hurried into the woods where the truck had been hidden. It was too dark to see much but he found no signs of a struggle or an emergency. They even appeared to have folded and stowed the scrim net rather than abandoning it.

So, what was Penny playing at? Had his men already overpowered the three Czechs and assumed control or were they lying in wait to do it all in a single *coup*? If it was the latter – especially if it was the latter – then why had he signalled Bradley to get out? But if he hadn't made his move, what gave with the breezy nothing-to-worry-about talk? Was this where Bradley was supposed to 'come in'?

Reaching into a hollow in a blasted tree, he pulled out the Pliofilm-wrapped M1 Garand rifle he had taken from the back of the truck and stashed there earlier, even before the car full of Russians had arrived. Mila's team had used some of the American weapons in the assault, but not all of them, preferring the German machine pistols for close quarters.

He checked the safety was on and locked the bolt all the way to the rear to press in one of several 8-round clips he had also stashed, carefully letting the bolt come forward to chamber the first round.

As he did so, all hell broke loose.

Shots rang out, muzzle flashes and tracer lit up the walls of the whitewashed outbuildings, and then an explosion sent a fireball rising into the night sky. Bradley's blood ran cold.

Biting his lip, fighting the urge to charge straight in, he worked his way around and approached from the direction of the ruined oil mill and the snowbound foothills. The first thing he saw as he emerged from the trees was not one but two trucks in the courtyard area that lay outside the monastery: the 'Jimmy' and what looked like a Canadian-built 3-tonner. The next, partly hidden by the trucks, was the Soviet car, in flames.

Between him and the trucks, almost completely silhouetted, was the bulky figure of a man who appeared somewhat like a British commando, complete with knitted cap comforter, blackened face and Sten gun. A lookout, presumably, but he had made the mistake of looking back at the fire. Before he had a chance to turn at the sound of boots in snow, the M1's buttplate connected with the back of his skull and he was already unconscious as Bradley stepped over him.

More shadowy figures, around the burning car. The flames illuminating the white stencilled letters on the 3-tonner: TTG. Bradley took cover behind the low wall of what had once been a pigsty.

Someone was dragging a body out of the car. Someone in a long coat. Not Elster. Mila. The body was caught in the back of the cabin, or what remained of it. Not Penny. Taller, thinner. Stas. On the other side of the car, in the rippling heat, Bradley saw Grigoryan standing hunched with his hands on his thighs, breathing heavily. As he watched, another black-daubed commando type stepped out of the shadows and put a pistol to his head.

The two shots – the commando's and Bradley's – sounded almost as one. Both men dropped.

Yet another figure moved out of the shadows towards Mila and her burden. Bradley was about to drop him too when he saw that it was Jack Penny. Together, the two of them managed to drag Stas away from the car.

Bradley took a moment to look for Elster and located an effigy of the man, slumped in the front passenger seat amid the flames that were spewing from the engine. Then another shape struggled back into the fire. It was Penny, with a frantic Mila trying to restrain him. Bradley thought he heard her cry of 'Leave it!' penetrate the noise of the fire and the echoes of shots that were either ammunition cooking off or another skirmish somewhere else in the compound. Penny shrugged her aside and re-emerged from the rear cabin hauling the smoking silhouette of box 7.

And then another pair of commandos, moving out from the arch that led into the quad and cloisters, one with a rifle, one with a Bren gun, preparing to lay down covering fire. Before Bradley could even take aim, there came the sharp double crack of two rifle shots and both men went down.

Some other faction was on their side, also hidden around the outbuildings or the woods. And there were at least two of them.

That was all Bradley needed. He moved forward again and beckoned to Mila and Penny.

"This way! Someone's covering us."

As they scuttled toward him, Mila called out:

"It must be Ludvík, with Marek... These soldiers killed Miro as we drove in, right in front of us, and threw a grenade under our car!"

"They shot Keeffe and Davies too, just like that," Penny gasped. "Fuckin' animals!"

When they joined him in the pigsty, Bradley had to resist the temptation to clasp Mila in a tight embrace of sheer relief. He had thought her dead.

"Stas is gone too," she said, and now he could hear the fury beneath the urgency. "Poor Stas. He would have liked a death scene. But things don't work out like that."

"How many of them are there?" Bradley asked.

"No idea. We were met by about six or seven when we drove in, but there'll be others."

"Well, now there's four less than there were," Bradley said.

Penny clapped him on the back.

"Stone me, mate! Talk about a sixth sense!"

"And what's happened to all our prisoners?" Mila said. "I'm guessing these aren't more of Elster's people, seeing as they just burned their boss alive."

"They aren't Elster's people," Bradley said. "I've run into these guys before. Friends of yours, Jack?"

Penny stared back at him, open mouthed.

"You ain't saying these are the buyers...?"

"I dunno pal. I dunno what scheme you had planned."

"Well..." he looked at Mila, who was glaring at him accusingly. "Not this! Oh shit..."

"What?"

"We forgot the box again – back there."

"I said leave it!" Mila hissed. For the first time, the insistent voice held a note of desperation. She blinked and shook her head. "What scheme, Jack?"

Penny looked up to see her G.I. issue .45 pointed at him.

"Fuck! If Keeffe and Davies did what they were told before these bastards blew their brains out, that truck of ours is now fully loaded with weapons from Elster's caves. Yeah, I know, we lied about them being empty… When me and Bradley got back from the castle, we was going to leave you here to make your own way back."

"What?"

"Come off it, love, you can't tell me you wasn't cooking up something similar!" Penny gazed wistfully at the shape of box 7, lying in No Man's Land between the outbuildings and the vehicles.

Before Mila could say anything, if she was going to say anything, they were startled by a kind of hoot and a strained voice, close behind them, saying: "Coming in!"

There was a flurry of disturbed dirt and snow as Marek leaped the low wall and slid to a halt on his backside next to them. He was in his American uniform, caked in snow, and had his Garand wrapped in a whitish cloth that Bradley recognised as the tablecloth Elster's men had used as a flag of surrender.

"'Uncle' Ludvík is somewhere back there in the trees," he said. "Stas is dead?"

"Yes. And Miro."

"We saw that. We've been watching since these British arrived. But Slečna Slavík, we never imagined that they would do that! To the Germans, yes…"

"The Germans?"

Marek looked sick.

"All of Elster's people. They have been lining them up, one by one. Asking them questions. Doing things to them. Shooting them."

"What questions?"

"We could not hear. We only heard the screams. But after most of them were dead, someone must have talked. The British found something, buried in one of the other buildings, and loaded it into their truck. A big, long box, like a footlocker."

"I don't think they're British soldiers," Bradley said. "This TTG outfit might be part of the British Army, but it looks like they're a rogue unit. I think they're Jews, from British Palestine, and they're over here to take revenge. I also think that they're your precious buyers. So, if anyone was counting on stiffing them – or anyone else – I'd say they beat you to it."

Mila nodded and gave a bitter laugh. Then she leaned forward and squeezed Bradley's arm.

"Thank you. You have done well."

Penny was aghast.

"You mean you was putting it on, the falling out with him – so's you could find out what I was up to?"

"You, or anyone else," Mila offered, by way of consolation. "We were worried that Keeffe and Davies were Lonsdale's."

"And let's just say I wasn't necessarily going to take your side if it came to it," Bradley added.

He heard the girl make a frustrated sound that was somewhere between a sigh and a sob.

"But none of us saw this coming..."

She peered over the wall again. The shooting inside the quad had stopped. Presumably the rest of the prisoners had been finished off, which most likely included Grigoryan's two MGB men in their underclothes and blankets. But regardless of the TTG folks' intentions and their attitude to the Soviets, the Soviets would surely be coming to investigate. Even if a local farmer or woodsman hadn't yet reported it, Bradley suspected that on a still night like this the firefight had been heard miles away in Blankenburg. It was time to get moving.

The girl had read his mind.

"They have their weapons. They have whatever else it was they came for. I don't think they'll bother tracking us if we just melt away."

"I ain't leaving them *that*!" Penny gesticulated miserably towards box 7.

"Jack…"

"Not after everything we been through! I mean…"

"Jack!"

It wasn't just Penny who looked. Bradley watched in disbelief as she dug into her coat pocket and pulled out a cloth-wrapped object.

A small cloth-wrapped object.

"No effin' way!"

"They took a bit of artistic licence in that portrait you showed us," Mila said. "I worked it out when Elster smirked at the idea of our needing his help to carry it."

Carefully she unfolded the chamois to reveal an intricate assembly of silver and diamonds that sparkled like the fresh snow in the moonlight. It was undeniably gorgeous and quite plausibly priceless, but even with the arches and the cross on top, it couldn't have been much more than four inches tall. The small nuptial crown so beloved by Queen Victoria was really just a miniature headdress, designed to be worn atop a wedding veil.

"Find the Lady!" an awed Penny muttered at last. "So the boxes – both bottles of bubbly?"

"I told Stas it wouldn't matter which one they chose."

"And I burnt me arse hairs off getting it out of the motor!"

"I told you to leave it." Mila wrapped the crown again and returned it to her pocket.

"Yeah, you did." Penny let out a snort that clouded the air. "Well, if he's right about these being the clients, I reckon they've broken the bloody terms of the contract – so yeah, I'm all in favour of leaving them to it and getting this back to Gerry, somehow. I suppose you got a way to get us out of here and across the border?"

Mila glanced at Bradley.

"Did you hide the dressing-up box?"

He nodded.

"When I stashed this rifle. It should still be buried in a snowdrift near where the truck was parked."

"Then we go out that way," she said. "Oh, shut your mouth for goodness' sake, Jack. I didn't know everything that was going to happen, but as a contingency I wrote Sam a note suggesting that he take charge of our civilian costumes when we got to our destination. It was tucked inside the lighter. You handed it to him at the Herrenhaus."

"We gonna walk out as refugees?" Bradley asked.

"I think it's best, especially if we can link up with a genuine group before the border. It's going to get bitter, but we've plenty of clothes in there for five of us…" Her face fell. Then she shook herself out of it. "First we get 'Uncle' Ludvík…"

They were rising to signal for him – and to check the lie of the land – when there came the sound of another vehicle speeding into the complex. Immediately the remaining TTG men opened up on the pigsty from positions inside and around the abbey. As he ducked, Bradley caught sight of the vehicle skidding across the fire-lit courtyard. It was a jeep, with Vickers machine guns mounted in the fashion of the British special service units, manned by more commando types. Jumping off as it came to a halt was a tall, rigid-looking figure who made no attempt to seek cover.

A cry from behind. Marek had taken a ricochet in the leg. Mila yelled for the unarmed Penny to tend to him while she levelled her .45 in both hands and squinted through a gap. But it was a trick shot at that range. This was Bradley's job. He rested the Garand on the broken wall and flicked off the safety, knowing he had only used one round and had seven left in the clip. He took aim at the tall man and pulled the trigger.

He never saw where his bullet went. It must have been the cumulative effect of butt-stroking the sentry and firing two shots of full-power thirty-ought-six. He saw stars as the kick of the rifle knocked his shoulder out again and left him paralysed.

Machine gun fire began to disintegrate the walls around them.

CHAPTER SIXTEEN

The command was so forceful that Mila heard it even over the shooting.

"Stand down! Cease firing!"

But for one solitary shot in dissent, they did.

"Hold your fire, damn you!"

The voice had all the lofty disdain of a British officer, yet it was thickly accented in English and repeated the orders more fluently in another language she recognised as Hebrew. There was something about hearing words in that language barked as commands, here of all places, that was dizzying.

Or perhaps it was the effect of being blown up and machine-gunned. Her ears were ringing and her head splitting.

All at once she became aware of two important matters. They had to be important because they overrode the siren call to lie down and rest her eyes, which was almost overwhelming. The first was the sound of injured men breathing heavily: Marek, Bradley, with the seething of Jack Penny, himself injured, as he struggled to treat them.

The second was another voice from the other side of the wall, raving furiously in Hebrew and getting nearer. It sounded like one of the Jewish soldiers was in no mood to obey his officer.

Fearing another grenade, her initial impulse was to ready the Colt. Instead, she laid it down, took a deep breath and stood up, showing her hands.

"Nazi *zanah*!"

That word she did know. Harlot. The man who uttered it

was nearly at the other side of the pigsty wall and from the look of him about to take it in one bound. He was huge, red with sweat and fire, and protruding from his massive fist was what looked like a British fighting knife.

Mila took a step back and fell into the best defensive posture her heels, skirt and coat allowed. There was no point in saying anything. The man wanted blood.

He cleared the wall as though it were a kerb stone, raising the knife in his right hand with the blade extended upwards and forwards, ready to slash down at her. Mila had nothing to wrap around her arm to deflect the strike and little hope of blocking anything with such force behind it, so she hopped back as it came down, just out of reach. But immediately she lunged forwards again with both hands and all of her own weight, grasping his wrist and twisting it to use the kinetic energy in the continuing movement to help him push the blade into his own armpit. As he flinched and lost his balance, she locked every muscle and settled hers, preventing him from pulling out the knife or even dropping it. He roared and his wild eyes glared at her in disbelief.

With maximum effort, piling her body against him, she worked the tip of the knife in another inch. Now any attempt to wrestle free would cause him to do serious damage to himself and she could tell that he knew it. The fight went out of him.

"I'm alright," she hissed to an agitated Penny. "Keep pressure on Marek's wound. How is Sam?"

"I think he just put his shoulder out again," Penny said, almost giggling with relief, and Mila heard Bradley grunt a confirmation.

The man she was grappling with seemed to come out of a trance.

"Eng-lish…?" he said haltingly.

With his bulk sagging over her, he was suddenly more like a drunken date than a deadly opponent. Mila's frustration got the better of her and she swore.

"Bloody near enough!"

"Eytan!" It was the officer who had driven in moments ago in the jeep, a rangy figure with a stiff leg that had delayed his arrival at the pigsty. He said something in Hebrew, not unsympathetically, and added in English as he negotiated the wall: "I have told him you are not the enemy. There has been a misunderstanding."

Mila maintained her grip on Eytan's wrist, now slick with his blood.

"We have three wounded men here. Four, if you count this one."

"They will be treated. We have a medic. Please, Miss Slavík, you can release him now. I promise you that you are safe."

"You know me?" Her fingers, clamped for so long, tensed rather than eased. Eytan yelped.

"I have been watching you."

"You were at the Herrenhaus," she said.

"Yes. And before. My name is Abba Levas. I am a captain in the Jewish Brigade. My men are here on a secret mission. When they saw you arrive with the criminal known as Elster, they decided that you were also Nazis. I apologise for this."

"We had captured Elster's people!"

"This was not fully understood. They thought it was the other way round. It was an easy mistake to make…"

Mila felt a wave of fatigue sweep over her. She released her grip and Eytan let go of the knife to clutch at the wound.

"It's easy to do anything if you decide people are Nazis," she said.

"My men exceeded their authority."

"They're your men."

Abba Levas nodded.

"I take responsibility."

Three soldiers had joined them now, including the medic. When Mila indicated Marek as the priority case, the medic looked to Levas, who nodded again. He spoke quietly with one of the others and then laid a consoling hand on his shoulder.

"You killed two of them," he informed Mila without expression. "Yonaton's brother and Eytan's... I suppose you would call him a blood brother. Another two are wounded, one with a cracked skull. It is by no means certain that either will make it."

Mila sat down on a broken section of wall. She pulled out her cigarettes to make it look intentional, but in fact the only other option had been to collapse in a heap.

"What were their names, the dead men?"

"Yehuda. Gideon."

"The ones of mine you killed were called Miro and Stas."

"And Keeffe and Davies," Penny growled. "Which makes four. In cold blood."

"I am prepared to call it even," Mila said. She searched for her lighter before giving a resigned shrug as she remembered.

Abba Levas leant forward, cupping a lit match.

"We cannot join forces, Miss Slavík. I think my men might still kill you. And we need all the space in both lorries for ourselves and our haul. But we can show you the best route to take on foot: the route others are taking."

"Ask him," she heard Penny say.

"Ask him what?"

"If Gerry set us up. If he always planned for these buggers to turn us over once we'd got the gelt..."

Levas lit two further cigarettes, one for the fierce-eyed Penny, the other for himself. He shook out the match with a look of amusement.

"Jacob Pieniazek – they told me all about you!"

"I reckon that's a yes," Penny muttered.

"You've got your guns," Mila said. "And what, some of Elster's buried treasure?"

The man laughed, but not meanly. His delight was obvious.

"Oh, it's treasure, Miss Slavík, but its price is far above rubies. We dug up his records. The new names of escaped Nazis. Details of their escape routes and the networks of sympathisers that they have set up to support them. Locations of further caches of documents."

"Then you can let us take the crown back to the Lonsdales, to fulfil our part of the bargain. If you are the buyers, you will still get it in the end."

He smiled but shook his head.

"The crown is our passport to *Eretz Yisrael*. And there is no guarantee that Lonsdale will honour his arrangement with our sponsors. It appears he is quite capable of betraying anyone. We may need the crown as a bargaining tool."

Mila gave a snorting laugh.

"If you were thinking of taking it for yourselves instead of paying for it, you should know that Gerry Lonsdale doesn't just betray his people, he expects his people to betray him too."

"What do you mean by that?"

"He took out insurance," she said, looking to the others, who nodded soberly. "The box is booby-trapped. If you hadn't just burned Elster to death he would have been able to confirm that earlier tonight, in the Schloss Blankenburg treasury, he helped me pack the crown with more than a pound of Composition B, together with – let me see if I can remember correctly – *six* detonators triggered by any attempt to open the case. Apart from me, only Gerry Lonsdale knows where you can drill into it safely to deactivate the mechanism. So, if you try to cut him out as well, all you'll get is a face full of the world's most expensive shrapnel."

"That's a desperate charade!"

"Is it? Ask your men back there if Jack Penny didn't just risk his hide to pull the box out of the car before the flames got to it. Ask yourself if you think I'm the sort of woman who fails to take precautions. And while you're at it, ask yourself this…" she cocked her head towards the moonlit forest and gave a world-weary sigh, expelling a thin, discontinuous trail of smoke. "Ask yourself where my other sniper is – because you were third on that match."

Abba Levas froze, which was just as well, for at that moment something plucked at the point of the woollen cap comforter he wore high on his head. They heard the crack of the rifle bullet – and the shot echoing from the woods a second later.

Mila gave thanks for 'Uncle' Ludvík and his years as a poacher. She gave thanks for his time with her in the resistance, and that he still remembered her personal twist on the BBC propaganda broadcasts which had used the opening of Beethoven's Fifth as Morse Code for V-for-Victory: *dit-dit-dit-dah*. In Slečna Slavík's MERCURY circuit, it was V-for-*Výstraha* or Warning, be that as a graffito to indicate that a safe house was compromised or the casual tapping of her finger on her knee in a café, alerting them to the presence of a Gestapo informer. Or, indeed, a broken jet of smoke, like one of Polybius' encrypted signals in the Punic Wars, inscrutable yet visible from afar.

But mostly she gave thanks that he had not aimed his warning shot two inches lower and killed Levas outright. That would not have improved their situation.

She leant on the wall to look down on the courtyard, where the other commandos, busy with the burned-out car and bodies, had taken up their arms again at the sound of the shot. Box 7 lay where Penny had left it. An ashen Levas joined her, pulling off his hat and waggling a finger through the new holes.

Mila put her cigarette to her lips but paused before drawing in any more smoke.

"Would you like him to put the next one into the box, just to prove that I'm making it all up?"

He gave a faraway smile and swung a stiff leg over the wall, leaning back to shake her hand.

"Head north before going west. There is a route, Langeln-Abbenrode, that will get you to the demarcation line and over it. Our people run it."

"For refugees?"

"For what we call the remnant."

"They don't have trucks to transport them, like your weapons…"

"No." He spread his hands in a helpless gesture. "On the other side, yes. This is what the rest of the Jewish Brigade is doing when the British generals aren't looking."

"But not TTG?" The strained tones were Bradley's. Penny and the medic had got him on his feet with his arm in a sling and Penny, freed from his nursing responsibilities, was following the conversation with a look on his face that Mila had not seen before. A bandaged Marek was standing too, using his rifle as a crutch, but if they were going to cover any ground, they would need Ludvík to help carry him.

Abba Levas beckoned for his medic to leave them as well. As he strutted back down to the courtyard, he looked over his shoulder.

"*Tilhas Tizig Gesheften*," he said. "It is pretty untranslatable, but it's something like 'in this business, you can kiss my arse'."

*   *   *

From the hayloft of the half-timbered barn, looking south beyond the pallid fields and sugar-iced treeline, she could just make out the structures on the summit of the Brocken. Crystals in the moonlight. The bombed weather station and hotel, they must be. And that faint blade of light was the television tower that had once broadcast the Olympics, in a different age.

A day had passed – the rest of the night and a whole day of cold and hunger, of trudging on numb, blistered feet through the frozen mud and snow and having one's face, hands and lungs scoured by the bitter winds. She, Penny and Ludvík had taken turns to carry the two ends of the stretcher they had constructed for Marek. For variety, where the snow was deep enough or the ground firm and bare, they took turns to drag it like a Red Indian travois. Bradley, wrapped like the rest of them in layers of ragged, mismatched civilian clothing, had shambled on behind as walking wounded.

She watched him now, gingerly removing his sling and testing his shoulder as he slumped against the bare wall of the derelict barn.

"I think your sniping days may be over, Sam."

He gave a grim nod.

"I have a couple of vacancies in my group now," she went on. "But as you will have gathered, these are short-term positions."

"Don't beat yourself up, Mila. We all signed up for this, and we know why we're doing it."

She shook her head despairingly.

"Why, Sam?"

Although he was just a collection of shadows in the reflected light through the narrow window, she saw the brightness in his eyes as he met hers.

"Didn't you hear? We're on the side of the angels."

Careful not to appear to stare, she surveyed the dozen other shadowy figures clumped around the meagre fire in the hayloft: the refugee group they had joined up with just past Langeln. Perhaps because of the presence of the Brocken, that fabled site of the witches' sabbath, she gave in to a string of gloomy thoughts. How could anyone suppose that any side in this everlasting conflict was in any way guided by the divine? Even these people, the persecuted 'remnant', hid their faces, conversed in monosyllables, told no tales. How could any of their sacrifices be worthwhile? How could any good come from any of this?

Lost in such meditations, she did not at first understand what Sam was saying. Her first thought was of something between Pandora's Box and the Sixth Seal.

"What?"

"Will he take it back?" he repeated. "Or do you think he's opened it already?"

"He'd better not have tried…"

"You didn't really booby-trap it, did you?"

She laughed, despite herself.

"That would be telling."

"Now you sound like Jack."

Penny was on guard duty with Ludvík. She and Bradley would take over from them in an hour. They ought to have been sleeping, but this was a recuperation too.

"I like him, in spite of everything."

"I'll like him better when I know he's finished with his tricks," Sam said.

"Oh, he'll never be finished with those." She shuffled closer to the American, so as not to disturb the sleeping refugees. It would have been nice to have leaned against him, as she had that first time they had talked like this, on a lonely Sudeten mountaintop at the war's end, but there was his injured shoulder, among other things. After a few minutes of companionable silence, she kicked at his foot.

"One of the German smoke grenades – rigged with a big nail and a spring. I thought it might buy us a few precious seconds if it came to it."

"And the rest of the weight is champagne bottles?"

"Yes. I don't know what will happen if that all goes off inside a sturdy ammunition box, but it could be quite dramatic."

She could tell that Sam was picturing the sequence of events. She heard him snigger.

"Jesus, he'll crap himself!"

"I'd say that was very possible. But he won't come after us for that."

"Not to get even – he'll probably laugh it off. But if he figures you had the crown on you all along, then he will."

"Mmm, we need to be ready to run at the first sign of them."

"And if he takes the box back to Gerry – I'm assuming you didn't really warn him in advance how to disarm it?"

"No, of course not. And when Abba Levas discovers that, he'll open it there and then in front of him."

"Gerry won't find it funny."

"No, he won't. But I'm hoping he'll come round when we show up with the real crown."

The derelict farmhouse and barn stood at the centre of a

sparse coppice that occupied a hummock amid the barren fields. Unlike the conifers on the high ground to the south, here the trees were deciduous, mostly young beech for fuel and woodworking. The owl call through their bare branches was startling.

"That's Ludvík," she said, already on her feet. Putting out her free hand to stop Sam from rising with her, she whispered: "Stay here. Watch Marek and the fire."

He pulled a face but nodded. He knew he couldn't get down the ladder quickly.

When she got to the outside door, another call from Ludvík allayed her fears. Peeking out, she saw his familiar silhouette under the trees, in the company of two others. As she put away her pistol and tiptoed across the moonlit clearing, she saw that it was a young, dark-haired couple in civilian attire not much smarter than hers. They carried bulging haversacks but no visible weapons.

"This is Estera, and Kalev," Ludvík said carefully.

"Not our real names," the girl shrugged, speaking a simplified form of Polish that sounded more like Slovak and seemed intended to be intelligible to a Czech.

"We are *Khalutsim* – Pioneers – sent by the 'Joint' to get these people across." Kalev had opted for a mixture of English and Hebrew.

"The Joint?"

"Oh, sorry. The American Jewish Joint Distribution Committee – the JDC."

"Among others," Estera grunted.

Mila's heart went out to them. They were so intense, and so young, and so obviously in love. The girl's acerbity, the boy's politeness, were first and foremost to convince and impress one another.

She smiled and shook their hands.

"*Shalom.*"

"Here is food for the group," Estera removed her haversack and Kalev did the same. Yet neither moved forward. They were waiting for an explanation.

"We are not displaced people, and only one among us is a Jew," Mila confessed. "But we were directed here by an officer of the Jewish Brigade. Captain Abba Levas."

The moonlight caught two grins beneath the piercing eyes. Clearly that name was shibboleth enough.

"Who is the leader of the remnant group?" Estera wanted to know.

Mila was hesitant.

"We haven't really spoken. They just let us tag along."

Kalev nodded as though it all made sense to him, but it was Estera who spoke.

"These people, you understand, are wary of all strangers, even each other. Are there children and old among them? Yes? Then they have come from somewhere like Uzbekistan or Kazakhstan, where the Soviets have had them working on collective farms. They return to their homes in Poland and are driven out again."

"I understand," Mila said.

"And the ones that weren't on *kibbutz* in the east, the ones without their children, without their *babushkas*..." Kalev added. "They were probably *ka-tzetniks*, in the Nazi camps, yes? Miracles, you might call them. Maybe some were even Kapos and that is how they survived. They too have gone home to find there is no home left for them."

Estera poked Mila in the chest with righteous force.

"They do not speak to each other because for them there is nothing that can be spoken about."

"Except – there is," Kalev said, hugging Estera to him.

"Except there is!"

For a moment, the tough mask slipped. Mila saw the tear of passionate emotion in her eye.

She also became aware that 'Uncle' Ludvík had slipped away, presumably to change places with Jack Penny, who came strolling around the side of the barn to meet the newcomers, already ebulliently joining the discussion.

"An' that's *Eretz Yisrael*, yeah?"

Astonishingly, without breaking stride, he flung wide his arms in an avuncular gesture and the two *khalutsim* ran in to embrace him, one on each side, like children. It was as though they had been magnetically attracted, or perhaps enchanted: all the years of hardship and the toughness falling away. Somehow, whatever small part of the unprincipled London gangster had remained a champion of the underdog, and especially the Jew, it had come to the fore and they had spotted it immediately. But it was more than that. It was written on his face in the moonlight, in that near-rictus grin, like an athlete's at those Olympics: the blend of personal fulfilment at the journey made so far and boundless determination for the journey yet to come.

"Chin up, girl! Chin up, sunshine!" As he wrapped his beefy arms around the two of them, almost lifting them, he caught Mila's eye and held it, and nodded – as much to himself, she thought, as to her. "We're gonna get you there, don't you worry. All of you. You can flippin' count on it!"

CHAPTER SEVENTEEN

With the help of the pioneers, getting out of the Soviet Zone proved no more difficult than getting in. At first light the young couple led them past the slumbering Abbenrode and through a wood that sat on the line of demarcation. Only a crude sign and an unmanned barrier across the track stood witness to their return to the British Zone.

Getting beyond the border area, however, was a different matter. Whether they had tripped an alarm or been observed from the church tower, before they reached the next hamlet, at Lochtum, they were intercepted by a buttoned-up jeep containing the customary cold pairing of British redcap and German *Feldgendarm*. After a half-hearted attempt to turn them back for having no papers, the MPs used the field telephone in Lochtum to summon transport and at length an UNRRA truck arrived to take them all to the Assembly Centre at Lebenstedt, a former labour camp that had been part of the Hermann Goeringwerke factory complex. Goodbyes were said before Penny and Mila used a mixture of bluff, bravado and their phony British Army IDs to get back on the road for the Sennelager proving grounds and Lonsdale.

"Stay with Ludvík," she had told Bradley then. "Help him get Marek some proper hospital treatment. Get some yourself."

"Nuts to that," he had replied.

And so here the three of them were, weaving through the ruins of Paderborn on Reichsstraße 1, still in civvies and driving a little soft-top DKW they had commandeered along the way. They had ditched their American weapons at various stages of the trek, but that didn't stop Penny producing a pair of British Sten guns before they reached the warning signs delineating the military ranges. How he had come by those at a Displaced Persons camp was anybody's guess.

"No, not for you, 'Oratio," he winked, passing Bradley a .38 service revolver instead.

Seeing his confusion, Mila mimed tucking an empty sleeve into her coat front.

"Admiral Nelson," she said sheepishly, adding: "Just let him have his fun."

Bradley coloured. Although he had regained most of the mobility in his arm and a good part of its strength, it was humiliating to know they were only partly joking and that they must have decided, independently or together, that he could not be trusted with the work of an able-bodied man.

Fighting to control his anger, he thumbed the lever and carefully broke the revolver open at the top, so as to check and retain the six live rounds without automatically extracting them. With a flourish he snapped it shut again.

Penny grinned.

"I think he's got it!"

Up ahead, according to an old German road sign showing years of neglect, lay the settlement of Haustenbeck. Instead, Penny turned off onto the unmarked dirt road that would lead to the airstrip and the smelting operation. Military detritus was strewn everywhere – broken concrete obstacles, oil drums, vehicle carcasses – and every open patch of land was criss-crossed by tank-tracks.

At the sight of the stacks of aircraft parts and the chimneys, Penny brought the car to a halt. Several trucks had been parked alongside the smelting house. One was the TTG 3-tonner from four nights ago.

It seemed to take an age for the clatter of their two-stroke engine to die down. Then all at once they heard the gunshots and baled out over the sides. Somewhere in the shallow

211

depression down there, among towering metal stacks like a giant's graveyard-shift of dirty trays and dishes, someone was fighting a desperate battle.

Bradley saw Mila, hunching over the Sten in her bedraggled fur coat and headscarf, scurry into the undergrowth to the left. Penny had broken right and gone to ground behind a rusted-out Kettenkrad motorcycle half-track. Cursing, Bradley crouched beside the DKW's passenger door and raised the revolver with both hands, resting it on the front mudguard. It looked like his job was to cover them if they went forwards.

But then there came another, isolated shot and a tall figure tottered out from between the stacks. Bradley recognised that stiff-legged gait. He was in service dress now, not his commando gear, but the manner was the same: that of a man who was never going to duck or kneel.

He watched helplessly as Abba Levas fell back against one of the stacks. The Jewish Brigade captain tried for several seconds to straighten his peaked cap, before sliding down into an awkward seated position as his legs gave way, the stiff one twisted out to the side. A shadow fell upon him and he tried to raise his hand to greet it – a hand that held a British service revolver like Bradley's – but even as Bradley's finger tightened on the double-action trigger, Levas' arm dropped.

The figure that had cast the shadow came into view. It was another tall British officer in matching service dress.

'Captain Prentice'. AKA Gerry Lonsdale.

Bradley took a long, deep breath and relaxed his grip.

He heard Penny call out and saw Gerry react. Cautiously, the other two rose from their hiding places and showed themselves. When Mila beckoned for him, Bradley did the same, pocketing the pistol. Mila and Penny had lowered but not put down their Stens.

Another two REME-types emerged from behind the stacks, each carrying one of Penny's silenced carbines. That meant the sounds of gunfire must have come from Levas and his men. And the shot that felled him had been fired by Lonsdale's service revolver. Recognising them, Penny had harsh words with the REME-types. Bradley heard the names of Keeffe and Davies invoked. But these were stony-faced and loyal to their new 'guv'.

"Miss Nightingale. Bradley. Jack…" Gerry was still out of breath but fast recovering his composure. He gave a sly grin. "'ang on a tick…"

Before they could say anything, he had vanished between the stacks again. A moment later there came a pistol shot. A moment after that, another.

At their feet, Abba Levas sighed. They crouched around him.

"Miss Slavík…" Despite the life in the pained smile, his face had lost all its colour. They could see the bloody bullet hole in his chest.

"I'm here." She took his hand.

"I must thank you for the champagne…"

"Ah. You opened it."

"In front of Gerry Lonsdale. He was not amused." He coughed blood and tried to sit up, eyes gleaming fiercely. "Don't worry, that is not why he turned on us. He has found other buyers, you see…"

"For the crown?"

"Crown, weapons, everything. His brother is coming here to seal the deal."

"Jimmy Lonsdale! Here?"

Abba Levas fell back.

"Ah, Jacob Pieniazek, there you are. *Shalom aleichem.*"

"Peace, 'e says! Not while them Lonsdales is breathing!"

"No, hear me, brother…" Levas' other hand sought Penny's and clasped it. "You know what a *sabra* is? It means one born in *Eretz Yisrael* – like the desert plant you call the prickly pear. Prickly on the outside, but sweet inside? Well, I am not a *sabra*. I was born in Vilnius. Only later did I escape the Iron Wolf to *Eretz Yisrael,* to fight her battles, under the noses of the British. Our sort, you see, we are prickly on the outside all right, but there is no sweetness inside."

"That's not true," Mila said. "You sent us to the pioneers…"

Levas managed another smile.

"Those. The children of the first *Khalutsim*. They are true *sabras*. Aren't they magnificent? Now listen to me…"

But at that moment Gerry reappeared from the stacks. He was holstering his revolver.

"That filthy Yid still alive? You can tell him his mates ain't."

Mila and Bradley rose instinctively to shield the dying man from the psychopath and his sidekicks.

"Dunno why you're sticking up for them, after they done for your mob!" Gerry stepped up to Mila, brushed the Sten aside as though it were a Salvationist's collecting tin, and took hold of the thick fur collars of her coat, hefting it, straightening them. When Bradley moved to intervene, one of the sidekicks levelled his carbine at his head. The other took the Sten from Mila's acquiescent hand and did the same with Penny's.

"I'll have that pistol, too, Bradley, if you don't mind… And then I'll have that crown."

"You will not," Mila said, almost with amusement.

"Not in the motor, then?"

"I'm not that stupid."

"No…"

The gangster turned his head away as though to scent the air and Bradley felt sure that the time had come for action. Although the sidekicks had taken their weapons, the effect had been to overburden them and hamper their ability to use their own. Yes, Lonsdale had a pistol, but it was fastened away now, whereas Abba Levas' pistol still lay next to his hand. If it had any rounds left in it. And if…

"Oh well," Gerry said brightly. "Not to worry, eh?"

"Not to worry?"

"I'll get it in the end. I am going to have to finish off the captain there, though. His tribe bears grudges worse than any of us."

"You're too late," Penny grunted as he reached out to close Abba Levas' eyes. "*Aleichem shalom*, pal."

"Ha! Okey-dokey…" Gerry was practically rubbing his hands with glee. Watching Penny get to his feet, he extended a lower lip to imitate his gloomy expression, like an abusive adult mocking a child. "Now we're all back together again, here's the next part of the forfeit…"

"We're finished with that," Mila said.

"No, you ain't. Jack here wants his old lady back, and contrary to the little act you was putting on at the Herrenhaus, you're gonna want to save *him*…" At his boss's nod, the henchman behind Bradley jabbed the muzzle of the carbine into the back of his skull. Bradley muttered an obscenity but did nothing, looking only to Mila. Short-term or not, made ironically or rhetorically or whatever the goddamn word was, he had wholeheartedly accepted her offer of a place in her group. It was what he had always wanted.

"So, what would you have us do now?" she asked, before Penny could utter anything more confrontational. He had borne witness to Levas' final words, but that wasn't mourning in his face now. It was intent.

"Jimmy's on his way to shut this operation down. Yeah, I know, Jack, it was a nice little earner, but 'alf the Tank Corpse is coming 'ere to test their new Centurions against the panzers. Jimmy'll take the gold back with him, but we need you to transport the rest of it to a certain map reference at a certain time on a certain day: the silver and copper, the weapons, and, yeah, the crown."

"For the new buyers…"

"That's it, missus. And they'll be coming for a shufty 'ere any time now. I think we've all had our fill of sight unseen."

Presumably that was a reference to the champagne crate, although it was sometimes hard to tell with the solecistic Gerry Lonsdale, as Bradley had realised. Tank *Corpse!*

"You can give us the details for the delivery?"

Gerry drew a folded sheet of paper from his hip pocket and

fluttered it. He gestured for one of his overburdened sidekicks, who managed to produce a pencil stub and a pocket diary. The two men set to comparing notes and calculations.

"'Pliers' 'ere was gonna set it up on 'is Tod," Gerry grinned as he handed over the amended papers. "But this is so much neater – it's like it's fate or something."

"And Marjorie?" Penny said through clenched jaws. "And Bradley?"

"They'll be there at that location – if you are, with the merchandise."

"And if we're delayed?"

Gerry rounded on him and the veneer of merriment vanished like breath on cold glass.

"See, I don't think you got it, Jack. That rendezvous ain't just a pacific place – it's a pacific time an' all. You ain't there…"

"We'll be there," Mila said. "With your merchandise."

"See that you are – for his sake."

At that, the gun tapped twice on the side of Bradley's head and he realised they were about to lead him away.

"Mila, I…"

"I'll see you soon, Sergeant Bradley." She tossed him a brisk, efficient smile, which was fair enough if she was his boss now. He cursed himself for sounding too familiar. Really he ought to have called her Slečna Slavík.

But then her look lingered, just for a moment, but long enough.

"Our secret," she said. "You can count on it."

As well as echoing Penny's messianic promise to the pioneers, which she had told him about, he realised it was her way of reminding him of her old entreaty, *I'm going to be counting on you.* Her way of telling him she remembered too.

And 'our secret'? Perhaps her way of saying Application Accepted.

"Right then," Gerry said. "The gear's in them three lorries back there, so I'll 'ave to leave you 'Pliers' to drive the third one. Still got some of your crew to take over?"

"Some," Mila said.

"Still got your forger for the movement orders?"

She met his gaze without expression.

"No."

"Dearie me! It's a long way to Antwerp. Well, you'll think of something."

He was about to add some further taunt but stopped instead to cock an ear. Sure enough, there was the drone of a twin-engine airplane approaching from somewhere over the rise to Haustenbeck. Bradley noticed a flush of genuine elation in Gerry's face at the thought of his brother's arrival, but it was quickly subsumed by a calculating frown.

"Right… they'll want to 'ave a butcher's at the loot, so you two better stay by your motor until 'Pliers' tells you. We'll be back up in the air by then. Come on, Yank…"

The other sidekick dug his carbine into Bradley's lower spine and they threaded through the maze of stacks without looking back. Stumbling to keep up with Gerry as those long legs strode eagerly ahead, Bradley was confused. Abba Levas had said that Gerry's brother Jimmy was coming here to seal the deal with the new buyers. Gerry had hinted at the need to display and examine the merchandise. But still it seemed an unnecessary risk for them to fly in and out of British Army territory like this. Inspections could have been conducted later, at Antwerp, when there was more chance that the crown had been secured as well. What was he missing?

The smelter was still in operation, for appearances now, Bradley presumed. He counted five REME-types engaged in feeding torn-up segments of airplane fuselage into the arrangement at the front of the furnace. They would be Lonsdale men too, of course.

On the way to the overgrown dirt airstrip, Gerry led them past the trucks. Parked between the TTG 3-tonner and a Bedford he recognised from the last day at the Herrenhaus, Bradley spotted the deuce-and-a-half that had taken them to Elster's base, now with its phony U.S. markings painted over.

It was a raggedy-ass convoy to drive halfway across Germany and Belgium smuggling weapons and other treasure, but Gerry was right, she would find a way.

As the sound of the airplane got louder, Gerry raised his voice to call out an inventory. Perhaps he was practising, but the relish was obvious.

"Jack's last-ditch rifles in that one – that was a nice little bonus. Plus his special service DeLisle carbines. Then we got a dozen boxes of MG 34s from Czechoslovakia, 'alf a ton of silver and two tons of top-grade shiny copper. There's already another five or six tons of that waiting in Antwerp. And, last but not least…" They had come to a stack of four crates, each a bit shorter and narrower than Mila's champagne/ammo box had been. These were guarded by a further pair of REME soldiers armed with the folding silenced carbines. Gerry gave Bradley a nudge. "But that's coming with us."

At last, the plane appeared in the murky air above the treeline. It was a stubby little passenger aircraft with two prop engines mounted close together on a high wing. Bradley saw British camouflage and roundels. As it bounced a couple of times and settled onto the runway to go past, he noted the peculiar shape of the lower hull, the side-door positioned unnaturally high on the fuselage and the tanks on the wingtips that didn't quite look like auxiliary fuel tanks. He realised that in other circumstances, those tanks would be able to fold down to become floats. The aircraft was an amphibian.

It taxied about and drew up adjacent to the smelter and the trucks. That side door, designed to remain well above the surface on water landings, opened up and out in two sections and a ladder was hooked in place for the passengers to descend.

Or rather, the passenger, for there was only one: a large, ungainly figure bulging from his humble REME craftsman's uniform. Revealing too much undershirt beneath his battledress tunic, and too much flesh below that, he descended the ladder backwards and turned around slowly, seemingly relieved to have his feet on terra firma again. From the look of him he had been cramped in the cabin of the amphibian as well as in its doorway, for it was only after a few seconds, and carefully, that he allowed his head, neck and shoulders to extend out of their stooped posture, but when he did so he turned from an out-of-shape fat man to something far more imposing.

Jimmy the Shiv was every bit as tall as his younger brother, and nigh on twice the width. The wonder was he'd had to use a blade at all to earn his nickname. He could have brought anyone into line just by crushing them. He was dark where Gerry was fairer, and the lower half of that formidable face was swarthy with stubble that far exceeded Jack Penny's unmilitary five o'clock shadow. From its upper half glinted two small, sharp eyes like lumps of coal on a snowman.

"Ger'," he said with a half-smile of greeting as he rolled towards them. "Who's this twat?"

"This is the Yank 'Special Agent' what jabbertised the 'ole operation, Jim."

The coal lumps blinked.

"Jeopardised, you pranny. Well, put a fuckin' bullet in him!"

"No, he's an 'ostage, to go with the other one. I'll fill you in."

"It's your funeral, bruv… And 'e's a copper, eh?"

"Sort of. A Yank one."

"Filthy rotter!" Suddenly as light on his feet as a boxer, Jimmy stepped up, spat in Bradley's face and danced back, grinning. "Didn't like that, did he?"

Bradley stared straight ahead and let the warm gob run down his cheek. Another dose of humiliation and a bit of saliva was a better option than a shiv. He tuned himself out, knowing that if the shiv were to follow there was nothing now that he could do about it. It was only distantly that he registered Gerry saying: "Get 'im on the plane."

As his escort herded him forward, he made out the sound of a car over the idling airplane motors and the general racket from the smelting house. It was thundering across rough ground, its engine and transmission screaming. His heart was in his mouth as he half-turned. Surely she wasn't going to crash in and finish it like this!

But then he saw it, dodging the outlying stacks, rounding the corner of the lorry-park in a cloud of dust: not their DKW cabrio but an olive green staff car.

Neither Jimmy nor Gerry showed surprise or alarm when it skidded to a halt at the edge of the runway. Of course not. This was the answer to the puzzle. The buyers weren't coming by air at all. They were already here.

Bradley stared open-mouthed as the day's second lone passenger emerged from the rear of the car. This one he had met before.

Doyle went through the hoopla of lighting his pipe before giving a cheery wave.

CHAPTER EIGHTEEN

MV Heliopolis was a modern tramp freighter of 2,200 tons. She had cargo holds, masts and derricks fore and aft, and a 9-cylinder diesel engine amidships that in her youth had pushed out more than 2,000 horsepower, good for a cruising speed of 15 knots. But her ten years had been hard on her. Built for a private Norwegian line, she had put into a neutral port after the Nazi invasion of her country and been pressed into service by the exiled government as part of the Nortraship fleet, spending most of the war on Atlantic convoy duties. One of the few charmed vessels to survive four years of bombs, mines and torpedoes, she had limped into liberated Antwerp for a much needed refit, only to be half-wrecked when a V-2 missile struck her dock. With the status of the Nortraship survivors still under renegotiation, and the hard-pressed marine insurers holding off in the meantime, *MV Heliopolis* was just one more rusting, unseaworthy hulk, tucked away at a forgotten berth behind burned-out warehouses and seized-up cranes.

At least, that was the impression her new owners sought to maintain.

Lieutenant Leonard Hoffman of the U.S. Army Counter Intelligence Corps – among other masters, he reflected bitterly – wiped condensation from the cracked window of the wharfinger's office and peered out at the quayside. Not that there was much to see. The lamps were mostly broken here, and any light in the sky from the city was blocked by the huge bulk of the unladen ship.

Frowning, he mopped at the window again, before doing

the same with his eyeglasses. He really wasn't cut out for fieldwork. The blazing stove in this little office was steaming him up like the stove in that snowbound Bohemian police post where he'd first encountered Stransky. That guy and his buddies had gotten him pretty steamed up too, especially when Berman had started nagging him via the SCRT radioteletype.

"WAT R U? CIC? BSC? OR DFENS?"

"2B HONEST," he had replied, albeit in the same simple cypher. "ALL B4."

"RPLY NT RCD. AGN WAT R U?"

He had known that protestations of divided loyalties would not be well received. Even from people who traded on them.

"DFENS."

The Defence. AKA *Haganah*. Lately, the term had been broadening its meaning.

Now his spectacles were clear again, Hoffman kept his breath off the window and looked over at the two TTG men. Both were sleeping like babies, although that was a most inappropriate expression for men like Haim and Aharon. What was the other? Sleeping the sleep of the righteous? Possibly. Of the innocent?

Definitely not.

They would sleep, he knew, until someone came. If that proved to be their unofficial commander, Abba Levas, all would be well. If it were anybody else, especially the British Field Secret Service agents who had been tasked with investigating the Brigade's unauthorised activities…

No, definitely not.

Hoffman thought back to the Bohemian police post. There, seeing the Nazi collaborator and the gendarmes who had collaborated with his kind, he had wanted to open fire with his submachine gun, even if it was doubtful that he would have hit the right targets. But then his blood had been up, after their encounter with the half-frozen refugees in the forest, the Remnant, as they were now calling them. What had followed had been different, and what these men had done – to

Stransky, and all the others – had been done as coldly and as cruelly as he could ever have imagined. He had been a part of it. That blood was on his hands also. And other misdeeds, less clear-cut. Other wrongs done to people, because they were Germans; sometimes simply because they were not Jews. Other injustices, and other undeserving cases. Like the MERCURY group. Like Bradley.

That was why, while the others slept, he could not.

Something – a blurred movement or a muffled noise – drew his attention back to the window and the frosty quayside. Two figures had appeared beyond the furthest of the ship's iced-up mooring ropes. A couple, or rather, a familiar sort of pairing. The stocky male figure would be an AB returning from shore leave, and his uncertain gait suggested he was in no condition to tell one ship from another. The female… well, there was no mistaking what she was. From the swing of her hips to the clouds of obscenities that she was emitting, visibly, into the night, her profession announced itself in tawdry neon letters. What other reason would she have to be around the merchantmen anyhow?

Perhaps the swabby had promised her a crack at his shipmates. If so, they would both soon be disappointed. The *Heliopolis* had only a skeleton crew aboard and they were battened down out of sight.

In dismay, Hoffman saw the pair pause by the chained-off gangway. The AB was fussing with it in an uncoordinated fashion. The hooker kept on at him, alternately pressing herself against him and pushing him away, her jibes growing more and more strident. Hoffman realised he was going to have to go out and send them packing before the shore patrol arrived.

When he did, shrugging into the same kind of unremarkable peacoat and beanie that the AB was wearing and wrapping a filthy old scarf around his face, he found that his warm breath on his rapidly cooling eyeglasses steamed them up again. By the time he reached the couple at the gangway, he had wiped the lenses clean but was still fitting the wire loops around his ears. Perhaps that was how he failed to register in time that neither of the newcomers looked very drunk or smelled of drink, that the girl was too fresh-faced to be a waterfront whore, and that the man had turned his back not to urinate into the harbour as he had supposed but instead to draw a large, threatening revolver.

"No sound, no sudden moves," the girl said in accented English.

"Just want to 'ave a bit of a rabbit," the man added in a far more accented version of the language, which Hoffman suspected marked him out as a Londoner.

"A rabbit?"

"Blimey, another Septic! Yeah, a rabbit an' pork, though by the looks of you…" The tough expression eased and a half-smile broke through. "I'd say less of the pork!"

"Look, I'm sorry…?"

The girl smiled too. Both of their guns disappeared.

"You get used to it," she said. "We want to have a talk with you. And my friend Jack here seems to have decided that as well as being what he calls a Septic Tank or a Yank, you're Jewish, like him. Which means that we've come to the right place…"

"An' we got a message for you," Jack said in a solemn tone. "From Abba Levas, Gawd rest 'is soul."

"Oh, he's dead?" Hoffman blinked, startled and more than a little unsettled. What was this news going to mean, with two of Levas' trained killers eagerly awaiting their commander's arrival and this angry-looking Londoner, a Jew no less, fixing him with a piercing glare? "Er… *May his memory be a blessing.*"

Jack looked at the girl, at the light emanating from the windows of the wharfinger's office, and at the weather-beaten iron superstructure towering above them.

"It fuckin' better be."

Hoffman went first. Sure enough, Haim and Aharon were awake by now and had armed themselves, but he managed to pacify them with a gesture and a name.

"These people have come from Captain Levas."

"My condolences, lads," Jack said at once. Surprisingly, he sat down in front of them and extended two blunt hands. Even more surprisingly, each of the TTG assassins took one in his own. The three men closed their eyes and Hoffman saw the clasped hands shake with emotion as they squeezed one another. He wasn't particularly observant, in that sense, but he didn't think it was a religious gesture as such, more an instinctive kind of communion. A communion of the irredeemable, perhaps. Whatever it was, Hoffman had never felt more left out.

"And the men who were with him?" Aharon asked as soon as they opened their eyes.

"Also killed. By the Lonsdales. But they couldn't stop Abba Levas passing his message to me. For you."

Hoffman snapped out of his idle thoughts.

"You had better give that to me. It's my boss we're all working for."

Jack regarded the other two. They didn't look very happy about it.

"I thought we was all working for *Eretz Yisrael*," the Londoner said.

"Give us message," Haim growled and Aharon nodded. Since one had a Sten and the other a German *Sturmgewehr* – and since it was in no doubt that they would be able to hit their targets – Hoffman surrendered with a shrug.

"S'the same fing anyway," Jack said. "Levas had made 'is own mind up – but 'e told me the word come from the top."

Side-lined again, Hoffman thought. Circumvented. Typical.

"And what is it?" he said.

"Ditch the weapons. Take the Remnant instead – many as you can. Get in touch with the *Khalutsim*. There's two what Abba Levas knew 'ow to contact: Estera and Kalev. They'll put you in touch with the Pioneers running training *kibbutzim* among the DPs 'ere in Antwerp. Training for *Eretz Yisrael*."

"You're crazy!" Hoffman said. "These guys have already got

the British Secret Service breathing down their necks for smuggling refugees around Europe and down to the Med – and all they're doing there is passing them over to people who can get hold of small boats. That's what the Escape is – a small-scale smuggling operation, under the noses of the British. But a big ship with hundreds of illegal immigrants? They'll start up a whole new organisation just to close us down!"

Aharon laughed. From their demeanour, he and Haim looked receptive to this new imperative. In fact they looked like a weight had been taken off their shoulders.

"It seems that our bosses have already started a new one to make sure they don't."

It was then that the girl spoke for the first time. As soon as she did, Hoffman kicked himself. No, he definitely was not observant!

"My name is Mila. You may have heard me referred to as Miss Nightingale or Miss Slavík, and possibly as MERCURY. That was the underground network with which I fought the Nazis, but now all I want to do is to rescue two friends of mine from the clutches of the Lonsdale gang and then to find my son. My fight is not your fight and I do not expect you to help me. Yet, for the moment, I believe our interests run in parallel. In the burned-out warehouse at the end of the wharf are three lorries that we have just driven across the British Zone. Inside them are your weapons, as well as some other loot. We are supposed to take our cargo to another location on the other side of the Scheldt, where Lonsdale's people will load them onto sailing barges for us to take to England. But Abba Levas told Jack Penny here of your plans to smuggle the weapons to Palestine on the *Heliopolis* and so I have come here to give you his last message and to make a request of you. Do as Levas said. Don't take the weapons. Let me take them to the Lonsdales, in return for my friends' lives."

Although he had apparently followed this appeal, Haim hadn't the English to counter it. He muttered something scornful sounding to Aharon, who interpreted.

"In what way, madame, does this line up with our interests?"

She stood and thrust her hand into her coat pocket, pulling out a wrapped object and tossing it to Haim. A heavy wrapped object.

"That will keep the British off your backs," she said, when they had unwrapped and gazed in astonishment at the little crown. "And there's something else…"

Taking his cue from her, Jack Penny cackled.

"You bet there is!"

But Aharon had his own objection to raise first.

"You said you drove *three* lorries across Germany…?"

"That's correct. Another of my group is out there. In fact, he has been covering us all this time."

Aharon grinned.

"I thought perhaps you were not serious, madame. Now I see you are."

Hoffman had been doing some arithmetic of his own.

"You said there were two ways in which our interests aligned."

"At least. If you let us take the weapons as we ask, my men and I will cross the Scheldt and deliver them to Lonsdale's contact. As well as the sailing barges, he has a warehouse of his own, we have been informed, in which he is storing the rest of the copper they have amassed and possibly other valuables. I don't see why you shouldn't come with us and take what you want. I'll even throw in the silver we have brought with the weapons. I daresay that will open doors for you in Antwerp, since the diamond trade has yet to resume."

"I thought you said you were going to make your delivery…?"

"We are going to make the rendezvous as agreed – it's not quite the same thing."

"And where is this rendezvous?" Hoffman asked.

It was Penny who answered.

"We was given a map reference that puts it in the Thames

estuary. And a date, four days from tomorrow morning, and a time, just after first light. A 'pacific' time, as Gerry Lonsdale called it. Perhaps the arsehole only got the wrong ocean! These coordinates are well out to sea and the specific time makes it most likely a rendezvous with another craft. Miss Slavík reckons the people we want to trade for will 'ave to be aboard that."

"So what happens then?" Aharon asked, sounding genuinely concerned as to how any confrontation would work out. "And how does that fit with our interests?"

The girl sat down again and shrugged. It was true that close-up, despite the excessive make-up that was part of her disguise, she looked much fresher and younger than the local hookers. But Dear God she also looked tired of it all.

"Your desire for vengeance," she said, putting a cigarette between blood-red lips and flicking a little gold lighter with a click like a safety catch being let off. "We intend to kill the Lonsdales."

* * *

Gerry leaned on the platform of one of the 40mm Bofors guns and grinned.

"They'll be thinking of pulling something. Prob'ly reckon we'll turn up in a few barges like theirs and they can jump us. They're gonna get a shock!"

Bradley shielded his eyes. This was the first time in days that he'd been allowed out of his darkened cell and despite the wintry overcast the light rebounding across the battleship-grey panorama of cloud, sea and steel was blinding. Although the structure on which they stood was securely anchored to the seabed, his legs felt numb and his head still spun with the same sensation of disorientation and exposure he remembered from the Atlantic crossing, and from the meeting that had followed on the R.C.A. Sky View.

That meeting had been the source of much disorientation, he reflected.

Reaching up, Gerry gave one of the operators' crank handles a lazy twist, which smoothly traversed the entire mount of the anti-aircraft gun towards him.

"So? I brung you up 'ere for your verdic' on what she'll do – her being due in a couple o'days and you being her oppo all along, crafty bastard…"

With his Sten-wielding escort in tow, Bradley took several steps back from the cantilevered gun platform towards the comparative solidity of the bunker in the middle. He stepped down again and went over to the parapet to survey the rest of the fort, affecting a casual air. The way his fingers gripped the salt-corroded steel and macadam armour would have told any sharp-eyed observer otherwise.

They were on the roof of one of a cluster of three-storey steel coffins perched high atop concrete legs out in the Thames estuary. The grey-painted towers were laid out like a spider, with a central control and radar tower linked by precarious suspended catwalks to four gun towers mounting 3.7-inch heavy guns and a fifth, this Bofors tower, with its two rapid-firing autocannons. One of the main gun towers led by a longer walkway to a similar searchlight tower, positioned further out.

The fort was one of several army-operated versions that had been constructed here as a second line of defence for London, closer in than the larger navy forts out in the open sea. According to Gerry, it had proved its worth against German bombers navigating up the estuary, as well as the odd E-boat or submarine. Lately it had been particularly effective against the robot V-1s. But it must have been a cold, lonely posting for its hundred-plus complement of reservists from 'Ack-Ack' Command: stuck out on the sandbanks, barely in sight of shore or the other forts on a clear day. As soon as the aerial threat had vanished, so too had the gunners, to be replaced by much smaller REME maintenance crews. Infiltrating their own men onto one of these had been a doddle, Gerry boasted, and so long as you kept an eye on the tides, and knew how to sneak a small craft through the boom defences, you had a perfect staging post for smuggling into Kent, Essex, or up the river right into the Smoke.

With all kinds of fancy automatic targeting and fusing involved, the 3.7s called for smart-arse know-how, Gerry acknowledged, and although the ammo was still in the bunkers in the gun tower parapets, someone – no names, no pack drill – had already spirited away the hush-hush computers that would deliver it magically to the point in the sky where an incoming airplane or a flying bomb might be. But no matter: the two Bofors guns on their elevated platforms could still make mincemeat of anything in the vicinity. Hence the shock that Mila and Penny were about to get.

Bradley nodded to himself and shut his eyes to clear his thoughts.

Like one of those computers, Gerry wanted him to predict Mila's plan of action. There didn't seem any merit in suggesting she'd play it straight. Having been forced into this never-ending forfeit, and having seen the Jewish Brigade betrayed, only a fool would expect the Lonsdales to accept the merchandise, hand over their hostages and leave it at that. Mila was no fool and they knew it. Crucially, compared with most other transactions in their line of work, they also knew she hadn't a rival crime syndicate waiting in the wings to declare war on theirs if things went south. Nor had Penny now, since most of his men had gone over to their gang. If Bradley dummied up entirely, the chances were he'd remove the only reason they had for keeping him alive. He couldn't do that yet – not just for the sake of his own skin but for his fellow prisoner's.

She had been here at the fort when they had made their hair-raising arrival by the amphibian. Once the heavy crates had been winched up, he and Jimmy had climbed gingerly into the fort's clinker lifeboat to be deposited on the control tower's landing stage, which was accessible at high water. Since the bottom of the sinister octagonal structure still hovered thirty feet above him, he could only imagine how imposing – and inaccessible – the towers would be at low tide, when thanks to the estuary current there might be another thirty feet of weed-encrusted reinforced concrete to scale.

With a dozen muted consultations to be conducted with his subordinates, Jimmy had paid Bradley no heed in the airplane or afterwards and soon disappeared with his boxes aboard the REME tender that came and went from Sheerness, leaving his brother firmly in charge. That was a pity, for if Jimmy was all business, Gerry liked to have his fun.

Bradley could think of no other reason why the latter had summoned Marjorie from what he termed 'storage' upon Bradley's arrival – if not to amuse himself by dashing her hopes with the evidence of his capture and the news of Penny's subjugation. As soon as she was ushered into the galley area where he'd been cuffed to a screwed-down mess table, Bradley had gone cold.

In the weeks since he had seen her, the poor woman had clearly suffered. Although she had made an effort to brush and shape her distinctive, grey-streaked hair and to dress in her familiar Sunday best, Bradley had hardly recognised her. The hair had more grey in it, and so did her face. The frayed and grimy clothes hung off her and she moved haltingly, the air of confidence and rectitude quite extinguished.

Or not quite.

"Please don't gawp, Mr Bradley, these men have not been abusing me." Ignoring Gerry and his cohorts, she had eased herself into a seat across from him. "The fact is I've been ill. This place is not exactly unaffected by the motions of the waves or the weather and I'm afraid I haven't been able to keep anything down."

"What the hell is 'storage'?"

"That, Mr Bradley, is something I suspect they're about to demonstrate…"

And abruptly, after only a few moments together (because unsettling and demoralising them had been the point of this), their captors had done just that.

Shut away in solitary confinement, in a plywood-lined storeroom with no window, no heating, no light source except a louvred blackout panel in the door and only a bucket and an army sleeping mat for comfort, it hadn't taken very long for him to understand how hard it had been for Marjorie. Bad enough even if you could force yourself to swallow the dry rations they provided once a day, unimaginable if you couldn't. But even that wasn't the worst. After a day and a night in the cell that mirrored the one she occupied across the lower level of the control tower, Bradley was certain that what had broken Marjorie's spirits, or at least come close to it, was the constant, clanging noise from the rest of the fort as the solid fuel boilers heated the radiators in the living areas and caused the panels to expand and contract, as the generators chugged unceasingly to power the lights and equipment, as fuel, fresh water and saltwater was pumped up and down, back and forth, to accommodate the men's various needs, and as booming voices echoed and army boots rang on hollow steel and paper-thin blacktop – shifting loot to the winches and the visiting Thames barges – to the accompaniment of the gulls and the wind and the waves. There was no chance to think, let alone sleep.

"Bring Mrs Jessop up," he called to Gerry now over the noise of the gulls.

"Why should I do that?"

"Because then I'll tell you what I think they'll do – Miss Slavík and Penny."

Gerry glanced over his shoulder and nodded. Bradley saw stars and fell to his knees as the man with the Sten clouted the back of his head with it. Hopefully there wasn't enough metal in that cruddy skeleton buttstock to do permanent damage, but it still hurt like hell.

"I think you'll tell me now, actually, if I say so."

He got to his feet again, rubbing the back of his neck. Without Marjorie, without Mila, he knew what he would have done. The fellow behind him was there to blast him should he make a false move, but had reversed his weapon to butt-stroke him. Provoke another nod from Lonsdale and Bradley could step back into him next time and seize the Sten. Even if the guy held on tight, Bradley was confident he could get one of their fingers on the trigger to drill the boss-man, and after that all bets were off.

But there was Marjorie to think about. And there was Mila – counting on him.

"All I'm saying, Gerry, is that Mrs Jessop spent more time talking to Miss Slavík than I ever did – you saw her yourself at the Herrenhaus. And she's the one who knows Jack's mind too. I'll give you my best guess, but hers might be better."

Gerry moved close, as his brother had done. Bradley braced himself for another gob of spit – or worse. Instead, with that animal sniff and a twist of his lips, Gerry turned his head sharply aside to address one of his other henchmen.

"Go get her. Bring her to the roof of the middle one..."

"The control tower, guv?"

"Yeah. The middle one." Still standing uncomfortably close to him, he gave Bradley a sly, knowing smile. "Okey-dokey, Yank. Let's see what she says."

Bradley found it tough not to shudder. Men like this were the worst: it was all a crooked game to them and they thought nothing of suddenly changing the rules. There had been a blatant challenge in the way he'd stepped up to him just now. It suggested that he had seen through Bradley's desperate little plan to snatch the Sten, had been amused by it, and was sure to see through any other ploy he might come up with.

Descending two levels inside the Bofors tower to reach the bridge to the control tower, they passed men asleep on bunks, playing cards and cleaning weapons. Perhaps in case of snap inspections, or because Jimmy prized efficiency above indulgence, at least some degree of military discipline had been maintained. Bradley hadn't had the opportunity to check the other towers, but he had seen and heard them coming and going and judged there to be at least twenty-five gang-members on the fort, with enough firepower between them to take on a company.

He set out ahead of Gerry and his men across the walkway. Although they were now something like fifty feet above the choppy surface of the estuary, in fact the fort was solidly built and the transverse timbers of the caged-in catwalk barely moved underfoot. When they reached the two armoured doors of the control tower, one of Gerry's escorts gave a piercing whistle and another henchman let them into the dingy lower service area that included 'storage'. From here, two flights of steps led to the roof. As with the Bofors tower, the basic octagonal shape had been extended with two cantilevered platforms, here for the crane hoists, but in place of guns it was equipped with a plethora of radar, radio and range-finding equipment, plus the fort's riding lamp.

As he came out of the stairwell penthouse, he spotted Marjorie in between two gangsters in their REME craftsmen's uniforms. It looked like one of the men was having to support her.

"Bring a chair up, dammit," he said to Gerry.

While Gerry, momentarily taken aback, directed one of his men to do so, Bradley took Marjorie's arm and led her away from the henchmen.

"We gotta put on a show," he told her. "Are you up to following my lead?"

"Lead away, Mister Bradley!"

"You're shivering. Stupid of me…" He shrugged out of his 'refugee' coat and put it around her shoulders.

"I'm afraid I've become an awful burden," she said.

"Don't think like that," he said, surprising himself with the fierceness of his tone. He squeezed her arm apologetically as he led her toward the waiting mess chair. "It isn't any of your damn fault – it's all theirs…"

Gerry had perched on the housing of some piece of equipment opposite them. He had his hands in his pockets but his manner was anything but casual. It was time.

Bradley extended both hands, palms up, in a gesture of

honesty and helplessness.

"My guess is she'll want to come in sneaky, that's her style. But I can't tell you how. I told you, I don't know her that well."

Gerry turned to Marjorie and raised an eyebrow. Bradley's heart went out to her when he realised how well she was going to back him up, without any training or time to prepare.

"I should say so, yes. You have noticed, I'm sure, how she keeps her hair short, so as to be able to wear any wig or military hat without hairdressing… That is her modus operandi: disguise, pretence, trickery."

Gerry scoffed.

"It ain't Jack's way."

"Oh, absolutely not! A bull in a china shop is my Jack. But he will defer to her. He's in awe of her."

Gerry nodded slowly, but still looked unconvinced.

"Ain't much chance of working a scam seven mile offshore neither."

"I wouldn't know about that," Marjorie said primly. "I thought you simply asked for my prognostication of her preferred methods. But if you mean a grand villainous scheme such as telling an old lady you've come to read her gas meter, well, do you never receive visitors here? Someone from the coastguard perhaps, or the lifeboat service…?"

Bradley realised he was starting to smile and had to recompose his features. The woman was a natural at sowing doubt and distrust! As for turning the inarticulate bastard's taunting back against him, using a word like *prognostication* to puncture his self-assurance just when it mattered, that was the mark of a fighter.

"It's a thought," Gerry said. Except he didn't. Being Gerry, what he actually said was: It's a *fort*.

"It certainly is," Marjorie replied without so much as a blink.

Bradley winced. She had gone too far. Before the understanding sank in, he needed to get Gerry's thoughts onto a different track.

Doubt and distrust: she had shown him the way. And

Doyle, whatever the hell his game was, had given him the opening.

"Listen," he said urgently. "It's one thing speculating whether or not Miss Slavík is going to play fair at the rendezvous, but what about that guy at the proving grounds? Operating on behalf of the British Government, ain't he? If I was in a sweat about who's going to turn up on the next supply tender, it'd be the cops, after Doyle's turned you in. Or did he sell you some story about him reequipping the Irish Republican Army?"

If he was surprised, he didn't show it. Gerry seemed mostly irritated at the interruption.

"What? No, 'course not! Me and Jimmy've always known 'e's working for the Government. They don't want no one to let the weapons and the crown get to Palestine – and they need an unofficial channel to supply the Japs and Frogs they're setting up to fight the commies in South East Asia or something…"

From the way he parroted certain phrases before pulling up lame, it was clear he left that side of the business to Jimmy, or rather Jimmy kept his brother well away from it. That limited the extent to which Bradley could sow his doubt and distrust, which was a shame, but at least he had distracted him from noticing Marjorie's sarcastic response – and just possibly from deciding that his prisoners had outlived their usefulness.

"Yeah, well," Gerry said now, getting to his feet. "I ain't got time for this, I'm a busy man."

He gestured for his henchmen and pointed to the two of them.

"Take 'em below again and lock 'em up."

Without waiting, he headed off down the stairs. Bradley watched him go.

"I think you rattled him," Marjorie said.

"No, I think you did."

"I hope it was a good idea. He's not a very stable person."

"Mrs Jessop," Bradley said with a smile. "He's a goddamn

lunatic. And you're a goddamn revelation."

They were getting her upright and manhandling her towards the penthouse. Bradley clenched his teeth at the Sten in his back again. Marjorie caught his eye. Her strand of grey hair had come free and was blowing across her face. She brushed it back into place.

"My Peter would have been about your age." She reached out her hand to cup his cheek. Her fingers were freezing. "Do try to stay alive, won't you, Mister Bradley?"

CHAPTER NINETEEN

She had been dozing. That was the real surprise. Despite her conviction that she would never again sleep properly, the change in her spirits after having seen Mr Bradley – or perhaps it was just the accumulated fatigue – had enabled her to drift off at last.

The wonder was that she had come back from it. She would not have wanted to, but something had penetrated the precious oblivion and summoned her. What had that been? As she recovered her wits, she recalled the sound that had woven itself into her dreams. An alpenhorn, resounding from the cloud-darkened mountains menacing Namsos Fjord. An alpenhorn, blasting out six haunting notes.

She sat up with a start. She had not imagined that.

Six notes, but actually only three tones. The first three notes all the same pitch, with the first slightly longer than the others. Then up a half step. Up a step from there. Back to the first note again.

Un – der – neath – the – lan –tern.

Not an alpenhorn. Of course not. A foghorn.

She heard boots on the metal floors. Shouting. Doors creaking open and banging shut. Mr Bradley's voice, from what must have been his open cell. Others from one of the armoured doorways leading out onto the walkways. An explosion of daylight illuminated her shutters. A squall of cold, damp air blew under her door and made her shiver.

Then her door opening – and Mr Bradley was there, reaching down for her.

"They're here," he said, grim-faced. "And we are wanted."

Before she knew it, she was being ushered out onto the balcony and across one of the catwalks. Perhaps because of her dream, perhaps because of the freezing whiteness of the sea fret all about, the impression of being high in the mountains was hard to shake off. Her legs nearly gave way but the American kept ahold of her. Behind them trotted two of the gang members with two mismatched but equally evil-looking machine guns.

"Mr Bradley," she tugged at the sleeve of his ragged pullover, suddenly conscious of the fact that she was still wrapped in his overcoat. "Did you hear the horn?"

"Mmmm. Just a passing vessel in the mist."

"Yes, but…"

There wasn't time to say anything more. Marjorie gasped and nearly swooned as they were manhandled into the next tower and up its stairs to the roof.

This was the one with the two, smaller, anti-aircraft guns on elevated platforms hanging out either side. On the raised structure between them she saw Gerry Lonsdale surrounded by half a dozen of his cohorts. Gerry and two men were examining something through their binoculars. Another of the gang was manning a piece of equipment like a seaside coin-operated telescope that she recognised from countless newsreels as a signalling lamp. And what were they all looking at? She squinted in the bright light and thought she spotted a number of ghostly shapes rising and falling in a heavy swell, several hundred yards off to the side.

"Jacob?"

"Oh, it's 'im alright, Mrs Jessop," Gerry lowered the glasses to throw her an ugly sneer by way of a greeting. "But 'e's playin' silly buggers is what 'e's doin'!"

She saw a bright light flash intermittently from one of the low, indistinct forms and heard Gerry confer furiously with his signaller.

"Come on then!" Gerry gestured for her and Bradley to join

him on the raised section. "Soon as 'e turned up, 'e stood off and threatened to jettison the 'ole cargo, unless we produced you two... WELL HERE THEY ARE! Go on, give him a wave…"

When Gerry went back to his signaller, Marjorie pressed close to Bradley.

"The foghorn was a message too," she mouthed. "From Mila."

He stared at her.

"You're certain?"

"Yes."

"I just heard a few blasts. Do you know what it means?"

Marjorie pulled a face.

"Only that it's *Lili Marleen*. It was a private joke between us. 'Underneath the lantern…'"

She saw his mind working frantically.

"Our secret…" he said, but not to her. "You can count on it…"

"I don't know what that means."

He grinned, suddenly. Marjorie had the notion that if he had been that sort of man, he would have given her a peck on her cheek.

"No, but I do, now." Then he frowned. "How long ago would you say we heard the foghorn?"

"Heavens! I was fast asleep… I don't know. Perhaps three quarters of an hour?"

He nodded.

"Good enough for me. Then we have fifteen minutes left."

"Until what?"

"I don't know. Neither did she when she gave me the cue, but she managed to give it to me anyway. A countdown from an hour. We have to be ready."

"Do you think she's on one of those barges? Do they have horns like that?"

"I don't know. They're bigger than they look and the one at the front has a proper motor. Possibly."

"But what can either of them do from there?"

Marjorie saw that Bradley was surreptitiously looking around the fort: at the other towers, at least those he could see from here without turning right around; at the gantries that suspended the catwalks and the peculiar arrangements of braces beneath the towers; at the hazy surface of the sea.

"Maybe she's not on the barges anymore."

*   *   *

"Right, that's enough of that…" Gerry Lonsdale said.

Picking one of his men who had been watching the prisoners and another who had been watching the barges, he stepped up to the outboard Bofors platform and climbed onto the gun, choosing the left hand seat with the elevation controls and the foot trigger. The others took up positions in the traversing seat and standing at the breech, ready to fill the autoloader with blocks of cannon shells like giant Enfield rifle clips.

"Point it just be'ind the front barge," he yelled to the man in the right hand seat. It was hardly the way the gun was meant to be operated, with its electrical predictor taking charge of the gun-laying. But it would do well enough against slow moving targets and even better if they were stationary.

As the whole gun and mount swivelled around, he wound his crank handles rapidly, lowering the barrel to fire over open sights. He didn't quite understand the fusing, but it was sure to make a big enough splash if it hit the sea, and to go off if it hit something solid.

He pressed the pedal and the gun automatically discharged all eight rounds they had loaded so far in what seemed like a couple of seconds. With his heart thumping and his eardrums ringing, he watched wide-eyed as six impacts stitched the rising wave about ten feet abaft of Jack's barge. The first two must have gone over the top of it.

He dropped the handles and grabbed his field glasses. So bloody difficult to fix on the trio of sailing barges, let along focus on them. But wait a moment… yeah, there was Jack Penny stepping out onto the long flat superstructure of the Dutch barge and going over to cling to the mast. Presumably he was about to make some signal that he was coming to tie up and unload.

Except he wasn't. Through the mist and the spray, Gerry saw him swing a crooked arm and catch it with the opposite hand in a gesture he recognised all too well. Before he could react, Penny pointed to the rear of the barge, where two unidentified figures in sou'westers had lifted a long crate onto the gunwale. Triumphantly, he slapped his hand downwards and Gerry saw what looked like a dozen rifles tip into the sea, followed by the empty box, which floated. The rifles did not. In horror he realised that other hands were performing the same task with crates of machine guns and silenced carbines on the other two barges. Crate after crate after crate.

"Load it again!" he shrieked at the man behind the breech.

It was at that moment that he heard the ship's horn once more, shockingly loud and close. Leaping up onto the seat to look behind the gun, he saw the huge shadow loom out of the sea fog and resolve itself into the oncoming bows of a merchant vessel, canted over in a futile evasive turn yet bearing down on them at what seemed like breakneck speed. There was a thud and a crash as it swept past the outlying searchlight tower and the whole fort shook, causing the Bofors gun to traverse on its own. Incredibly, the first thing Gerry saw when he recovered his balance was the complete No.2 gun tower – a tower almost identical to this one – tilting over, twisting around and toppling like a barstool, its gun falling off into the water. The next was the ship still coming on, with the rigid steel catwalk that had linked the searchlight tower to the adjoining No.2 tower now draped across her prow like a snapped twig caught in the fender of a lorry.

He looked for the other men on the gun but they had disappeared, tossed into the sea when it spun around, most likely. Over the screech of rending metal and the echoing rumble of the earthquake that was shaking the whole fort, he heard another of his men yell out: "Guv! It's gonna hit the control tower and that'll pull us over with it!"

It was Andrews, the guard with the Lanchester submachine gun from the navy's locker. But where were the two prisoners he had been guarding with it? Nowhere to be seen. Escaped the instant Andrews had been distracted by an effin' great ship ramming into the fort, no doubt – as though prepared for it, as though forewarned.

The ship was slowing and turning in a turmoil of churning water and impossibly moving structures, yet still ploughing forwards under its own inertia. A word popped into Gerry's head, a word he had never felt confident to utter but which seemed to capture the motion perfectly. In – ex – or – bly.

He stared in mute dread at the tarnished, battered superstructure of the vessel. It had come from nowhere. Perhaps it had no living crew... But then he spotted darkened figures moving on the bridge.

"Shoot at them!" he called to Andrews, pointing.

As he raised and aimed his heavy, wood-stocked gun, there was a flash from somewhere above the ship's bridge windows. Just a blink of light, brighter and briefer than Jack Penny's signals, scarcely visible in the spray – but Andrews dropped the Lanchester and clutched his arm.

The bows crashed into the far side of the control tower and Gerry had to cling on for dear life as everything rocked.

She'll come in sneaky, he thought.

*   *   *

Mila clambered onto the fo'c'sle deck, which was strewn with broken rigging and wreckage from the fort. One cable, in particular, coiled violently as it snagged on the windlass and the foremost pair of cowl vents, now creased and bent over like cardboard. Wasting no time, she picked her way to the rail just aft of the tangle where the jackstaff had collected the walkway.

Although it was slowing now, the *Heliopolis* was not going to stop, that much was obvious – at least not until it had sliced through the connections to the two remaining gun towers seaward of the control tower, which it had just struck with a glancing blow. There would not be a better time to get onto the control tower roof.

She had misjudged the height difference though. As the ship's hull ground against the concrete legs and the encumbered bows butted and scraped the armoured steel structure, she realised that even at high tide and with a relatively light load, the fo'c'sle deck was going to pass beneath the upper storey of the tower, too low to jump across. She would have been better using the lifeboat deck or the bridge, but it was too late to change position now. Trusting to her tough gloves and boiler suit, she shinned up the remaining anchor davit and leaped for the outside edge of the tower's parapet. The landing knocked the wind out of her and one hand slipped, but the other held. Now all she had to do was to pull herself up by brute force, get a leg onto the ledge, and grab hold of the parapet proper.

When, somehow, she had completed this, she raised herself up and was met by the astonished face of one of Lonsdale's fake REME craftsmen.

His astonishment turned to anguish as 'Uncle' Ludvík, lying atop the bridge, put a rifle bullet in his shoulder.

Mila vaulted the parapet and made sure that the man was in no condition to cause further trouble. She raised her head again in time to see the bridge team go past at her level. One of them, dark-bearded, grimacing at the damage he was doing to his ship, gave a brief salute.

Captain Valerius. What an asset he had proven to be! It was he who had identified the coordinates as belonging not to the location of a rendezvous on the open water but that of an actual structure, which he was able to describe in some detail, together with the remaining boom defences and mine loops. It was even he who had proposed the course of action they'd adopted, with Jack Penny drawing the villains' attention toward the lee side of the fort while the *Heliopolis* turned in from the main channel, benefiting from weather which Valerius could not guarantee but had done a miraculous job of predicting.

And it was he, of course, who had agreed to the other aspect of the mission, although for that part he and his crew were to be handsomely rewarded.

She watched Ludvík go past as well, shuffling on his elbows to keep her covered. He raised a thumb.

No one else on the roof of the control tower.

Mila checked that her pistol was still securely holstered and picked up the wounded man's Sten.

*   *   *

The impact threw Bradley sideways against the staircase railings, nearly causing him to lose his footing and tumble into Marjorie, but then they were down on the bottom level of the Bofors tower.

"That was the ship hitting the control tower," he said.

"What happened to the lights?" Marjorie asked.

"I think the main generators were in the searchlight tower."

"Oh, so there's no power for anything…"

"We can lower the lifeboat by hand."

That was his plan, such as it was: to get off the Bofors tower and onto the platform beneath the control tower, in case they all went over like the gun tower, huge concrete foundations and all. To get away in the clinker lifeboat – or to help Penny come aboard and hand Marjorie over to his crew, whoever they were.

But to do that they would have to retrace their steps across the catwalk.

And hope that the control tower did not topple while they were heading for it.

"Mr Bradley…"

He put his good arm around her.

"We'll go together."

As he led her across, he wondered what he would do if one of Gerry's men appeared at the armoured doors ahead of them. He had no weapon and the element of surprise was of little advantage when your opponents were already in a state of alarm.

Just keep going, he supposed. The gang must be in complete disarray. Those manning the equipment in the searchlight tower were cut off. Those in the No.2 gun tower were most likely drowned. The last he had seen of the ship it had been set to slice off the No.3 and No.4 towers, which would maroon any men stationed on those. That only left Gerry and his few sidekicks behind them, plus whoever they were about to encounter in the control tower – possibly just two or three – and the few men, if any, from No.1 tower, which was used primarily for storing loot awaiting pickup. With only one sturdy lifeboat, and half the inflatable life-rafts inaccessible beneath the other towers, surely any minute now the survivors would decide it was every man for himself.

They reached the gantry by the double doors. There was a ladder leading down from the narrow balcony here, but Marjorie was in no state for that, so Bradley forced open a door and led her into the darkened service level where they had been imprisoned. Marjorie put her hands over her ears. Down in this confined area, the shriek of grinding metal as the ship elbowed past was deafening.

Bradley heard the shots though. A short burst of submachine gun fire. Propping Marjorie against the wall, he searched around and found a heavy wrench they must have used when the doors were proving hard to seal.

Another couple of shots from the level above. Bradley had just crept into the shadows of the stairwell when a body clattered down the last flight of stairs and landed at the bottom with a groan. A body wearing REME uniform, clutching bleeding legs.

He pursed his lips but could not remember the tune. His

eyes sought out Marjorie in the gloom. After a moment she nodded and whistled the first three of six notes.

The other three notes echoed down the stairwell.

"Mila?"

She descended cautiously, a Sten gun tucked close to her body. She was wearing thick dark coveralls and a woollen hat that looked like Abba Levas' commando cap comforter. Her face, gaunt as Marjorie's and smeared with grime, lit up when she saw the two of them.

"I see you got my message," she said.

"*Underneath the lantern…*" Marjorie incanted, as though in a trance.

"Well, we almost missed the searchlight tower but I'd say dropping me off right by the riding lamp was close enough!"

"On your own?" Bradley asked offhandedly.

"For the moment. The ship's not stopping – she's on her way to Palestine now, although she'll need to drop 'Uncle' Ludvík off somewhere, and make some running repairs."

"How many aboard?"

Mila smiled.

"Estera and Kalev told us two hundred. I wouldn't be surprised if it's three times that."

She was looking at Marjorie with concern. After a moment she went over and touched her arm lightly.

"Nearly over now," she said.

"Penny?" Bradley asked, although he could guess the answer.

"That's right. He and his men will be here any second. We might go down and signal them."

"His men?"

"Some of Abba Levas' men. They've rather adopted him. Or vice versa..." She threw Marjorie an amused look, but the older woman's reply was tense, almost distressed.

"Those other awful men will be here in a second too! Gerry Lonsdale and his thugs are just behind us."

Mila nodded and went to the open door with her Sten.

Bradley saw her study the sliding suspension bearings, the tubular steel sections of the catwalk and the joints between them.

She turned to him.

"Can you blow this?"

"With what?"

"With whatever we have to hand."

She swapped the Sten's magazine for one she had pushed inside her belt and presented the weapon to a dismayed Marjorie.

"For if they start to come across. I'm going to cock it now. Keep it pointed that way. All you need do is hide behind the door and pull the trigger. Short bursts are best."

"Where are you going? Can't Mr Bradley…?"

"I'm going down to see if I can help Jack come aboard. Mr Bradley will be busy rigging a bomb."

Bradley rolled his eyes and started racking his brain.

"With a timer, I suppose…?"

She looked up from the service steps that led down beneath the tower. There it was again, like before: that slow, fluttering, starlet's wink.

"I can always count on you, can't I?"

*　　*　　*

Taking the steps up from the landing platform three at a time, Jack Penny burst into the lower level of the control tower and looked around for Marjorie. Even so, it took him a moment to recognise the haggard, wild-haired woman clutching a Sten gun at the doorway.

"Oh, come 'ere you silly thing," he said, going to wrap his arms around her.

"Jacob!" she shrieked. "I have a job to do and *this* might go off at any moment!"

He saw the whiteness of her knuckles around the barrel jacket and the grip, or what passed for one, and was momentarily amazed that it had not done so already.

"'ere, I've got it. You let go, love."

He turned and handed the gun to Mila, who was right behind him. Then he took Marjorie's face between his hands.

"Let me look at you. What have they done to you!"

Her expression crumpled as tears came.

"Am I so frightful?"

Penny pressed her to his chest and pulled a face, biting his lip.

"No, love. I'm the frightful one for not saying 'ow gorgeous you look."

Her words were soft and muffled, by the onrush of a kind of drowsiness as much as his sou'wester.

"That's nice of you to say, anyway…"

He saw Mila take over at the door with the Sten.

"Gerry's mine," he mouthed to her.

She shook her head and indicated Bradley, who was coming along the corridor with something in his hands.

"Jack," he grunted with a nod, before holding the object out for Mila's inspection. It was the front part of a 3.7-inch anti-aircraft shell. "I got this out of No.1 gun tower – there's no one over there."

Penny grinned.

"There was four blokes downstairs trying to get away in the lifeboat. My chaps 'ave let 'em go – without oars."

"We've been lucky," Mila said.

"Not with Jimmy," Penny said, recalling the answer to the first piece of information he had demanded of the fleeing men.

"One thing at a time," Mila said. She turned back to Bradley. "You can use that as a demolition charge?"

The American nodded.

"Once you've detached the HE projectile from the cartridge, all you need to set the clockwork altitude fuse is a wrench… and an altitude fuse is basically a timer."

"How long?"

"I'd say forty seconds."

"And it'll take out the catwalk?"

"Maybe not the gantries suspending it, but in the middle, yeah, I'd say. If not, it'll make them think twice about crossing it."

Penny was shaking his head. Mila fixed him with a glare.

"We just need him bottled up while we get away, Jack. It can't be long before someone comes to see what all the fuss has been about."

"It'll be his people. Or he'll spin the authorities a story anyway – his unit's practically official."

"And if you go over there, you'll get caught with him. We have to go!"

He sighed and gave a reluctant nod.

"Go and set it please, Sam," Penny heard her say. It was enough. He was through with fighting, through with worrying fit to burst about Marjorie – and puking his guts over the side of horrible flat-bottomed barges that wouldn't have stood even a near miss from that flippin' Bofors gun.

That flippin' Bofors gun. And she was talking about getting away in the barges. With the *Heliopolis* limping away.

He kissed the top of Marjorie's head and ran after Bradley.

"Jack, no!" Mila shouted.

"He's still got the Bofors!" he shouted back.

Bradley was rising from the crouch, turning around, waving his hands. He had set the fuse. Penny tensed his muscles and shouldered past, hard enough to prevent the American from grabbing him but not so hard as to knock him off his feet when the poor bloody Septic was just trying to get back to safety.

He heard Bradley's exasperated cry but did not turn as he leapt over the artillery shell he had laid out on the timbers.

Forty seconds, Bradley had said. Give or take, Penny supposed. It was a bit arse-puckering at the end there, but he made it through the blast-proof doors of the Bofors tower and even had time to push them shut again before the explosion sounded outside. He allowed himself a butcher's through the armoured slats as the smoke blew away and saw that the catwalk had ruptured at the bottom and sides, leaving only the buckled remnants of the top rail connecting the towers. Bradley was right. You'd think twice about trying to shimmy across that, with the sea churning underneath you. More than twice.

It was as he was scaling the second flight of stairs to the roof that it occurred to him he ought to have hung onto Marjorie's Sten. He paused to wrestle out of the sou'wester, growling increasingly foul-mouthed insults at himself and every other impulsive fool with a barrel of *kak* for brains. All he had was a service revolver from TTG, of which he seemed to have become an honorary member.

Penny shook his head. Kiss my arse business, they called it. But this wasn't business at all. This was personal.

He ran out onto the rooftop.

*   *   *

Gerry Lonsdale had been loosening the tourniquet on Andrews' upper arm. He didn't really need it and having it so tight would likely do more harm than good. The blood was still seeping out from the bullet wound, despite Gerry's attempts to staunch and bandage it, but not in an arterial flow.

He looked up when he heard the penthouse door crash open. Out into the confined lower level of the Bofors tower rooftop tottered a familiar, stocky figure.

"Load a clip then get in the right hand seat," Gerry told Andrews.

"But guv, me arm…"

"You got another one. You can use that on the crank."

Gerry picked up the Lanchester that Andrews had dropped. It was heavier than the Sten, partly because it was better built and more reliable, partly because of the enormous 50-round magazine protruding from the side. But as far as he could tell, Jack Penny didn't even have a Sten, just a .38 six-shooter.

Jack had seen him and ducked behind the little penthouse. There wasn't anywhere else to hide. As well as hanging out over the sea, the two gun platforms extended inwards to accommodate the ammunition bunkers and the machinery to automate them, nearly meeting at the middle. The space between them, also raised, was the housing for the electronic predictors and served as the step up to either platform. The only cover was that far corner behind the penthouse.

Gerry fired a burst that hit the parapet at the back of Penny's hidey-hole, seeing sparks fly. With luck, his 50 rounds would be enough to get him with a ricochet.

Penny's pistol poked around the corner and fired blind.

"Not good enough, Jack!" Gerry shuffled backwards and checked that Andrews had traversed the Bofors far enough for him to slip into the left-hand seat. He could still cover the penthouse from here.

He raised his gaze momentarily and surveyed the remains of the fort. The ship must have yawed sideways or backed out after striking the middle tower, because the gun towers that had been in her path were still standing, albeit with their walkways busted down. Only the first gun tower had actually fallen, although one of the concrete legs of the searchlight tower had been chiselled away to its core and the whole thing was looking gimpy. The ship itself was chugging off smokily into the mist behind the cut-off towers. But it had not gone far and the mist was thinning.

Before he returned his full attention to the gunfight, his eye was drawn by two other wakes that were catching the rising sun. The first would be the barges, with all available motors pounding and sails set to claw off the lee shore and get back out into the channel. The second was pitching straight through the waves from the direction of that invisible shore: the steady advance of an armed trawler from Sheerness.

"I may not be able to hit the barges, Jack," he called out. "And I may only be able to load four at a time. But your ship's a sittin' duck!"

In the end, for all her strengths, she had been too soft. By only shooting to wound his men, she had left him the one extra hand he needed to scupper her plans. He wondered if she was on the barges or whether she had transferred to the ship by now and whether the ship was bound, as he suspected, for Palestine with the rest of the weapons. Jimmy's new sponsors wouldn't much like that. Tipping the wink to Andrews, he helped him lay the gun on target, copying the man's awkward one-handed cranking so as to keep the Lanchester free.

"I reckon that's about right, guv," Andrews slumped back from the sights with a groan.

Gerry depressed the foot trigger and the gun shook as it launched four explosive shells in a shallow arc towards the ship.

This time, when Jack's hand poked out again, half his face did too. Gerry emptied the magazine at the penthouse corner and looked back at the ship. From the little bloom of orange, one of the shells had hit something.

He wondered if he had too.

*   *   *

Aboard the *Lelie*, one of the little convoy's less effectively motorised barges, Bradley gave thanks that the steep angle of their turn into the wind more or less neutralised the angle of the peaked foredeck on which he lay prone, facing backward past the wheelhouse towards the fort. Curled up beside him on the other side of the shallow gable, Mila had a much harder job of holding on as the sails battered and the spray swept over them and the vessel pitched and rolled: not least because she was having to use both hands to keep the boat's ancient brass telescope trained on the target.

A moment ago they had seen the Bofors gun fire and the shells fly over. They hadn't seen the impact with the *Heliopolis*, but they had heard it, even before the sound of the Bofors reached them.

"I keep losing it!" she gave a squeal of frustration. "Then I pick up the nearer tower instead."

"If you figure there's no point any more…" Bradley began to say.

"No. As long as you think they're still in range, there may be something we can do."

Blinking as another freezing wave broke over them, he pulled a face that was half grin, half snarl. He knew she would never give up. He patted the rifle that was propped up on the hatch in front of him, a gift from one of the TTG men.

"I dunno what the Brits get from these No.4 Enfields these days, but back in the Boer War they say they made kills over a mile with the earlier versions. I just wish I had their sights."

"And perhaps some African veldt?"

"That might help."

"How far do you think we are from them now?"

"Coming up to a thousand yards," he said. "It's a little hard to tell…"

"I've got something! I've realised now that I couldn't see them when they were sitting down to operate the gun. But now one of them is standing up to look."

Even peering straight over the rifle's iron sights, all he could make out was the grey, spiky structure at the rear of the tower – and that was swinging up and down and back and forth. How he was supposed to factor in elevation and windage as well was a mystery to him.

"Look for a dark blob against the sky, to the side of the barrel."

"No blob. I can't even see the barrel – it'd be like spotting a hair at this distance. But I can see the shape of the whole gun and work out where the barrel is from that."

"Wait, he's moving – right in line with the top of the barrel now!"

He flipped up the long-range leaf, adjusted the aperture slider for 1,000 yards and made his best guess for windage. He tried not to tense as he pulled the trigger. They had done their best to cushion his shoulder, and had rested the rifle on the remaining cushions so that he had no need to grip it tightly, but there was every possibility that he would only get one shot.

It was probably one more than Jack had got.

*   *   *

Penny never heard the shot, but he heard the man cry out in pain. He heard the other's shout of alarm. He heard the thud and the clang as someone toppled off the gun platform, hit the railing and went over the side.

He did not hear the splash because he was already rolling across the worn asphalt roof and aiming his pistol from below the step that led up to the gun platform.

At Gerry Lonsdale, sitting upright in the Bofors gun, open-mouthed.

Penny's first thought was that the shot had come from one of the other towers. Bradley, maybe, had climbed back up the control tower to cover him. Except that made no sense. Bradley had been leaving with the rest of them, and if he hadn't, why hadn't he taken the shot earlier – or taken another shot now? Why hadn't they heard the shot?

No, the shot hadn't come from anywhere on the fort. It had come from the barges, more than half a mile away, or from the *Heliopolis*, even further out.

He couldn't help laughing.

"Told him to get up and reload it, didn't you? What you gonna do now, Ger'? You can't lay that gun on your own."

His pistol was empty. Gerry had probably guessed that. From the way he let it fall, his submachine gun was empty too. Penny watched him swing his long legs free of the gun and shuffle himself forward. When he was on the base of the mount and presumably shielded from the barges and the ship by the gun platform on the other side of the tower, he stood up tall, rolling his head, working his shoulders, flexing his hands.

"This has been a long time coming, Jack."

"You said it, pal!"

Penny was a scrapper, but that was what was needed against a natural hitter like Gerry. Get picked off boxing fair – or get in under those long arms and get dirty. He feinted with a left jab, blocked the counter, and ducked inside, driving stiff, blunt fingers into his groin and solar plexus. Then wallop, up with the head, aiming for a butt under the chin, missing, but snatching a short uppercut to achieve the same thing.

Trouble was, Gerry had snapped back his own head and ridden the punch, ready to tag Penny as he broke away. One-two, right in the kisser, then a step to the side, frighteningly fast, and a thumping hook to his kidney as his guard came up too late and left his body exposed. Penny sucked air and backed off. Gerry laughed.

This time Penny let his opponent come forward, shocked at the lightness of his footwork, even in army boots on tar and rivets. As he dodged and blocked, unable to put together a combination of his own, he realised Gerry was herding him into the corner by the penthouse and he had to skip past him at the last minute. As he did, Gerry caught him with another explosive body shot to his side, sending him staggering into the central unit between the gun platforms. Penny put his hands down to break his fall, made as though he was going to vault the obstruction, then kicked out backwards like a mule as Gerry came in fast with a kick of his own. He was gratified to feel the soft stuff on Gerry's knee crunch, even more gratified that it had stopped the nimble bastard pressing through with his attack while he himself was off balance.

"Not bad, Jack," he panted, rubbing his knee. "'Oo taught you to impervise like that?"

Penny spat blood.

"She did, of course. And it's *improvise*, you berk!"

On the last word, he went to finish it with a haymaker while Gerry's guard was down, but even as he put all his weight and momentum into the punch, he realised that he'd made a fatal mistake. Gerry was ready for it. He ducked under it and as Penny swung wildly he grabbed him from behind, wrestling his hands under Penny's armpits and then back behind his head. Penny felt himself being spreadeagled and lifted clean off the rooftop, unable to fight back. Then Gerry forced his head down at an angle in front and ran them both into the riveted steel frame of the penthouse.

Jack Penny saw flashes of light, flakes of rusty grey paint, and blood, lots of it, streaming down his forehead into his eyes. But Gerry wasn't finished. Now kneeling on his back, holding him by his hair, he banged Penny's face down onto the rooftop — once, twice, three times, four. Penny thought his head had caved in. He certainly felt his nose go. And something in his back, digging into his spine, nearly snapping it…

Gerry let go and staggered to his feet, giving Penny one last kick in the side of the head for good measure. Penny rolled over, gasping for air, inhaling instead a viscous mixture of blood and mucus and vomit.

Through the waves of pain and darkness that were washing over him, over the violent thudding of his own heartbeat, Penny became aware of a different sound: a boat engine, underneath them.

Leaning over the parapet to catch his breath before launching the final onslaught, Gerry let out a triumphant laugh.

"It's the navy! 'ard cheese, Jack – I can tell them what 'appened and they'll go right out there and stop your ship before it gets to Margate, let alone fuckin' Palestine!"

Penny was feeling under his back for the impediment that had dug into his spine. With his head hung forward, still dripping blood, he managed to get to his knees and then, shakily, to his feet.

His eyes had swollen almost shut. He wasn't even sure if that was surprise on Gerry's face as he brought the claw hammer down.

CHAPTER TWENTY

Spring was turning to summer. The breeze that propelled the sailing dinghies across the Dümmer See was fresh, the spray clear and cool, but on the dock, in the lee of the clubhouse, it was warm enough to sunbathe. Several of the younger C.C.G. women had unbuttoned their shirts and two had undressed to petticoats and brassieres. Those men who were not out on the water were stripped to the waist and larking about, pushing one another off the dock. The game only served to emphasise their rather puny frames and in most cases their acute reliance on their spectacles.

Having checked that her blouse was not bulging indelicately, Marjorie was regarding Mila with an odd, defensive look. Mila guessed that she had seen how she was scrutinizing her colleagues.

"Have you any idea how much goes into not losing a war after you have won it? We started planning for this phase while our armies were still retreating on all fronts. And when the outdoorsy types from school like you and Mr Bradley started winning the battles for us, these misfits were training night and day to take over from you."

Mila nodded. Point taken. And who was she to deny these men and women – the young ones, and the older volunteers, like Marjorie herself – their Sunday outing, when her own cause was so selfish by comparison? True, she had got them all caught up in something bigger, with unforeseen outcomes (the acquisition of Elster's records being a notable bonanza, she had been assured) but there was no escaping the fact that the others might still be alive had they not set out to help her in her personal mission.

Miro. Stas. With his fear and his paradoxes.

I hope you would have liked my solution to the immovable object problem, Stas; after all, it was you who proposed the unstoppable force.

Marjorie interrupted her train of thought – an overburdened train nowadays – with a more conciliatory note and a warmer tone.

"I am very grateful to you for what you did for me, Mila. To you and Mr Bradley of course. And Jacob."

"Have you heard from him, or been to see him?"

"They wouldn't allow it, our not being related. Or perhaps it is he who won't allow it. In any case, I have my job to do here, like any other serviceman or woman..."

Mila tried to read her face and gave up. She had learned long ago from Richard that the English rarely wore their hearts there, or anywhere else you could go looking for.

"There is still the appeal..."

Marjorie shook her head.

"They were always going to make an example of him – to be seen to crack down on the 'spivs' that were allowed to emerge during the war. And he was seen too, plain as day, by that naval officer underneath the tower."

"There were mitigating circumstances!"

"No, Mila," she said, her mouth a straight line, her gaze sharp and unyielding. "There are never mitigating circumstances for murder."

"Even for Jacob?" Mila said. It was not Jack Penny and Gerry Lonsdale she was thinking of, but other people, many of them nameless. Not least the hijackers on Reichsstraße 1.

"Oh, I understand it – his commitment to the Jewish cause – but no, I'm afraid I can't condone what he did. If I condoned it, I could not go on..." For a second, the worn face fell, the pained voice cracked and Mila was about to reach out for her, but she sat up straight again, regaining her composure. "I could not go on doing what I'm doing here."

"But he was manipulated. We were all manipulated, by the Americans behind the JDC, and by the British Government, or at least elements of it…"

Marjorie had turned to watch the horseplay on the dock. A man of about forty in pebble-thick specs caught her looking and waved. With his suntanned hands and face and his lily-white body hinting at a childhood pigeon chest or other illness, he appeared ridiculous. In his other hand he held an improbable cup of tea, which he also raised in a silent toast. Then one of his colleagues bundled into him with a roar and man, teacup and spectacles disappeared in a glittering splash.

"I love my country, Mila," Marjorie said. "I am often appalled by the way the upper strata of society behave, but I'm so proud of what ordinary people have achieved. Like Tony there. Do you know what Tony is thinking about today, since his promotion from the Registry? He is thinking that if the experts are right and this turns out to be a hot summer, Germany's fragile crops may suffer, and if those events were to precede a bitter winter, which is overdue, we ought to be making contingencies right this minute."

Mila sat, chastened. She adjusted her sunglasses and the summery headscarf she had chosen to hide her overly short hair, trying to look normal, feeling anything but. Although she accepted Marjorie's argument that these people were fellow combatants of a sort – and while she had personal reasons to be grateful for their attempts to save the Germans from starvation or further indoctrination from right and left – still she knew what she felt most like here, with her scars and her guilt: a wolf in the fold.

"Did you find anything out?" she said.

"Not at Bünde, no," Marjorie's reply was brusque, almost scornful. "But since I achieved a certain notoriety, everybody wants to talk to me, including the journalists – and they operate by what they flatter themselves to call the *quid pro quo.*"

"You got them to do a little digging for you?"

"To be honest, once they appreciated that it was an opportunity to set right some of the inaccuracies in a LIFE Magazine photo-story, they were only too eager."

Mila could not help but smile.

"You have learned some guile along the way!"

"Since I fell…" Marjorie started to say, then shook her head and produced a doubled-over buff envelope from her handbag.

"They ruled out all the likely foster families, save one. The family was killed in an air raid late in the war, but not the boy. He was taken in by another family. Here the details grow sketchy. But it is a location where a great many children live rough on the bombsites, part-time or full-time, and there is the name of a man in here, a former priest and some kind of unofficial charity worker, who can point each of them out to you."

Mila took the envelope but did not open it. Nor did she attempt to hide her tears from the other woman.

"Did they find out what Pavel's name had been changed to?"

Marjorie nodded, laying one hand on Mila's arm and lifting up her chin with the other. It was not the gesture of a friend, not anymore. But it was the gesture of a mother.

"Paul," she said. "They called him Paul."

*   *   *

Jack Penny sat at the table with his back to the door, a pair of unsealed letters in front of him. One of the two warders and the chaplain sat either side. He had been offered a rabbi days ago and had refused one, but now there was something he wished to confess.

"Yes?"

"Well, Father…"

The padre winced politely. The man was sixty if he was a day, soft-spoken and more than a little airy-fairy, though he must have had a toughness to do what he did.

"You don't have to call me that…"

"The thing is – that day I first became this Mighty 'ero of the Jews what I seem to 'ave been mistaken for – I was just telling Laughing Boy 'ere about it…"

The glum-faced warder thought for a moment and then said:

"The Battle of Cable Street."

"Bob's yer uncle," Penny said. "Blimey, they do pay you fellows to listen, don't they! Well, the truth is I was only there that day to turn over Gardiner's department store, not to fight them effin' blackshirts at all, beggin' your pardon, Father…"

"You really don't…"

"And I don't want that on my conscience. Nor these…" His grin faded as he touched the letters one after the other. The first was addressed to Mrs Marjorie Jessop, c/o Gasthof Lipke, Bückeburg, British Zone of Occupied Germany. The second bore only the name Jimmy Lonsdale. Although he was meant to be on the run after the business at the fort, the authorities would know well enough how to get Penny's message to him, should they choose to deliver it. Not that it was a message exactly. More of a curse, or his best attempt at one, drawing on his old mum's tales from the *shtetl*. It might only give the bugger a giggle, Jimmy the Shiv being a no-nonsense sort of pig. But then you never knew with gypsies.

The God-botherer mumbled something heartfelt and appropriate. Laughing Boy was looking grimly at the door.

"Oh, cheer up you two, it may never 'appen!" Penny said.

At that he heard the door crash open and what sounded like a hundred no-nonsense Jimmys stomped into the room all at once. The two men at the table rose and he did likewise, only to be seized from behind and pinioned around the wrists. Penny went cold as he saw the man who had done the strapping: a middle-aged, unremarkable civilian wearing a dark suit and a fair helping of Brylcreem on his thinning hair.

It wasn't just time now. Reality itself seemed to be slipping away. Penny watched as the man, without turning, walked straight towards the wardrobe… which two new prison warders had rolled magically to the side. Beyond was another door, also sliding open, and beyond that a brightly lit cell down into which hung three ropes, the two either side with a big knot at the end, the thick one in the middle looped up at head height and ending in a noose.

Warders were frogmarching him through the doorways. The civilian stopped abruptly and turned to face him, leaving him standing on something that had a fraction of give to it. Someone was strapping his legs from behind, someone else positioning a white bag above his head.

When the man reached out to tug it down, Penny managed to smile.

"I shared an aeroplane ride with you once."

"You'll go on this trip alone, sonny. But it's a short one, I promise."

As the hood came down, he said:

"I'll be waiting for you there."

*　　*　　*

Blinding light, exploding in his brain, scrambling his thoughts. With the incredible noise and the different waves of heat meeting in a pressure front, it really was like being caught in an explosion.

He pressed his hand over his remaining eye and warily separated the fingers.

A rectangle of bright blue, a border of flushed, foreshortened faces, clustered in concentric ellipses, like looking up from the depths of some human well in one of those phantasmagoric parables of the early Flemish masters. The moans and wails and angry cries inextricably entangled with the thudding of the engines and the calling of the gulls – and the endless scream, for surely that was what it was, of the explosive sky.

"Go on, go on!" yelled the *Shomer*, forcing him toward the ladder that led one level higher in the abyss. Up he climbed, step by weak, painful step. Here, between the feet of those leaning out over the balcony to snatch a breath of cloying air, lay dozens of sick and old people, some looking close to death. Like him, they had been allowed up from the hold for a short time, but they hadn't the strength to climb further.

He knelt beside a woman who was gasping her last, felt her forehead and took her pulse.

"Here!" he called for the *Shomrim*. "Water here!"

"Who are you to tell us our job?"

"Michal Wlasnowalski," he proclaimed. "I was a doctor, in Warsaw, when I was alive."

"Whoa, doc!" The Young Guard laughed, beckoning for his fellow volunteer with the water pouch. "We'll take care of her. I think you better get on up topside."

"I shall do as you say…"

Eventually he emerged from that enlarging rectangle into the screaming light. He was on the foredeck of the ship, but penned in a sort of up-and-down animal run between spiked stakes and barbed wire fences he did not remember from his previous trip topside, however many hours or days or weeks ago that might have been. What it did remind him of, and what, despite himself, he did remember, was the footbridge at Chlodna Street, where the normal rush-hour trams and traffic ran between the big ghetto and the little ghetto and one might spot the familiar face of a former colleague or friend, eyes studiously downcast. Two different worlds, folded together yet never meeting.

He looked for a view between the crowds, the palisades and the gleaming white structures but could see nothing. All he heard now was sawing and hammering.

"They are constructing battlements," said his neighbour at the rail, whom he vaguely recognised as one of the Hungarians who had been with him at Genoa.

"Battlements?"

"For the battle to come. We are nearly there!"

"Nearly there?" Wlasnowalski felt he would go mad if he

could not find a way out of this Piranesi prison. Although he was no youngster and far from healthy, he began to fight his way through to the next flight of steps. Just then, it seemed to him, it was more important to expend his last strength on seeing their destination than actually to get there – but first he had to climb from the plains of Moab!

The journey had been a long one. From Czechoslovakia to Tarvisio, then onward to Genoa. In Genoa, always dodging the authorities, there had been the Panamanian-flagged American corvette to take them out to their rendezvous with this ship, the *Heliopolis*, which had been resupplied with food, fuel and DPs all the way from Gibraltar without ever once putting into port, so they said. Certainly it looked worn-out. From down here he could see the twisted derricks and ventilators that made the forward hold even less habitable and suggested some violent collision in its recent past.

He reached the top of the steps and howled with frustration. Ship's crew, many of whom were American Jews who had transferred from the corvette, were welding a metal gate in place to block his way. Wlasnowalski seized the bars between powerless fists and pressed his head, with its homemade eye-patch, against them.

After a time when he could do no more than cling to the bars to prevent himself toppling back down the steps, he became aware of hushed voices communing on the other side of the gate. He opened his eye and saw that one of the deck hands had gone to fetch another pair of *Shomrim*, a boy and a girl. Perhaps they were *Khalutsim,* but he did not recognise them from Genoa. Perhaps they had been aboard from the start.

They were regarding him with concerned, respectful smiles. He realised that in clinging to the bars his sleeves had slipped down, revealing his emaciated forearms. The young couple were looking at the number tattooed there.

The girl was striking, with her wild bird's nest of hair tied back, her shirt unbuttoned and her long, suntanned legs in baggy shorts rolled up scandalously shorter. Her moist eyes flashed with outrage as she ordered the sailor to unlock the gate.

"I am Estera," she said, taking his arm and leading him through. "This is Kalev. Come and see where we are."

Peace be with you, ministering angels, he thought.

They led him between rusty-white superstructure and out onto the raised deck at the front of the ship, the fo'c'sle deck, he supposed it would be called. For the first time in a long while he saw the sea, a brilliant blue from horizon to horizon. Except, as Estera led him forward to the mangled railings, he could see that ahead lay not only more water but bright shapes and colours.

"Excuse me…"

He wiped his eye and made out ships, grey and black and white, and beyond them a rippling white town, and beyond it a hazy ridge of mountain.

"That's Mount Carmel," the boy told him. "And below it, Haifa."

"Palestine?" he mouthed.

"*Eretz Yisrael*," said the girl. Then her tone altered. "And those ships are British destroyers. Now we're into territorial waters, they mean to board us."

"But we will fight back," Kalev said.

Wlasnowalski thought about the barbed wire and wooden spikes.

"With what, with clubs?"

"If we have to," the girl said. "And with this…"

She put two fingers in her mouth and let out a piercing whistle. Another couple of *Shomrim* appeared with a wooden box. On the box lay a carefully folded white cloth. Setting down the box, they began wrestling with the cloth in the wind. It was a white flag bearing a blue Shield of David and they were fastening it to the jackstaff.

Kalev opened the box and brought out, most surprisingly, a miniature crown entirely composed it seemed of sparkling diamonds in this impossible light. Estera reached beneath her shirt and produced a small egg grenade of the kind favoured by the Germans in the Great War.

"They'll have glasses on us by now," she said, holding up the grenade.

Kalev did the same with the crown, and then together, taking their time, they inserted one into the other: two different worlds, interlocked.

"Just in case they get the idea of shooting us and fishing for it later," Estera said, taking the crown to the jackstaff and extending one long, muscular arm to hold it out over the sea at the ship's prow. "If I drop it now, they'll never find all the pieces."

Wlasnowalski sat down on the empty box. Whether because others on the decks below had spotted the shore, or because of the sight and sound of the *Mogen Dovid* fluttering to the fore, he could hear singing, clapping and stamping as groups of refugees formed up and linked arms to dance a *hora*.

Refugees? They were immigrants now, he told himself. Admittedly illegal.

And this *laissez-passer* of theirs? Clearly there was some significance to the crown that was intended to paralyse the British blockade. Would it work? It seemed unlikely, but whether or not it did, they would fight on regardless, that much was obvious. Should they be boarded, they would fight back. Should they be turned around, they would return. If taken into Haifa under guard, they would escape, again, as they had before.

He would do his best to stay alive to see it.

*   *   *

It might have been any north western German town, grown up to serve and manifest the creed of industrial entrepreneurship. Many buildings were still standing. Many were not. Missing blocks, along whose entire length the women had neatly stacked the rubble, gave little indication of the lives of those who had lived or worked and died there.

Bradley had grown accustomed to looking out across squared-away waste grounds and seeing in the middle distance the remains of larger structures that were not so easy to strip and salvage. Bridges. Cranes. Viaducts. Chimney stacks. Churches. Here they had the full set.

But slowly, life was returning to normal. The electric suspension railway, a smaller version of the famous *Schwebebahn* at Wuppertal, was running again. Barges plied the canals and rivers. And even if the *Gründerzeit* buildings were mostly skeletons, lights burned at lower storey windows, shopfronts displayed their wares, men and women stood in line for the *Kino*. Showing tonight would be the Warner Brothers western *Saratoga Trunk*, starring Gary Cooper and Ingrid Bergman.

And Charles S. Fisher, too, rode again – at least according to Leonard Hoffman, who had sought him out upon their return to Antwerp.

"I lost my false I.D.," Bradley had told him.

"We can fix you up with another one."

"And my Special Agent's gold badge…"

"Heck, you can have mine."

The erstwhile CIC officer – if he had ever truly been such – was once again as good as his word. Within a couple of weeks, Bradley's cover had been restored, complete with a replacement wardrobe and, yes, his own 'rat runner's' badge. He even had a jeep, with enough passes to enable him and any passenger to move freely throughout all the occupation zones.

What Hoffman had not supplied, however, was any kind of debriefing, beyond the news that Doyle and the successor agency to British Security Co-ordination were delighted with how he and MERCURY had done. Doyle in particular, Hoffman reported. He had known that Bradley and Miss Slavík would never let the gangsters get the guns or the loot. But given how close they had come, that was a stretch. And it left some big questions unanswered. Hoffman, struggling to explain, returned again and again to the mantra of 'long-term British interests in the Middle East', which were apparently distinct both from American policy towards Jewish immigration and the stated position of His Majesty's Government on the same issue.

"Meaning?"

"No good asking me, Bradley. I'd be the last to hear. But I wouldn't be surprised if it was about not being seen to help the Jews, in order to keep the Arabs sweet. Not the poor Palestinians. The ones with power in the region, not to mention a rather important canal. The ones who might otherwise be tempted to start leaning towards Moscow."

Stymying the Reds. Somehow it always came back to the same thing.

Now he turned the jeep off the main thoroughfare and headed for the rubble field on the fringes of the old town: all that remained of the workers' housing that had borne the brunt of the air raids. Here on a hillside stood the shells of mill workers' tenements, turned two-dimensional by unremembered tragedies. The barren landscape between him and this backcloth was one he also recognised from scores of other towns and cities. Jagged splinters of walls with oases of isolated relics – a fireplace, a bay window, a bathroom. Crazy slides and jungle gyms of twisted girders. Overgrown nooks and crannies. Shanties of pilfered boards and canvas.

The boondocks. No-man's-land. A leper colony.

A playground.

"There," Mila said.

Bradley stopped the jeep, adding to the general haze of dust. Where the track forked and all but disappeared stood a donkey cart. Beside it stood a man. Despite the heat, he was dressed in a sort of oversized work coat that resembled an artist's smock. His boots were coming apart. His bald head was bare.

"God Almighty! He looks like Brother Juniper!"

"*Guten morgen, Herr Pfarrer,*" Mila said.

Bradley sat in the jeep and watched the two of them as they

conversed. He saw the pastor's expression shift gradually from distrust to geniality, saw him introduce his ancient donkey and raise the tarpaulin on the cart to show the foodstuffs he had brought. Loaves and fishes, Bradley caught himself thinking, although it turned out to be cans.

This, of course, was what heroes really looked like: like characters most folks would cross the street to avoid. According to Mila, the little man had been a pastor of the Confessional Consensus that had stood up in opposition to Nazism and the German Christian movement. He had lost his church, of course, and then his liberty, imprisoned in Tegel and eventually in Sachsenhausen. Whatever else he had lost along the way, besides his teeth, God only knew; from the look of him he was half bonkers. Perhaps that was why, when his buddies re-emerged to start rebuilding the church and publicly re-evaluating the German soul, he had stuck to the places where nobody was going to see Ingrid Bergman tonight, where their needs for nourishment were more immediate.

Mila was back at his side. For a while she sniffed and said nothing. When she did, her breathing sounded as though she had just climbed one of the steeper rubble-mounds.

"He says there is a place, up there near the top of the hill, a flat concrete area where the children play football when they are not foraging. He says he thinks he is there this morning. Paul."

Bradley noticed the single tear in the corner of her eye. There had been others, which she had wiped away. There would be many more, one way or another.

"Pavel," he said.

"Yes…"

"Well, I doubt we'll get much further in the jeep. I'll walk with you."

"Thank you."

They waved to the pastor and set off across the rubble. Every now and then a carrion bird cawed or alighted on a stump. Bradley had the impression of eyes watching them from the cavities that had been created by the toppled apartment blocks. But any movement was probably rats.

When he took her hand to help her across a defile, he felt the tension in her muscles. Her whole body was shaking.

Was there really any chance that this was her kid and not another of the war's unnumbered orphans – or that she could even know for certain, now? Wasn't it more likely that somewhere dark inside herself, if not this time then the next, she would have to make a conscious choice to bury the doubts with all the other suffering?

Then, with a sudden gulp of the foul-smelling air, she stopped. The flat platform was ahead and there were only two small, ragged figures upon it. A boy and a girl.

Mila's foot slipped on a loose rock and the two children turned. The girl bolted. The boy did not. He just stood, blinking in the sunlight, sweeping the long fringe of dusty blonde hair off his face and shielding his eyes with one filthy, sun-bronzed arm.

"You go up," Bradley said, offering her a last helping hand, but she had already gone. He watched her climb to the platform and brush herself down before taking tentative steps towards the child. When she was a few steps away and the boy still had not fled, she sank to her knees in front of him.

Bradley turned aside to light a cigarette, making sure there was another left in the pack. She deserved so much more that he could not give her, but right now she deserved her privacy.

He could give her that.

AFTERWORD

I hope you enjoyed *The Herrenhaus Forfeit.*

I would love to hear what you thought of it, so please do consider leaving a review on Amazon. (And if you haven't yet read the first book in the Chasing Mercury series, *The Borodino Sacrifice*, you can find it there.)

You can also get in touch for news of Mila and Bradley's next adventure – or even an exclusive preview – by visiting www.bypaulphillips.com/chasing-mercury.html

As before, I am indebted to everyone who helped me link together a wealth of research material – too many and too much to name here – in shaping my fictional story.